SERENDIPITY

TEN
Romantic Tropes,
TRANSFORMED

SERENDIPITY

TEN
Romantic Tropes,
TRANSFORMED

EDITED BY

MARISSA MEYER

WITH STORIES BY

ELISE BRYANT • ELIZABETH EULBERG • LEAH JOHNSON

ANNA-MARIE MCLEMORE • SANDHYA MENON • MARISSA MEYER

JULIE MURPHY • CALEB ROEHRIG • SARAH WINIFRED SEARLE

ABIGAIL HING WEN

FEIWEL AND FRIENDS
New York

A FEIWEL AND FRIENDS BOOK
An imprint of Macmillan Publishing Group, LLC
120 Broadway, New York, NY 10271
fiercereads.com

Our books may be purchased in bulk for promotional, educational, or business use. Please
contact your local bookseller or the Macmillan Corporate and Premium Sales Department
at (800) 221-7945 ext. 5442 or by email at MacmillanSpecialMarkets@macmillan.com.

Library of Congress Cataloging-in-Publication Data is available.

Library of Congress Control Number: 2021917023

First edition, 2022
Book design by Michelle Gengaro-Kokmen
Printed in the United States of America
Feiwel and Friends logo designed by Filomena Tuosto

ISBN 978-1-250-78084-3 (hardcover)
1 3 5 7 9 10 8 6 4 2

FOR ALL THE INCORRIGIBLE ROMANTICS.

—M.M.

THE STORIES
(and the Tropes ♥)

BYE BYE, PIPER BERRY
(The Fake Relationship)

JULIE MURPHY

PIPER

*E*very iconic teen movie my dads ever made me watch prepared me for the moment a boy would throw pebbles at my bedroom window in the middle of the night. I just never thought it would be me throwing the rocks and at Gabe Rafferty's window at four in the morning. I guess it helps that to throw rocks at Gabe's window, I only had to open mine, and that instead of rocks I was throwing plastic beads from a beading kit my aunt Sylvia bought me because she thinks I'm still eleven years old.

"Psst, Gabe," I hissed. "Psst!"

A light flickered on in Gabe's room as his silhouette stumbled out of bed. After a minute, he pushed his bedroom window open for me like he had so many times before.

"He's sorry," Gabe swore for the hundredth time as he rubbed at his eyes and put his black-rimmed glasses on. "What time even is it?"

"Yes, I've heard him use that word many times, but I don't think he understands the meaning," I said as I leaned out the window into the dewy night air. "He can be as sorry as he wants," I told Gabe. "It's over for us. It was over the moment he even thought about sticking his tongue down Carolyn Daniels's throat."

Gabe's full lower lip turned into a frown. "This blows. It's the start of our senior year. We're supposed to be having the time of our lives. All of us together."

"Don't pretend like I'm the one who completely ruined our friend group here, Gabe."

"Well, if you're so dead-set on not forgiving him, why exactly are you throwing shit at my window like an angry squirrel on a mission?"

I scoffed as I sat in the frame of the window with one leg hanging over the side. "There is nothing 'squirrely' about me, Gabe!"

He yawned. "Out with it, Piper."

"I know that you knew."

Gabe Rafferty was never a good liar from the time we were six and he tried to cover for me and take the credit for the time I pooped in the pool at Victoria Treviño's birthday party. Mrs. Treviño saw right through his round, flushed cheeks then just like I did right now.

"I knew it!" I quietly shrieked. "Gabe Rafferty, you little piece of shit. You knew! You knew this whole time!"

"That's not fair," he said. "You know all my tells."

"Calling the full-body reaction you have when you're nearly caught in a lie your 'tells' would be generous at best. Your whole head turns into a flashing billboard."

"I'm feeling very victimized here," Gabe said as he squeezed his large frame through his open window. His body hit the grass with a thud, and he groaned as he stood. He used to keep a wooden crate between our two houses, so he could use it as a boost, but now he was so tall he could just lean right into my window like some giraffe at a drive-through safari.

"Gabe, I'm serious. How could you not tell me Travis was cheating?"

He ducked his head through my window and clasped both hands in a prayer. "He said it was a one-time thing, Pipe. I swear. Besides, they had that onstage kiss . . . I figured it couldn't be that much different."

"Well, it obviously was," I said, trying and failing to disguise the hurt in my voice.

Gabe would always belong to Travis first. In the same way that Maisie would always be mine, but Maisie was a year older and already well into her semester at the University of North Texas. The four of us had been friends since our bikes had four wheels instead of two. And even though his loyalty would belong to Travis before anyone else, it still stung to know that Gabe—sweet, reliable, chronically funny next-door neighbor Gabe—had known about Travis's transgressions and kept me in the dark this whole time. And now with Maisie gone, Travis turning out to be a cheating dirtbag, and Gabe covering for him, I had no one.

Tears began to well up as my chest tightened with a new kind of pain.

"Oh, Pipe, don't cry." He pulled himself up and ungracefully slithered through my window. There was a fifty-fifty chance my dads would hear and come crashing through my door to defend me from an intruder.

I couldn't help but laugh at the sight of him there on my floor, but it came out like a sob. "What are you doing? We have school in like three hours."

"You're the one who started it by throwing rocks or nuts or something at my window."

"Beads. They were friendship bracelet beads. And don't worry, I'll pick them up before Ziggy eats them," I told him, referring to his mom's Pomeranian, as he stood up.

He took a step closer and pulled me against his chest for the kind of hug that felt like a good wringing-out. Like Gabe's whole body was a sponge and he was soaking up all the pain and all the heartbreak.

"I'm so sorry," he said, his voice raspy and muffled against my hair.

"Good," I said with a pout before taking a step back, so I could look him right in the eyes. "Good. Because you owe me."

Suspicion passed over his face like a cloud. Just like I knew Gabe couldn't tell a lie, he knew I held on to a grudge like it was a life raft. "What are you talking about?"

"You know what I'm talking about. You let me go to all those *Bye Bye Birdie* rehearsals like a total fool. I'm literally Carolyn's dresser! I have to help the girl my ex-boyfriend of three years cheated on me with in and out of her costume so she can just go onstage and kiss him all over again."

Gabe winced. "Travis does make a good Albert Peterson."

Travis had explained to both of us several times during the lead-up to auditions that Conrad Birdie wasn't actually the best role in *Bye Bye Birdie*. Why name a whole musical after a character that's not even the star of the show?

"Could we just stop treating Travis like a god for a freaking minute?" I asked. "Yes, he makes a great Albert What's-His-Face, because he's good at everything. Including sneaking around! But not good enough to not get caught and humiliate me in front of the whole school. And you weren't good enough to at least warn me!"

He exhaled heavily. "Okay, okay. What do you want me to do?"

"Easy. Be my boyfriend," I said simply. I didn't actually know if revenge was one of the stages of grief, but it only took me a few days of tears before I decided I wanted to get back at Travis and I wanted to make it hurt.

Gabe's cheeks turned a bright shade of red as he wiped the back of his hand over his brows, and it was very clear that just the thought of seeing me as a romantic interest made him terribly uncomfortable. It was a real confidence boost to see one of my oldest friends find me so deeply disgusting. "W—what? What do you mean?"

"Not my *real* boyfriend," I clarified as I took a step closer, peering up at him. "Just my fake boyfriend for a few days."

"A, this is an awful idea. B, can this at least wait until next week when *Bye Bye Birdie* is done?"

"No," I told him. "In fact, that's exactly why it can't wait. So what do you say, Gabe? Will you be my boyfriend?"

GABE

According to Piper, boyfriends picked their girlfriends up for school. I knew that wasn't entirely true, because Travis only had his mom's Suburban on Tuesdays and Thursdays, but Piper made it clear that our arrangement was very much about appearances.

I shouldn't have said yes to begin with, but it turns out it's impossible to say no to the girl you've loved since first grade. I guess it probably seemed like my whole life up until this point must have been torture—my best friend dating the love of my life for so long that they were practically married in high school years. But I knew early on that Piper existed in a glass case for me. I could be near her and I could enjoy her company and her wry sense of humor, but she would never be *for* me. The chubby guy with a dad bod didn't really stand much of a chance when it came to girls like Piper, especially when I'd been in competition for her since the day she moved in next door and Travis and I trotted over to meet the girl with long brown hair, her know-it-all older brother, and two dads.

I fell for her first, but Travis was the first to let his feelings be known when in fourth grade, he gave her a mini box of chocolates on Valentine's Day with a stuffed monkey wearing a T-shirt that said *You're Ape Out of Ten*. To this day, it still bugs the shit out of me that the joke on the monkey's shirt didn't even make sense. Monkeys aren't even apes. Whatever. I noticed the awful thing still pinned to her bulletin board when I crawled through her window this morning. I was almost shocked she hadn't purged everything she owned relating to Travis, but the moment she asked me to be her fake boyfriend, I knew. This wasn't about getting revenge on Travis or making him suffer just as much as she had. This was about winning him back.

Piper was quiet the whole drive to school. Either she was exhausted from only getting a few hours of sleep or she was feeling just as awkward as I was by the prospect of what we were about to do.

I parked the car and turned the ignition, Taylor Swift's voice cutting out halfway through "Lover." (Swiftie till the day I die.) "You ready, Pipes?" I asked.

She nodded. "We should have gotten here earlier to get a better spot. This will only work if people see us."

I sucked in a deep breath and stepped out of my truck, preparing myself to fully betray my best friend. Piper met me halfway in front of the truck, and I did the stupidest thing I've ever done. I took her hand.

She looked down quizzically at our interlaced fingers, perfectly locked into place like they were finally right where they were meant to be.

"We gotta sell it, don't we?" I asked.

She nodded, and squeezed my hand lightly.

We walked into school, heads slowly turning and chatter beginning to hum. "Let 'em stare," I whispered as I pulled her a little closer.

She leaned her head against my shoulder and my heart . . . it soared.

It only took one class period for Travis to find out.

"What the fuck, man?" he demanded as he stayed close on my heels.

I couldn't let him see my face, because then he'd know. He'd know I was lying just like Piper had. I threw my hands up and shrugged. "It just happened, but you've got Carolyn, so it's cool, right?"

"That's no—not bro code," he stammered. "And I don't *got* Carolyn. That was a one-time thing! I even told you so!"

"Trav, you're into theater and I'm a bigger Taylor Swift fan than almost everyone at this school. Pretty sure 'bro code' isn't a thing for us. And explain to me how a one-time thing happened four times."

"Well, then, best friend code," he said as finally caught up to my long strides, gripped my shoulder, and spun me around.

I had about six inches on my best friend, but he was limber as hell from all those years of spinning and twirling dance partners across the stage of Martindale High School.

"I always thought there was something up with you two," he said.

My jaw dropped and I immediately tried to pick it up from the floor. "W—what?"

"You two always laughed at the same nonsensical shit and your bedrooms are so close you might as well be sleeping in the same room. Fuck. I can't believe I trusted you all these years, man, and all it took for you to turn your back on me was for me and Piper to take a break for a few days."

"I'd hardly call it a break," I spat back. "You *cheated* on her. You had it made, Travis. Piper adored you. She worshipped you. She showed up to every single one of your shows and even helped out backstage. She was your 'lucky charm' and you gave it all up for a sweaty makeout sesh in the costume closet. Sounds like a *you* problem. Not a *me* problem." The words were out of my body faster than I could stop them, like some kind of religious experience.

Ever since he'd told me about the whole ordeal with Carolyn, he talked about it like it was some kind of thing to gloat about. As if it was something to be proud of. Some sort of male rite of passage. I hated it, and holding on to the secret made me sick. In fact, when Piper had asked me just hours ago if I'd known all along, I would have told her if she hadn't figured it out for herself. Because deep down, for very selfish reasons, I wanted Piper to know. For so long I'd cornered her off in some part of my heart as someone who would always be there in my life—an unwavering presence I could feel but never touch. A constant reminder that I loved her fully and that I would have to find some sort of joy in just simply knowing she was near and happy, but never mine.

"I need her, man," he finally said. "I need her backstage with me. Mr. McCoy said she stepped down from the show entirely. But I can't go out there without her waiting in the wings for me."

"It was only a few weeks ago when you were telling me that

you felt like you two were growing apart, and now you suddenly need her?"

He shrugged. "She's my lucky charm."

"Don't you get it, Travis? Piper isn't yours. And people aren't lucky charms. They're just people. With feelings and hearts and their own wants and dreams. Break a leg, dude."

Piper and I didn't have the same lunch period. She had first lunch and I had second lunch with Travis. But today, Travis was nowhere to be found, which was just as well. I'd said what I needed to say.

I sat there with my sloppy joe from the lunch line, because I was too freaked out to leave school and get quizzed by a junior or senior on off-campus lunch about my relationship status. At least here with all the freshmen and sophomores, they were all too intimidated by me to look me in the eye. And I wasn't even a popular jock, but being a burly guy did come with a few privileges.

My phone lit up with a message from Piper.

PIPER "PIPES" BERRY: Hello, boyfriend.

I smiled into my phone, dipping my chin down into my chest so no one could see. Hello, girlfriend, I typed back.

PIPER "PIPES" BERRY: Date night tonight. You drive. I'll pay. Roma Trattoria.

Whoa, I typed back, that place is pretty fancy. We can always just hit up that taco truck you love on Fifth Ave. I like it low-key.

> PIPER "PIPES" BERRY: Boyfriends and girlfriends go to nice restaurants.

Your call, I typed.

> PIPER "PIPES" BERRY: hey... I was thinking we should set some ground rules tho. Just so no one gets hurt.

My heart deflated a little. Sure.

> PIPER "PIPES" BERRY:
> 👫 Rule #1 Physical contact for the sake of PDA only.
> 👫 Rule #2 Kissing on the lips is allowed in public, but NO TONGUE.
> 👫 Rule #3 It's over when I say it's over.

My fingers hovered over the screen for a moment. Rule #3 hardly seemed fair.

> PIPER "PIPES" BERRY: Don't forget. You owe me.

She was right. Maybe I wasn't just as bad as Travis, but keeping the truth from her definitely made me trash on the dirtbag scale. So I simply typed back, Does this place have a dress code?

There was, in fact, a dress code. The kind that meant I had to borrow a tie from Dad. All of his ties were covered in a thin film of dust, but I settled on a solid navy blue one, dark blue jeans, and a lavender button-up shirt Mom got me for Christmas last year.

Piper had called ahead and when we got there, the hostess led us to a candlelit table along the window that overlooked our little downtown of Goodnight, Texas.

"I've never even been to this place," I whispered as the hostess held the menu out for me to take, which was bound in leather and heavy enough that I misjudged its weight at first and nearly dropped it.

Piper grinned. "I only ever came here once a year for Travis's meemaw's birthday." She looked over the menu. "I just want literally anything with cheese."

She looked perfect tonight. Piper always did, but tonight she wore a baby-blue dress that fanned out around her waist and made me wish I knew how or had a reason to twirl her around a dance floor. Her hair was pulled up into a bun that was still just a little damp from being washed and she wore cherry-red lip balm. I couldn't help but wonder what it tasted like.

After we placed our orders, I leaned across the table and admitted, "I've actually never been on a date like this before."

She grinned again. "Travis only took me out like this for

birthdays or Valentine's Day." She shrugged. "We're in high school. Who has money for this kind of shit anyway?"

"Speaking of . . . you don't actually have to pay."

She reached down the front of her dress and pulled out a shiny credit card with the name *Parker Berry* printed at the bottom.

"You stole your older brother's credit card?" I asked.

"'Stole' is such a strong word. More like 'momentarily borrowed.' Besides, he still owes me for all those times he raided my piggy bank for gas money when I was in middle school."

"Well, I can get behind that, I guess."

She ripped off a piece of bread and dragged it through the plate of olive oil. "I like the tie."

"It's my dad's. He's not really using his ties much these days."

"I thought he found a new job," she said softly, her voice laced with concern.

I shook my head. "Didn't work out. But he's looking some more. At least, he says so to my mom."

"Something will come up," she said, with such certainty. Her gaze dragged along the window and then over my shoulder to the door. "Oh, oh, oh!" She scooted to the edge of her seat and reached for my hand, her soft fingers intertwining with mine, causing my heart to thrum. "He's here. Make googly eyes at me."

"Uh . . ." I glanced over my shoulder to see Travis, his parents, and his meemaw filing into the restaurant. "You didn't tell me it was Meemaw's birthday!"

"You're his best friend," she said. "You should know!"

"Was!"

"Was? What do you mean, 'was'?"

"We got into a fight," I told her. "I—I didn't like what he did to you, Piper. And I should have spoken up sooner."

Her shoulders sloped down, her whole body softening as her eyes widened and her lips formed a soft "Oh."

She leaned forward with her elbows on the table, and I felt my body move to meet her in the middle until the two of us were just barely sitting out of our chairs and hovering above the tiny circle table. The candle flame flickered beneath us as the shadow danced along her lips. She closed her eyes and I followed her lead. And then it happened.

Her lips pressed against mine, and I had to beg my brain to remember Rule #2. The feeling of her lips melting into mine was electric, and her cherry lip balm tasted like the rose tea my grandma used to drink.

"Piper? Is that—is that you, Gabe?"

We both dropped back into our seats to find Mrs. Fletcher, Travis's mom, lingering at our table as Mr. Fletcher and Meemaw had gone on to their table and Travis drifted somewhere in between the two parties, looking back at us with nostrils flared.

But Piper's eyes were on me, her cheeks flushed and her lips slightly parted as though something had just stunned her. It took just a few blinks for her expression to shift as she turned to Travis and his mother. "Hi, Mrs. Fletcher," she said through a wide grin.

"So nice to see you both," Mrs. Fletcher said as her eyes darted from us to Travis.

"Tell Meemaw we said happy birthday," Piper said as she looked over Mrs. Fletcher's shoulder and directly at Travis.

Travis stormed off toward a closed-door dining room at the back of the restaurant and Mrs. Fletcher quickly followed.

"She always hated me," Piper blurted the moment Mrs. Fletcher was out of earshot. She inhaled deeply and then let a long breath out. "Okay, sorry. Back to our date."

"If that's all you came for, we can just go," I said. "No point wasting money on a fake date."

"Psh, no way. This date is sponsored by Parker Berry and we are going to eat like kings, damn it."

PIPER

Gabe and I got into a routine. He picked me up in the mornings and would walk me to first period and, at night, we would both lie in bed with our blinds open as we talked on the phone.

That first night after our date, we talked on the phone to make a plan for the rest of the week, and I guess I just liked having someone to talk to so much that I called him the next night too. And then the next and the next after that until it was Thursday— the night before *Bye Bye Birdie* was set to open.

"Big day tomorrow," Gabe said. "You got your game face ready to go?"

I could hear his sheets rustling. I watched his silhouette as he pulled his blankets up to his chest. "If by 'game face' you mean Travis's favorite dress of mine, then yes."

"Why his favorite dress?"

"You know why," I droned. "I want him to remember what he did to me and what he's missing out on."

"Are you sure that's it?" he asked softly.

"What do you mean? Like, am I trying to get back with him? Hell no."

"So then why not wear *your* favorite dress? Isn't this about you getting the final word?"

I didn't like where this line of questioning was heading. "It's just a dress," I said firmly.

The phone went silent for a moment. "Okay."

And in that moment, I could feel all the things we'd left unsaid for the last week. My mind was doing somersaults trying to keep up since the moment I leaned across that table and kissed him on our so-called date. My heart felt like it had leapfrogged into my throat and then suddenly Travis and his family were there and I had to force myself to remember what I was even doing in the first place and that Gabe was playing along out of the goodness of his heart . . . or the guilt I'd burdened him with.

Since then, I felt the way my body hummed when I saw him and the warmth that spread from the tips of my fingers to the tips of my toes every time we held hands.

"Gabe." The sound of his name was breathy on my lips. "I'm— I'm really thankful to you for doing this for me. It's . . . You're a good friend. I promise when we have our breakup, I'll tell everyone you broke up with me and that you're a great kisser."

"I haven't *really* kissed you, so how would you know what kind of kisser I am?" he asked with a chuckle.

"I can imagine," I said with certainty. "But you just can't go out there giving out sloppy kisses after I tell everyone how wonderful you are."

"I'll do my best to live up to your praise."

I laughed a little, but there was no ignoring the jealousy that bubbled up at the thought of Future Gabe with a Future Mystery Girl. "I bet I could write an excellent letter of recommendation."

He groaned. "College . . ."

"Shh, shh, shh. Don't say it again and definitely don't say it in front of a mirror in a dark room three times."

"The only thing worse than being haunted by your past is being haunted by your future," he said.

"Ow." I clutched my chest, even though I doubt he could see the subtle movement. "That stung."

He yawned into the phone, but didn't say he had to go. He never hung up first, no matter how tired he sounded.

"I better go to bed," I said, finally letting him off the hook. "My dads make breakfast burritos on Fridays. Come over a few minutes early so you can get one."

"Exactly how many minutes? I don't mess around when it comes to breakfast food wrapped in tortillas."

In a small town like Goodnight, every event was an Event with a capital *E*, so the fall musicals always ran for three nights to packed houses. It helped that the theater schedule always coincided with the football team's bye week.

As Gabe and I took our seats in the front row, thanks to two tickets Travis had put aside for me weeks ago, Gabe turned to me and said, "Nice dress."

When I got dressed earlier that evening, I'd laid two options out on the bed. One was a body-hugging black dress that Travis had picked out on one of the few times he'd gone shopping with me, and the other was a burgundy sweaterdress with a U-shaped neckline that always made me feel both comfortable and cute. I couldn't help but hear Gabe's voice ringing in my ears when I picked the burgundy. "Thanks," I said. "It's my favorite."

The lights began to go down, and even though no one could probably see, Gabe's hand drifted over the armrest, searching for my fingers.

I took his hand in mine and pulled his thick arm even closer so I could lean my head there. I'd been with Travis for all of high school, but I had to admit: There had been multiple occasions when I'd seen Gabe across a room and wondered what it might feel like to simply rest against his broad shoulders.

As the stage lights came up, a chill of delight ran up my spine. Travis had always said the audience was a black hole to him and the only reminder that they were there was the sound of their cheers or laughter. But from where I so often stood in the wings, waiting for him, I'd noticed the way the light spilled out into the first few rows, almost inviting those select few audience members to break the fourth wall and become a part of the spectacle. But I'd written it off, assuming that the lights on the stage were much too blinding once you were under them.

But it turned out that Travis could see the audience—at least some of us. Because the moment he entered the stage in full character and costume as Albert Peterson, his eyes briefly scanned the crowd before widening for a moment as he noticed me there curled into his best friend's arm. This was more than a stab in the gut. This was twisting the knife. And it felt good.

Travis rounded the edge of the stage and Gabe pulled back from me just a bit, and it was enough for me to tighten my grip on his hand. We'd kept up this whole charade for an entire week, and by the time we had our very amicable "breakup," I was going to be even more of a wreck. Girl got cheated on by Boy. Girl faked relationship with Boy's Best Friend. Girl started to maybe fall for Boy's Best Friend? There was no script for how to survive this emotional double whammy.

But all I needed from Gabe was tonight. We just had to string this along for one more night, and then he could set things right with him and Travis and he'd be free of me and my messy drama.

Gabe's fingers eased against mine as Travis exited the stage. "This is so weird," he mumbled.

"Yeah, it is a pretty deranged musical."

"You know that's not what I mean."

We were quiet for most of the rest of the first act, and Gabe didn't pull away from me again. He even laughed a few times, and I did too. For a brief moment, I even forgot that I hated Carolyn. It was almost as if we were on a date. A very normal date.

It was the last number before intermission, the reprisal of "Healthy, Normal, American Boy," one of Travis's favorite songs from the show.

"I want you to kiss me," I whispered to Gabe.

He turned to me, his brow furrowed with uncertainty. "What?"

"Kiss me."

His eyes widened as he searched my expression. For a moment, everything felt quiet. There was no musical or audience. Just me and Gabe. I tilted my head back and he crushed his lips against mine.

I sighed against his mouth as he hooked his fingers around the side of my neck and his thumb brushed up and down the length of my jaw. Persistently, my lips opened against his as I slid my tongue in his mouth. Everything stood still for a brief second before Gabe pulled me closer to him as his tongue moved against mine, sending chills through my body. When all this was said and done, there would be no lies coming out of my mouth when I talked about what a great kisser Gabe Rafferty was. All I wanted was to feel this kiss with my whole body. I wanted to rip the auditorium armrest out from between the two of us, so I could press myself against him. It felt urgent. It felt necessary. It felt—

A loud crash broke us apart, and we came up for air just in time to see Travis tumbling off the stage and into the orchestra pit. Behind him, Carolyn let out a piercing scream.

Oh. My. God. My first inclination was to run toward the pit and check on him, but in a matter of seconds the music came to a screeching halt and the auditorium went dark.

All around us, stagehands fumbled to navigate this unrehearsed catastrophe as the audience rumbled with whispers. Soon the orchestra began to play intermission music and the lights came up.

I clapped a hand over my mouth to stifle my laughter. "Oh my God, Gabe, did you see that?"

But when I turned to Gabe, he was already standing up, his shoulders pushed back and stiff. "I'm leaving," he said as he maneuvered through the crowd and up the aisle.

"Wait," I called as I tried to keep an eye on his unmistakable head of chestnut-brown hair.

He couldn't leave. We hadn't broken up. I wasn't ready.

"Excuse me, excuse me," I said to anyone in my path until I broke free into the lobby and out the front doors.

He was walking too fast. His legs were too long or maybe he'd just magically made the crowd part for him. "Gabe!" I yelled. "Gabe!"

Finally, with his hand on the door handle of his truck, he stopped and turned to me.

I ran to him, my cowboy boots splashing through puddles. "You can't just leave."

"I can and I am," he said, leaving little room for argument.

But where there was a Berry, there was a way. "It's not our fault he fell." I reached for his arm, but he took a half step back. Okay, I could see the boyfriend act was totally over now. That stung.

"It's not just that. I mean, that was awful and I'll probably feel shitty about it for the rest of my life, but you—you broke one of your own rules, Piper."

"Wha—" It dawned on me. "No tongue? This is about no tongue?" My nostrils flared as my temper got the better of me. "I'm sorry, okay? I'm sorry you find me so disgusting that I forgot about the rules for half a second and kissed you with a little tongue. I'm sorry that was so awful for you."

He rushed forward then, closing the short gap between us. "Don't you get it, Piper? Don't you see what's happening here? What's been happening since the day I met you? I'm in love with you, Piper Berry, and it's the kind of curse I'll have to live with for the rest of my life, which was fine. It was fine! I'd gotten used to being your friend and seeing you in love with Travis . . . it was enough. But this last week has been *heaven*, Piper."

My heart swelled against my rib cage and my throat was thick with all the things I didn't know how to say. He *loved* me? Gabe Rafferty *loved* me? "Gabe . . ." All I could manage was his name.

He shook his head and pursed his lips. Everything about his expression and the way he held himself was painful. "Please, don't. Please don't say you're sorry or that you don't have feelings for me. I know it's true, but that doesn't mean I have to hear it, okay? I thought I could survive this week and being some kind of chess piece between you and Travis, but it's gone too far. Besides, you got what you wanted. Travis humiliated himself. You got him where it hurts. And now it's done."

He didn't wait for me to respond, and honestly, I didn't know what to say. Gabe shook his head and got into his truck. "And just so you know, that ridiculous stuffed animal Travis gave you in fourth grade is a monkey, not an ape. So the awful joke doesn't even work." He sighed heavily as he started his ignition. "Goodbye, Piper Berry."

I watched the rest of the show from the last row as sadness and disappointment hit me in waves. Gabe had been in love with me since we were kids. How could I have missed it? Our jokes always synced up (to the annoyance of everyone else). He always gave me these apologetic looks any time Travis and I were fighting. He always waved from his room when both of our blinds happened to be open. He checked in on me when I paced my room angrily or was crying so hard he could hear me.

In the second act, Travis appeared to make a full recovery onstage as though nothing had happened, and I couldn't decide if that made things better or worse.

I knew I was getting into dangerous territory with my own

feelings. I knew I'd never look at Gabe the same way again, but I hadn't once stopped to think what this would mean for him. Sure, he and Travis would resolve things. Maybe even bond over their shared history with me.

But I never meant to hurt Gabe. I never meant to toy with him. And yet, it didn't matter what I meant to do. It only mattered what I did.

After the final ovation, the lights of the auditorium lifted, and I slowly made my way through the crowd to the parking lot. I'd texted my dads to see if one of them could pick me up after their double date with Mr. and Mrs. Gupta, but I hadn't heard back. That was fine. I could walk and be even more alone with my guilt. I deserved that.

"Piper!" a voice called behind me.

I turned, hoping for Gabe even though I knew better.

Travis, still partially in costume, sprinted out of the stage door exit toward me.

Even though I wanted to hurl a million insults at him, the only thing I could manage to say was, "Mr. McCoy's going to kill you for not getting out of costume first." The theater teacher was a real stickler for his rules and preserving the magic of the stage was first and foremost, so all actors had to be out of costume before they ventured out from backstage after a show.

"I don't care," he said breathlessly as he drew closer. "Piper, you have to know how sorry I am. Me and Carolyn . . . it was a huge mistake, and I know you're with Gabe, which I don't even understand. It makes no sense to me. But I would do anything to have you back and to put all this behind us. I don't know who I am without you."

And there it was. The apology I'd been waiting for. The whimpering. The begging. But nothing about it satisfied me. This wasn't who or what I wanted. I knew that now.

"I forgive you," I finally said. "But I don't want you back. Not even a little bit." I held a hand to my mouth, as if I could somehow erase the words. But there it was. I didn't want Travis back and I think maybe I never did.

"Oh," he said, surprised. Maybe he expected for me to tear into him, or maybe his ego was so bloated that he expected me to take him back, but whatever Travis thought I would say, that wasn't it.

"Just because we were together for so long doesn't mean that what we had was working, Travis. You were kissing other people. That's not exactly a good sign."

He nodded uncertainly. "I . . . I could feel things changing, but I thought we would make it until graduation, at least . . ."

"I don't regret what we had," I said softly. "But we can't go back. There's nothing left to go back to."

He thought about that for a moment, and then nodded. "I suppose this is all for the best in some weird way."

"I better go," I told him as I turned back toward the street. "Better start figuring out who you want to be without me, Trav. Don't worry. You've got time."

"Piper?" he said, calling my name one last time.

"Yeah?"

"Would you mind skipping the next two shows?"

GABE

I spent the rest of the weekend with my blinds drawn and my cell phone off. Travis. Piper. Whoever. I didn't want to hear from them. By Sunday morning, I was starting to freak out my mom. She didn't say so, but I could tell. I think I reminded her a little too much of my dad and the funk he'd been in since his losing his job back in January.

Which is why I guess it wasn't such a huge surprise when she called down the hallway to my room on Sunday night, "Visitor incoming!"

I braced myself as the door creaked open and let out a quiet sigh as Travis stepped inside.

"What are you doing here? Shouldn't you be at the cast party?" I asked with a growl, not moving from my desk and the huge queue of YouTube videos I'd been burning through. (I was currently on a lake scuba-diving kick where this guy just filmed himself diving and finding weird stuff. It was as anticlimactic as it sounded. Perfect depressive episode entertainment, seeing as my life felt as murky and awful as the bottom of the lake where he'd just found an old iPhone.)

"Checking on my best bud," Travis said. He still had little bits of makeup caked to his skin, including eyeliner, which always took him days to fully remove. "Besides, the cast party starts when I say it starts." He paused for me to laugh, but I didn't, because it wasn't funny. "I heard that . . . uh, things went south with Pipes."

I shrugged. "It was never real to begin with. Just a big show to make you jealous."

"It worked," he said with a snort.

"A little too well," I muttered. "I'm sorry. It was a shitty thing to do."

"Asking you to lie for me was also a shitty thing to do."

"Yeah. Can't say you're wrong about that."

He sat down at the edge of my bed. "I guess I should thank you, in a way. The last two shows were great. I guess the lucky-charm thing wasn't real. It helped that Piper didn't make out with someone in the front row."

"How thoughtful of her."

"You're pretty hung up on her, huh?" he asked.

I shook my head. "Just a bad situation."

"Really? Because it looks to me like you caught feelings."

"I didn't catch feelings," I told him. "They were always there."

"I know," he said in that asshole, smartest-person-in-the-room voice.

"You knew?" I turned fully to face him. "You knew I liked her and you didn't care?"

He shook his head. "I couldn't change the way you felt about her, but I knew you wouldn't try to swoop in and steal her."

"Why?" I asked. "Because your fat best friend could never steal your girl?"

"No. Because my fat best friend didn't think he could, but I saw Piper on Friday after the show. You're in her head, Gabe." He paused for a moment as he stood up and began to pace. "Listen, this is some weird territory for us, okay? I'm not trying to set you up with my ex-girlfriend or something, but what I am going to say is that you gotta see yourself how I see you, man. You're funny. You're not bad looking. You're fat, but who cares? That's not even a bad thing, and I hate when you act like it is. Maybe all those years ago, Piper would have gone for you instead of me if you'd just had a little faith in yourself."

I wanted to bite back and tell him he was wrong. It was more than that. But I thought about that silly stuffed monkey more than I cared to admit, and I couldn't help but wonder what might be different if I'd been the one to give her a valentine that hardly made sense.

"Maybe you should put yourself out there," Travis said. "You can't get the role you don't audition for."

I grinned at his cheeseball line. "Alright, enough with the inspirational drama department bullshit. Go to your party. I'll see you tomorrow."

"We're cool?" Travis asked.

"We're cool," I said. "But don't be a dick again."

I rolled over, pulling blankets with me as a sharp thud hit my window. It almost sounded like hail. I drifted back to sleep, and then I heard another sharp thud.

Rolling over, I checked the time on my phone. Six minutes after three in the morning. I'd only just fallen asleep, but it was enough for my head to feel groggy and my eyes to feel crusty.

After a third thud, I sat up in my bed and rubbed my eyes before putting on a pair of shorts.

I pulled up my blinds to find a human-size squirrel standing there in the narrow space between our two houses. Was I high? Or worse, dead? With a grunt, I opened my window.

"I don't know what you want or who you are," I said, "but my mom's dog is tiny yet vicious and has been known to eat squirrels."

The giant squirrel gripped its head and pulled it off. "I'm not scared of Ziggy, and most of the squirrels on our street are bigger than him," Piper said as she tucked the squirrel head under her arm.

"What the hell are you doing outside my room dressed like a squirrel?" I asked, even though what I really wanted was to dig a hole and hibernate in it until Piper went away to college so I would never have to see her again after confessing my love for her. And it was all because I couldn't handle a little bit of tongue.

"I'm throwing nuts at your window," she said, opening one hand to reveal a fistful of acorns. "Like a maniacal squirrel."

"Oh okay, well, that sounds perfectly sane," I said, my heart silently skipping at the callback to that night a little over a week ago when she first woke me up in the middle of the night to hatch her plan.

"Gabe, I'm sorry. I'm so sorry. This whole thing started out for the wrong reason, but at some point last week, it just started to feel . . . right. *We* felt right."

My anger melted away so quickly at the sight of her. Especially in that damn squirrel suit. "I shouldn't have agreed to it in the first place," I admitted. "It was a bad idea."

"That's fair."

"And I knew it would go too far . . . in more ways than one."

"It was petty of me," she said. "I wanted Travis to feel pain like I had . . . but I never meant to hurt you. In fact, I was trying to figure out how I could possibly get over both of you. With

Travis, it was easier. I was angry. But with you, Gabe . . . I wake up every morning and see you. The last two mornings with your blinds shut . . . And I could barely fall asleep without our nightly phone calls."

"I missed those too," I said quietly.

"Gabe, you . . . you said you love me, and I can't stop hearing it over and over again in my head. I can't walk away from this without knowing what's between us. I can't. Please give me another chance. I want you to be mine. I want you for real." She held up a paw, dropping her acorns to the ground. "Squirrel Scout's honor."

I leaned over the sill of my window into the damp nighttime air. "Where the hell did you get that costume?"

"Rented it," she said with a shrug as she eyed the head tucked under her arm. "It's pretty impressive for a last-minute find. All thanks to Parker Berry's credit card."

"Piper." Her name came out like a laugh, and it felt like cold water on a sore throat. "You have got to stop stealing your brother's credit card to finance our relationship. That's called identity theft."

"Our relationship?" she asked, the glee in her voice rising with each syllable.

"Identity theft," I said again.

She tilted her head skeptically. "It can't actually be identity theft if you share DNA with the person, though, right? Then it's only partial identity theft."

"My girlfriend is a criminal."

"Your girlfriend?" she asked as she stood up on her tippy toes, bringing us so close that our lips nearly brushed.

"Only if you keep the costume," I said. "The costume makes it."

"That can be arranged," she said as she pressed her lips to mine. Wasting no time, I parted my lips against hers, our tongues meeting. I'd dreamed of this exact moment so many times. Kissing Piper Berry good night and good morning in this little sliver of space between our two houses, the moment was just as perfect and heart stopping as I always knew it would be.

"I guess we should go to bed," I finally said with a groan.

Her nose nuzzled into mine. "Are you giving me a ride in the morning?"

"Only if you wear the squirrel costume."

"Oh, really? Would you say you'd give it an ape out of ten?"

My nostrils flared as I tried to look annoyed, but all that came out was a deeply embarrassing snort-laugh. "You're on pun probation."

"Hmmm, I do have the costume for a full forty-eight hours," she said as she smiled into my lips. "I needed it for my backup plan in case you didn't forgive me."

"Do I want to know what the backup plan consisted of?"

"Way more credit card charges."

"I'm going to have to save you from a life of crime, aren't I?"

"You can try," she said with a laugh. "Good night, Gabe Rafferty."

"Bye bye, Piper Berry."

ANYONE ELSE BUT YOU
(Stranded Together)

LEAH JOHNSON

DATE: FRIDAY, MAY 12, 8:45 P.M.
Location: Party Palace Superstore Wholesale Warehouse Parking Lot
Hour: 1

9 don't expect much out of Jada Baxter, I really don't.

But I thought that maybe, this once, she would do the bare minimum and actually live up to the duty the class copresident title entails. Because this is *Senior Send-Off*.

It's the biggest event senior class officers put on every year. The night before graduation, Ardsley throws a huge party for the entire class. One last hurrah before walking across the stage and leaving this place behind for good. We've been planning for months. Picking up some party supplies for the table-toppers, trinkets for the photo booth, and renting the pump for the balloons we'll drop at midnight tomorrow is the last step.

I look down at my watch again, hoping that I won't see what

I know I'm going to see. We have fifteen minutes until the Party Palace closes, and my copresident is nowhere to be found with our student accounts credit card and tax-exempt forms. I knew I shouldn't have let Jada convince me she could be responsible for, well, anything. I text my best friend, Carmen, a selfie of me rolling my eyes, and she shoots back six skull emojis almost immediately. Jada's chronic lateness has killed us both.

I check my watch one more time, and huff out a laugh when another text appears saying, the princess strikes again, along with a GIF from Real Housewives. I've never related more to a famous-for-snark, millionaire reality queen than I do right now.

But when it starts sprinkling, the warm summer rain dotting my green-and-white Ardsley Academy Key Club T-shirt, that's when my low-simmering annoyance explodes into full-blown indignance. I march inside to avoid the rain, and instead of slowing down to allow myself to be greeted at the door by one of the employees, I slink straight to the back in hopes of finding a restroom to get dry.

There's no way we'll have enough time to collect everything we need now, so the least I can do is be dry and angry instead of soggy and angry. There's something deeply undignified about being pissed off while resembling a Labrador retriever who got carried away playing in a puddle.

The Party Palace is massive—dozens upon dozens of rows of cheap, themed junk for all of your party needs as far as the eye can see—so it takes me a while to find the employee restroom in the back. I dry myself off quickly with the rough paper towel, and check my face in the mirror. Same plain dark brown eyes.

Same puff with the same baby hairs. Same diamond studs in each ear I've been wearing every day since the ninth grade. I sigh. Nothing spectacular to see here, folks.

When I open the door, I practically jump out of my skin when I see Jada leaning against the opposite wall.

"Jesus! Where did you even come from?"

Jada smiles, and as usual, it lights up her entire face. She's wet from the rain outside, her loose curls a little frizzy from the humidity, but even her flyaways frame her cheeks in a cute way. Her perfection is unbearable.

"You didn't answer your phone." She waves her pink Otter-Box case in the air. "I tried to tell you I was pulling into the parking lot, but you should get inside before they do the whole 'Sorry, we're closed' thing and then neither of us can get in."

I look down at my phone and realize that I have zero bars visible. Stupid Sprint.

"I don't have a signal in here! And what 'Sorry, we're closed' thing? The thing where there's a *closing time* and employees expect you to *respect it* because their time is valuable and you're *stomping all over it*?"

My voice is pitching higher and higher as I speak and I would be embarrassed except for the fact that Jada is the absolute worst, okay? And somehow, I'm always the person on the receiving end of her terrible habits.

She waves her hand around like she's shooing an annoying fly away from her general vicinity.

"I just mean that sometimes, if you come in right before closing, they get snippy about letting you in. And I know how you are so—"

"What do you mean, 'you know how I am'? You don't know anything about me—"

"You're always so blah, blah, '*Be on time,*' blah, blah, '*Let me check my watch*'—"

"Oh, so that's what I sound like, huh? Real nice, Jada—"

"Why do you take everything so personally? It's like you want to live your life in a perpetual state of clenched butt cheeks—"

We're talking over each other, and Jada is rolling her eyes while I'm throwing my hands up in the air and she's pointing her pale blue manicured finger at her own chest and I'm tapping my foot on the ground and the walls shake with thunder from the storm that's picked up outside and then everything goes black.

Not right away, which is how I know it's not a power outage. Aisle by aisle, the lights flicker off until we're left in relative darkness. Only the auxiliary lights above illuminate the long, runway-like row we're currently standing in. Jada turns to me, eyes wide, and I look down at my watch. It's 9:02. The store is officially closed.

And we're still inside of it.

Here's what you need to know about Jada Baxter: She's never been on time to anything in her entire life.

She told a story during a "Who Are You?" essay presentation in fifth grade that they had to induce her mom's labor because Jada still hadn't decided to make her way into the world a week after her projected due date. And in seventh, when we were scheduled to visit the polar bear exhibit at the Indianapolis Zoo—on

the morning they were expected to emerge from hibernation—
she held us up by an hour because she showed up to the buses
late, and we completely missed them waking up.

Most of the time, she'll appear with a wide smile and some
gifts or flattery that sets whomever she's inconvenienced at ease.
But she doesn't even try it with me. She must already know
I can't be swayed by her ridiculously symmetrical face and a
throwaway compliment about my shoes or whatever. Not that
Jada would compliment my shoes, obviously; they're just regu-
lar old low-top Chucks, but still.

Which is why I know better than to assume any of the respon-
sibility for us being trapped inside of the Party Palace Superstore
Wholesale Warehouse after hours. This is 100 percent her fault.

"Jada."

She's pulled the student account credit card out of her pocket
and is trying to finesse the lock on the front door. But I know
it's no use. The employees locked this place up from the outside,
and even if we were able to get past the door, we'd still have to
find a way to defeat that Final Boss: the sliding gate. They've got
this place locked down like it holds national security secrets of
the highest order, and not just an unseemly collection of expired
hard candies and *Sesame Street* piñatas. We're well and truly
stuck.

"Give it up," I say, checking my phone again, hoping for a
signal. I lean my head against the glass and sigh so hard it fogs
it up. I was supposed to be home by now watching *iCarly* reruns
and eating junk food on the couch while my parents were away.
This is so far from fair. "We're going to have to call someone to
come and do this the old-fashioned way."

The thunder claps outside, and this time it's loud enough that the walls shake a little on impact. I walk over to the corded phone plugged in behind the counter, and Jada starts clicking around on the computer behind one of the registers. But I don't even get a dial tone when I pick up the receiver.

"This relic doesn't even work."

Jada sighs. "The Wi-Fi is down too."

"Must be the storm," I groan out.

I'm struck with the idea to run to the back of the cavernous warehouse in hopes that maybe I can find a spare set of keys in the manager's office, but even that door is locked. By the time I make it back to the front, Jada is leaning against the counter, scrolling on her phone.

"I thought of something—we could just call the police! Emergency calls work even without a signal."

I roll my eyes. "Don't you read the news? Do you have any idea what's going to happen when they spot two Black girls just casually hanging out inside of a locked store? No thanks."

"Okaaaaayyyyy." She drags the word out so it's three times as long as it should be. She perks up immediately. Her brown-green eyes literally *sparkle*. "But isn't this kind of cool? I mean, you had to have had that fantasy as a kid of what you might do if you got stuck in, like, a Walmart after hours, right?"

"No, actually." I press my hands over my eyes. She's just so . . . glass half full. "Like most normal children, getting marooned on a deserted big-box-store island didn't top my list of dream scenarios."

"Has anyone ever told you that you have a distinct habit of

sucking the fun out of a situation? Because you do." She honest-to-God pouts. "You're a world-class fun-sucker."

"Real mature, Baxter." I look around and try to come up with other solutions, but short of breaking down the door and risking at the very least a misdemeanor charge and getting my college admittance rescinded, I've got nothing. No phones, no internet, no keys. Just me, Jada, and the unholy weight of eight years of mutual resentment festering between us. It's my worst nightmare come to life.

We're stranded together until morning.

TIME: 11:45 P.M.
Hour: 3

We've only been stuck in the Party Palace for three hours, and I'm already beginning to feel like a caged animal. I'm pacing back in front of the front doors like one of those bears from our seventh-grade field trip to the zoo, and honestly, I'm even managing to freak myself out.

I don't do well without structure. It's why I'm so rigid about keeping the time. Control is how I've managed to keep my sanity in this too-small city and my cliché-to-the-point-of-tragic school. Control has kept me safe. I'm not built for this type of scenario. Not the way Jada is, apparently, evidenced by her casual lounging on the counter next to the register, playing some sudoku game on her phone that doesn't require Wi-Fi or a signal.

It's like when we had to come up with a presentation to request more money for the Senior Send-Off from the student funding board a few months ago. Jada was perfectly content to let me stress about the plan by myself, while she just waltzed into the meeting with the board five minutes late, charmed their pants off, and went back to rehearsal for the spring play. Everything is so easy for her. Including facing down a night inside of a warehouse party store in a storm with no cell service or internet to get us out.

"So . . . you know where you're going yet?" I decide to try to make conversation. It's a pretty dumb question, all things considered. I mean, graduation is in less than forty-eight hours at this point. Even the biggest slackers in our class knew where they were going a month ago, including most of Jada's circle.

"IU, I bet," I continue. I lean on my hands and let my head flop back so I'm staring at the ceiling. "You guys *love* IU."

When you grow up going to a private school that spans from kindergarten to high school, you know way more about your classmates than is reasonable. You know who peed their pants during that one tornado drill in first grade; whose parents got divorced after a dramatic fight in the parking lot after a PTA meeting; who ate glue way later than they should have.

So, I know Jada Baxter. We've been linked by last name—Barnes and Baxter—since the day she showed up at Ardsley in fourth grade. At nine, she was already more charismatic than anyone I'd ever met. She was the first to raise her hand to volunteer to run attendance down to the office, affable and kind to even the most withdrawn kids, and just plain excited to be at school. And everyone else was excited to have her there.

But the two of us never quite meshed. Even though she was always Miss Congeniality, we didn't play together at recess or choose each other for partners during science class. I watched as she floated from group to group, making friends with everyone like the social butterfly she is, but she never made her way over to me. Which was for the best. Definitely.

Jada represents everything about this place I don't understand and am not interested in figuring out.

"'You guys,' hm?" She pockets her phone and hops down off the counter. "You make me laugh sometimes, Perry, you know that?"

"Huh?" She strides toward the back of the store, so I do too. I practically trip over my feet trying to keep up with her. "What's funny about me?"

She steps into an aisle that's lined on both sides with party favors, all arranged by color. Red napkins and tablecloths and plasticware neatly positioned next to green napkins and tablecloths and more plasticware. On and on until the entire rainbow has been completed. There are even feather boas in every shade.

Jada picks up a green-and-gold Saint Patty's Day hat and tries it on.

"Have you ever considered that maybe you're not the only one who wants out of here?"

I don't know if she knows where I'm going to school, but she has no idea what she's talking about. Whatever she's interested in getting away from is nothing like what I'm trying to escape.

I didn't even want to be class president. I ran because I knew how good it would look on college applications, and that I could probably manage to convince a generous section of the student body to vote for me if I promised actionable items like a bigger, more Instagrammable Senior Send-Off than ever before. I've never been all that interested in school spirit and all it entails.

That sort of thing—the face-painting and the pep-rallying and the bake sales to raise money for new baseball uniforms—falls directly under the purview of Jada and her ilk. Jada is the first one to cut her gym shirt into a crop top and pull on a pair of knee-high socks to cheer the boys' basketball team on at State, or throw herself into the running for Winter Ball court, even though it's less glamourous than prom or homecoming but somehow even harder to win. She loves the limelight, and she genuinely loves our school.

When I'm a college freshman in a few months, I'll be going to parties, getting swallowed up by the city that never sleeps, and only thinking about Ardsley in the romantic way every alum thinks of their high school experience: *Oh, I was so young and foolish then! If only I knew at eighteen what I know now!* And that's just one more reason why the Venn diagram of Jada plus Perry has always been two separate circles. She'll fit wherever she goes, meanwhile all I can do is run.

I'm not just going to New York because I visited NYU once on a family trip to the city and I fell in love with everything about it. Sure, the heartbeat of the drummers in Washington Square Park, and that crappy one-dollar pizza you can get around any corner are great. But it was also because even though I'm not from some hick town in the middle of nowhere, I'm still from Indiana.

And if my anecdotal research has taught me anything, it's that this isn't the place to be a gay Black girl. So, nobody knows.

Not my parents. Not my best friend. And I intend to keep it that way until I'm far enough away that it won't matter. It's not the most original plan, but it's the best one I have. Me and Jada couldn't be more different.

But still, I can tell when I'm being reprimanded, so I try to change course.

"So where are you going, then?" I ask, a little chastened. "I just figured you'd be heading to Bloomington with the rest of your friends."

Instead of responding, she runs her hand over one of the racks of feathered boas and pulls down a rainbow-hued monstrosity to wrap around her neck. She flips one end over her shoulder with such flair that on anyone else I'd be tempted to laugh. But it's Jada, and I never know quite what to do around her, so I default to my usual defense mechanism: annoyance.

"Or don't answer; that's cool too."

She looks at me through her lashes, the corners of her lips ticked up in a smile. For some reason, that knocks me off my game even more. I cross my arms over my chest.

"Everything always has to be the way you want it." Her voice is almost amused. She grabs another boa, a lime-green one this time, and winds it around her waist twice before tying it in front like a belt. "Perry says it, so it must be law."

"What?" Is she seriously insulting me right now? After she's the reason why we're in this mess to begin with? "I don't think that at all."

"Yes, you do." She practically hums. "Perry Barnes, the girl with all the answers."

She walks around me to pluck another boa from the rack,

this time in hot pink, to twirl from her wrist to her shoulder. She does the same with a bright blue one on her other arm.

"National Merit Scholar. Key Club treasurer. Future NYU freshman." She rattles off my achievements like they're dominoes she's setting up to knock down. It feels like a rock is settling in my stomach at the sheer visibility of it. My face must betray my shock at the fact she knows all of those things—any of those things—about me, because her smile shifts from sharp to something softer as she meets my eyes. "You want to know why you don't like me, Perry?"

I swallow. I focus on a spot on the carpet so I don't have to look at her while she tells me that I'm jealous. That I spent too many years with my face in a book and my nose turned up in the air at everything and everyone. I'm afraid she's going to be honest with me, and the thought makes me want to evaporate where I stand. But she doesn't say any of that.

"I'm the one thing you can't quite make sense of."

She pulls the boa from around her neck and drapes it around mine. She stands there holding both ends for a moment without pulling away. My heartbeat is so loud I'm convinced she must be able to hear it. I want to move away but I can't bear the thought of trying. She flips one end over my shoulder like she'd done for herself just a few minutes ago, and turns to walk down the aisle.

I look down at the rainbow boa, and get so lost in it that I barely hear her as she drops one last match on my internal kindling.

"The one thing besides yourself."

TIME: 1:05 A.M.
Hour: 5

Without making any formal declarations, after the boa incident—
what I've taken to calling it in my head—the two of us seem to
retreat to our separate corners of the store. I've been slumped
against the luau section with a tiki torch digging into my back for
the past thirty minutes before the silence begins to be too much.

I try taking a nap, but I can't shut my brain off enough to
sleep. All I can think about is what Jada said before, about what
she might have meant, and what that could mean and—

I take a breath. I try to remember what Carmen always says
about not being able to control everything. I mean, she'd probably quote the *Lion King* musical at me or something, but I
know the best course of action is to do something productive.
Something mature.

I find Jada in the back of the store after wandering through
the aisles for about five minutes. She's blowing bubbles while
humming the tune to a song I've heard on the radio before but
can't remember the name of. I clear my throat but she doesn't
look up. She just keeps blowing bubbles and humming.

"Jada, I really don't want to fight with you. I shouldn't have
made all those assumptions about you, okay?" I'm unused to
the sensation of apologizing, because I'm usually pretty good
about keeping a cool head. Except when it comes to Jada. And
I'm big enough to acknowledge that. "I'm sorry."

"You have a funny way of showing you don't want to fight. It
seems like all you've ever wanted to do is get me to be as mean
to you as you are to me."

She looks up at me then, and her frown makes me feel like the biggest asshole in the world. I don't know how to explain it. That it's her, but it's not her at the same time. That something about her reveals something about me that I don't like. But it only really makes sense in my head.

"You've never liked me, I get it." She straightens her back and shrugs. She blows some bubbles up in my direction, and I try to resist the urge to start popping them right then and there. "How about we just call a truce until we get out of here?"

She sets down the bubbles, pushes herself to standing, and dusts off her leggings. She looks like she just came from working out: ratty T-shirt, leggings, sneakers. And somehow still model-flawless. She's so close to me I can see the little flecks of gold in her eyes. I realize I've been staring at her too long and my face heats up. Luckily, she gives me an out. She nudges my shoulder.

"You know what? I bet they have music in here somewhere."

She marches up to the front of the store and I follow. She hops over the counter easily and kneels down until she finds what she's looking for. "Aha!"

"What do you think your parents are thinking right now?" I ask, leaning my elbows against the register. I feel like I've finally gotten some sense of language back, and I wonder how Jada is going to explain this to her parents—how she could possibly keep them from sending out a search party when she doesn't come home tonight. "About you being gone?"

"Nobody knows I'm here." Jada fiddles with the controls until the speakers crackle above us. She finds a CD case full of unmarked discs and slides one out before pressing a button to pop it into the player. "My mom isn't around and my dad travels for work pretty much nonstop." She shrugs. "An empty house doesn't call to check in."

She says it so matter-of-factly that I don't know how I didn't have this tidbit of information about her tucked away already. I want to ask her how that feels, if she's okay, if she ever gets lonely, but music cuts through the air almost immediately, and she claps wildly in celebration. Whatever moment we might have been heading to is derailed. She shakes her hips a little as she jogs around the counter toward me.

"This is the perfect montage soundtrack music. Let's go!"

Jada grabs my hand and pulls me to the costume aisle and starts pulling whatever looks silly or fun or adorable off the rack and shoving it into my hands. She snorts as the stack of cheaply constructed clothes are almost toppled by an adult-sized taco shell. Jada's enthusiasm is contagious. I can't help but laugh as she poses in a Jessie from *Toy Story* costume.

And just like that, it's like once the crappy nineties music starts blaring out over the store, a switch is flipped between us. We don't have to be enemies, or rivals, or the popular girl and the nerd or whatever it is we are outside the confines of this building. We can be pirates or doctors or giant foods. But we can also, maybe, for a little while, be friends.

"You know we've gotta pay for all of this stuff, right?" I fall over as I try to squeeze a leg into Buzz Lightyear's space suit. Jada saunters over in the bright yellow chaps on top of her leggings and pushes me so I have to hop on one foot to regain my balance. We're both breathless with the childishness of it all. "We're the worst copresidents ever."

I'm talking about the money we're throwing away on opening

these costumes, but also not, and I hope Jada gets it. That I'm sorry for spending a year at her throat, and eight years before that resenting her. That I know one night doesn't change everything, but I hope it's at least a start. She waves a hand around, that same wave she always does that signifies water under the bridge, and I smile even wider. It means a lot to me, suddenly, that the two of us leave high school on good terms.

"Oh my God, I love this song!" Jada practically squeals as the song over the intercom switches. I've never heard the soft-voiced lead singer crooning over a light guitar riff before, but that doesn't seem to stop Jada.

She drops the red cowgirl hat that would complete her Jessie costume on the floor and rushes over to where I'm still struggling to pull the space helmet over my puff. She tugs the helmet off my head completely, and when I try to argue she just smiles.

"Dance with me," she says, placing both of her hands on my waist and pulling me close. She giggles as I flail my arms, unco-ordinated, before I wrap them around her neck. "This is in— Haven't you ever seen *How to Lose a Guy in Ten Days*? Matthew McConaughey was, like, still average hot in that movie before he became, you know, Zaddy hot."

I don't have any opinion on Matthew McConaughey's various stages of hotness, and I'm pretty sure I've only seen like ten minutes of the movie she's talking about anyway. All I can think about is how warm her hands are through the thin fabric of my T-shirt, and how it feels to be this close to her. I've never danced with anyone before, at least not like this, and especially not someone like Jada.

Someone smart without being boastful about it. Someone with soft curves and even softer skin.

"So, I didn't see you at prom," she says softly. It feels like she's throwing me a life jacket, and I try to grab ahold of it with both hands.

"Yeah." I am swallowing, trying to keep my mouth from feeling so dry, but it's not working. "It didn't really feel like my scene." I shake my head. "Carmen went, though, and reported back."

"Carmen Gilbert, right?" I nod. "She's in my Econ class. A little obsessed with *Dear Evan Hansen*. But mostly cool."

I laugh a little. Yeah, that's Carmen. A cynic with a not-so-secret love of musical theater. A strange contradiction, but my perfect counterpart.

"Are you guys, like . . . a thing?"

My head snaps up quickly. It feels like all the air has been sucked out of the room.

Once, when we were freshmen, I thought I might have a crush on Carmen. I was still trying to figure out all the complicated feelings I was having about other girls that my furious Google searches couldn't answer. But it only took holding her hair back after our first house party and her first Jell-O shots to realize that the love I felt was strictly, immovably, platonic.

But no one knows that. And if I have anything to say about it, no one ever will. I shake my head quickly. "No, she's just— We're just—She's my best friend. That's all."

"Oh, okay. Cool. You guys are always together so I just wondered."

I swear her face relaxes then. I try not to feel insulted by that reaction, that she's only comfortable being this close to me—holding and smiling and cracking jokes with me—as long as she knows I'm not queer. She wouldn't be the first person to feel that way, obviously. But for some reason it smarts more than usual this time.

I untangle myself from her and take a step back as the song switches to the next. I smooth down my shirt and try not to shiver as I run my hands over where hers just were. Whatever I felt, whatever I was thinking for a split second when she grabbed me, doesn't matter. None of this does. I have to remember that.

"I'm, um. Going to use the restroom. I'll, uh, see you in a second."

I backtrack away so fast, I almost manage to miss the look of confusion on her face, and the twist in my gut that follows.

Time: 4:15 a.m.
Hour: 8

Ardsley isn't like a lot of Indiana schools. We have a Pride display near the front office in June and everything. But it's still the small stuff that you notice. Like the things girls say in the locker room about anyone they suspect might not be totally, 100 percent straight. As if queer people are predators waiting for a chance to snatch their virtue so you shouldn't change in front of them in the locker room. Or the GOD MAKES NO MISTAKES bumper sticker on the back of the principal's Chevy.

I've learned to just get over it, mostly. But there's stuff I miss—like prom. Stuff I'm going to look back on in ten years and maybe, a little bit, wish I'd experienced like everyone else. I'm thinking about all those missed moments as I lie on a bed made of tablecloth packages with Jada.

After we danced together, I splashed some water on my face and promised myself I would let it go—I wouldn't let a bad moment ruin what was becoming not a total nightmare of a time together. When I came back, we picked up where we'd left off. We danced to NSYNC while draped in Valentine's Day banners; we raced down the Christmas aisle with tiki torches between our legs like witches on broomsticks; we reminisced about Ardsley's greatest hits—all the biggest scandals of our high school careers.

It's nice, thinking about my classmates less like still-life yearbook photos and more like big, colorful, complex people. I wish I'd done more of it over the past twelve years.

"Do you remember when we met?" I ask. I stretch my arms over my head and yawn. I'm in that sweet spot between sleep and waking where nothing feels quite real anymore. It makes it easier for me to bring up the memory that I thought I'd buried a long time ago.

We found mermaid costumes earlier with tails that make for acceptable stand-in sleeping bags, so I settle my legs more securely into mine.

"Yes." She wiggles her way into her tail. "You took one look at me and practically threw up all over my sequin backpack."

I turn on my side to face her and I shake my head. She's misremembering.

"No way, *you* hated *me*. You were always so nice to everyone else, but I don't think we said more than five words to each other that year."

"I never hated you, Perry. You avoided me. If I was playing four-square on the playground, you made sure to play kickball with Carmen. If I asked you to borrow a pencil, you wouldn't even make eye contact as you shoved it at me." She sits up and brings her knees to her chest. "It was obvious that you didn't like me. I wasn't going to keep pushing myself on you."

I'm speechless. That's not the way I've thought about that year all this time. I try to recall all of the instances where I was most convinced Jada had a personal vendetta toward me, and come up short.

Jada has always had an issue with tardiness at meetings, but she's at least done her job as my copresident. She never asked me to make our presentations in front of the student funding board when I was too shy to push for more money for the Senior Send-Off. She nudged me to take my credit in front of the rest of the class officers when I'd come up with a strategy for sustaining our budget from year-to-year instead of claiming it for herself, even though I'd asked her to make the official pitch to them.

I don't know what to make of this moment between us, or the fact that if Jada isn't my enemy, I have to find a new way to categorize her. I know then exactly what new category that is, what I've been trying to ignore for longer than I understood what the feeling even was, and the realization terrifies me.

"I was always paying attention to you, Perry," she whispers, voice impossibly quiet in the huge store.

She cups my cheek with one hand and my heart nearly stops. Everything outside of this moment no longer exists. Everything in my universe is narrowed down to the softness of her palm caressing my face.

"I think you were just too scared of what you might realize if you paid attention back."

DATE: SATURDAY, MAY 13, 7:30 A.M.
Hour: 11

In the light of day, I expect every revelation from the night before to come rushing back in a crush of awkwardness. But in true Jada fashion, Jada is unflappable. When she wakes up just before the employees are set to arrive, she hangs up all the merchandise that can be salvaged, and gets the rest ready to check out. We do our best to erase any trace that we were there all night, and hope that the brief power outage took care of the security cameras. She chatters about how excited she is for the party, and the new skirt she plans to wear that just arrived in the mail two days ago. Everything is overwhelmingly . . . normal.

I try not to be disappointed by that.

We duck behind a huge Earth Day party display and try to blend in with the fake tree, so no one sees us. We sneak to the front once the store officially opens and try to act as casual as possible about the fact that we're here at the crack of dawn, with arms full of random junk. I hand over the student accounts card to pay and force a smile at the girl at the register with a confused expression.

All the while, Jada talks about everything and nothing. I want something more from her than this artificial niceness. I want her to explain why she touched my face like that last night, why she draped that rainbow boa around my neck, why she looked relieved when I told her me and Carmen weren't together. But she doesn't, and I'm too afraid to ask.

We carry all of the party supplies outside and she helps me load them into the back of my mom's van. I check my watch as she deposits the last bag in the trunk and lowers the hatch. We're due at the school in fifteen minutes to set up, but I don't want to go yet. Jada steps away and offers a little wave like she's going to walk to her car and she just—she can't. Not like this.

"Hey," I start. She turns to face me and raises her eyebrows. "Can I ask you something?"

"Anything," she answers.

It's something that's nagged at me for years, but now that I can see Jada more clearly, like the film of antagonism that's layered all of our interactions for all these years is gone, I suddenly have to know.

"How come you're always late?"

She bites her bottom lip before answering, like she's deep in thought.

"You remember the year we went to the zoo?" she finally says. I nod. "My mom had taken off the week before. My dad was such a wreck afterward he hadn't left his room for days. He forgot he was even supposed to take me to school that morning. He forgot I was even *there*." She shakes her head. "But then I got to school, and you know what happened? Everyone was relieved to see me. Everyone was excited I'd finally arrived."

She smiles, almost sadly.

"I guess it's just . . . nice, sometimes, knowing that people have no choice but to notice when you show up." She looks at the store over my shoulder. "Or when you don't."

My heart breaks a little bit, then, and I want to wrap my arms around her. I want to tell her I noticed her in every room we ever shared, and felt her absence when she was gone, even when I told myself I didn't want to.

"See you in a bit?" I ask instead.

"Just don't expect me to be there on time," she says with a light laugh.

The weight of all the things I can't say sits heavy between us, so I don't say anything. I just follow my instincts. I close the space between us, unlatch my watch from my wrist and wrap it around hers. I hold on to her for a beat too long before I finally take a step back. It's not everything, but it's something.

"Later, then."

"Yeah." She looks down at my watch with a faint smile and taps the face once. "Later, Perry."

DATE: SATURDAY, MAY 13, 8:35 P.M.
Location: Ardsley Academy Gymnasium
Hour: 24

"Why do you look like you're one jump-scare away from peeing your pants?"

I do, in fact, jump at the sound of Carmen's voice. And I try, unsuccessfully, to play it off. "What? I'm not! I'm just making sure everything is in place."

I didn't tell Carmen where I was last night, or who I was with. I thought about it this morning as we set up, but it felt like a violation somehow. And it's not like I'd know how to describe it anyway. I mean, nothing happened. Except for a handful of moments where my ridiculous emotions just decided to make themselves unignorable.

Right?

"Ugh, you're such a control freak." Carmen laughs and throws an arm over my shoulder. "Everything is perfect, Madam President." She hip-checks me and smiles. "And guess what? After tonight, you're finally free from Jada's talons. We should be celebrating."

I duck from under her arm. I know she's just joking, and it's a joke we've made a thousand times over the past eight years, but I feel . . . bad about it now. She's not what we thought she was. I'm not who I thought I was, either.

A lot can change in a night. And a lot can be revealed in a night about how maybe we haven't changed that much at all. That somewhere deep down we're all still those kids from fourth grade: scared and a little foolish and just trying to survive each day without embarrassing ourselves in front of our crush. I don't know how to explain that to Carmen, though.

Yesterday, me and her were a duo—two cynics against the world. But nothing feels as simple to me now as it did twenty-four hours ago, thanks to Jada.

Who still isn't here.

The longer I go without seeing her, the more unsure I become. We didn't really talk when she came to set up this morning—we were both putting out fires and helping direct the other officers and the people delivering the bigger attractions—but maybe we should have. Are we back to being essentially enemies? Was last night a brief but incredible blip on the radar of our relationship?

"Where is she?" I mumble and look down at my naked wrist. Of course, Jada still has my watch. I look at Carmen as she clicks away at her phone, Jada already forgotten. "Class officers were supposed to be here five minutes ago."

I can see Vanessa Andrews and Reece Reynolds, our treasurer and secretary, posing in the photo booth by the entrance. Kelly Lewis, our VP, is batting a stray balloon back and forth like a beach ball with our class historian, a constantly giggling Maggie Caletti. Everyone is present and accounted for except for my copresident.

"Well, I wouldn't worry about it." Carmen shrugs. "As usual, she's flaking and you're actually doing your job. One last gift from the princess."

"She's not—" My voice comes out sharper than I intend, and I try to dial it back. "Jada isn't that bad."

She's actually kind and hardworking and more considerate than either of us have ever given her credit for and I might just be in over my head already with how I feel about her, I think.

"Yeah, and Ali Stroker actually deserved to beat out Amber Gray for Best Featured Actress in a Musical in 2019. Be serious."

I don't know what Carmen is talking about, but it's enough

of a distraction to get me to focus on other things that need to be done. I rally the other officers and tell them the plan for the evening: Have fun and be safe. It's our last job of our high school career, so I thank them for their work, and even get a little emotional when Vanessa insists we do a group hug and a selfie.

Before I know it, the DJ has kicked on the music, and our classmates are pouring into the gym. There's a totally appropriate amount of fawning, given the amount of work we put into it. People are even amused by the random Jessie and Buzz costumes, and keep putting them on to jump into the photo booth to smile cheesily at their friends and immortalize the kind of corny, innocent fun that we'll be saying goodbye to soon.

I dance with a group of my friends from Key Club when a One Direction song we all loved in elementary school comes on. I face-plant into the ball pit with Carmen and we laugh so hard our sides hurt. I watch a dance battle between Kevin Kilbourne and Greg Han and cheer them on like we're at the Super Bowl. I kill hours with my classmates, saying goodbye and making some final memories. And it's good. But it's missing something. Some-one.

It's eleven thirty before I know it, only thirty minutes until we drop the balloons and send everyone on their way, and Jada still hasn't shown up. I know she's chronically late, but her absence leaves a knot in my stomach. Even if she were avoiding me, she wouldn't skip Senior Send-Off. There's no way. I finally cave and send her a text.

Where are you? Everyone's wondering about their fav president lol

I don't get a reply until five minutes before midnight:

Meet me in the greenhouse

The lack of an exclamation point is unlike Jada, but so is all of this. I duck out of the gym quickly and wind my way through the halls until I reach the glass enclosure that belongs to the horticulture club. I push open the door and am met with humid air, but also a scene so breathtaking it feels like a page out of one of Carmen's sappy musicals.

I look around the greenhouse and my mouth drops open. The enclosure is lined with fairy lights, wound around the stems of hanging planters and dangling from the roof. I tiptoe closer.

"Jada, what are you—what's going on?"

Jada smiles from where she stands in the middle of the room, surrounded by overgrown vines. She's dressed in a red corduroy miniskirt, a white crop top, and a pair of white high-top Chucks. Her hair is slicked back in a low ponytail, and she has rings on every finger. She's as beautiful now as she was in leggings and a threadbare T-shirt last night, but my mouth still goes dry at the sight of her.

She taps her phone where it's lying on a table near the entrance and the same guitar riff overlaid with the wispy voice from the store last night sings about kisses in bearded barley or something.

"Our first dance didn't end the way I wanted it to." She smiles and holds her hand out to me. "I thought we should try a redo. You wanna?"

She twirls me once, and the whole scene is so strange, so

unexpected, I laugh louder than I can remember laughing in months. Jada wraps an arm around my waist to pull me close and we sway slower than the music calls for, but I don't mind.

"I don't get it." I shake my head. "You did all this instead of going to Senior Send-Off?"

"I've made lots of memories with the rest of our class. I want more of them with you, and I want them right now." She smirks. "I guess I'm a little greedy like that."

"Jada . . ."

She shakes her head.

"Perry, in fourth grade, I didn't avoid talking to you because you were mean to me." She looks serious for the first time since I found her out here and all I can do is nod. "I avoided you because you never raised your hand, even when I saw you had the right answer. Because you always stayed after with our teacher when you needed help with a math problem but were afraid to ask in front of the class."

There's no way. There's no way she was noticing me like I was noticing her, even back then. I am scared to believe that maybe I don't have to run to get what I want—to get this moment with this girl and not have to do it on borrowed time.

"You were so intense and smart and I wanted you to like me, Perry, because I thought you were special. And last night was the first time I thought you actually might." She looks down at the floor and then back up at me. "Was I wrong?"

I shake my head and I can feel the way the smile that's blooming is wide enough to practically split my face in two. But I don't care. This is better than a ball pit or a photo booth or any of the spectacles we've set up in the gym. This is the only way I can imagine saying goodbye to high school now. Here, in this humid greenhouse, listening to an annoying song from a million years ago.

"But we're gonna be late for the balloon drop," I say, because what I'm really feeling is too big to voice.

She smiles but doesn't respond. Instead, she leans forward and my eyes slide closed of their own accord. Her lips meet mine in the gentlest touch, and everything feels like it snaps into place at once. Despite all the chaos that got us here, there is something very right about kissing Jada Baxter. Every one of my senses comes alive under her hands.

When she pulls back, she brings her wrist up in front of her face to check my watch.

"I happen to think we're right on time."

DATE: TUESDAY, SEPTEMBER 5, 2023, 10:59 A.M.
Location: Silver Center for Arts & Science, New York University
Hour: 2,774

I tap my foot on the ground and sigh. She just couldn't help herself.

"We're almost late to our first class, thanks to you."

Jada strides toward me and shoves a small black coffee from the cart on the corner into my hand. She laughs at my pinched expression, and the sound of it is so beautiful, so new and free,

I can't even be mad about the fact that class starts in less than a minute.

"Okay, P," she says, smiling. "Let's do this."

She kisses me on the cheek. She squeezes my free hand. And we step through the doors of our new life. Together.

THE IDIOM ALGORITHM
(Class Warfare)

ABIGAIL HING WEN

1

The Lee kitchen was full of afternoon sunlight, candy, and the sizzle of scallion pancakes frying on the stove. Tan tore a sheet of foil to wrap two for Rebecca, who was meeting him at the mall soon. He checked his phone; she'd said she'd text him when to head over. He wasn't looking forward to their errand, but Stanford Shopping Mall would be decked out for Christmas and perfect for walking around with his girl.

"Give us a hand, Tan?" Winter spoke around her mouthful of pancake.

"Sure."

Tan joined her and four-year-old Sana at the dining table. They were building a gingerbread house. Winter Woo and her mom had been renting out the Lees' spare bedroom for the past year, since Winter's dad passed away and she started as a sopho-more with Tan at Palo Alto High.

Tan held a cookie corner in place as the frosting hardened, while Winter picked through a bowl of gumdrops with fingers dusted with confectioners' sugar. She lined the roof in peach and orange as Tan's sister planted frosted trees and gingerbread people in the yard.

A dress of gumdrops slid off the gingerbread girl, landing in a heap at her feet.

Sana was distressed. "She's naked!"

Tan covered his eyes, mock horrified. "Tell me when it's safe to look!"

"No stripteasing in mixed company, young lady," Winter scolded the gingerbread in a mock-gruff voice. "We'll have to give you a talking-to about modesty."

Sana giggled. Winter was always playacting for her. "What's a striptease?"

"Hmm . . . tell you when you're older? Tan, it's safe."

Tan opened his eyes to Winter replacing the gumdrops. "Thank God."

Winter snickered. "Speaking of clothes, Tan, why do you have to buy a suit just to meet Rebecca's parents?"

"Because I don't have one."

"You never wear suits."

"Which is why I don't have one!"

"Soy sauce for Rebecca, Tan?" Mom tossed him a plastic packet, which he deftly caught.

"Sure, thanks."

Tan braced for Mom to weigh in on the suit, too—*Be yourself, the rest will follow.* But Mom merely returned to flipping pancakes, her daily break from her quantum computer startup. And a habit that benefited all of Tan's friends.

Tan pocketed the hot, foil-wrapped pancakes. "Rebecca says these remind her of home."

"She's welcome to dinner anytime." Tan's dad heaved a black pot of oxtail stew onto the stove. He also worked in tech, but his true passion was gardening.

"I'll let her know." Tan already had, but Rebecca was shy. "Once I meet her parents next weekend, it will be easier for her to come. We'll be more official. In her eyes, at least." He was eager to introduce them. Most people loved his family—they were warm and welcoming.

"What were her parents thinking, dropping off a child to fend for herself an ocean away," said Winter's mom. Her gray-streaked black hair was tied back with a scarf and she was chopping carrots.

"Their jobs keep them in Shanghai."

"No supervision," Tan's mom said. "I'd worry."

Rebecca had come two years ago to study at Palo Alto High School. She lived on her own in a luxurious apartment on University Avenue.

"You always say we need to respect other cultures," Tan said. "Catch, Winter." He shot the sprinkles bowl, hockey-puck style, across the table into Winter's hand.

"That could have broken," Mom chided.

"Not with Winter as goalie."

"Saving your ass as usual," Winter said.

He grinned. Kids at school sometimes called him and Winter

the Odd Couple. It *was* a little odd to go home with your classmate who'd found you on Craigslist. Her mom was in night school for her counseling degree. Renting the Lees' room was perfect. Tan's family needed the income to support their three-bedroom, two-and-a-half-bathroom house, and Tan's parents and Winter's mom spent sunny afternoons together in the garden.

As for Winter and Tan, she was an artist, he was a nerd. She illustrated and wrote for the yearbook; he coded artificial intelligence. But Winter was a sister to him and Sana. A twin, with a birthday a week from his in February.

Rebecca buzzed his phone: On my way.

"Gotta go."

"You're afraid of her, aren't you?" Winter sprinkled candy bits on the roof.

He raised an eyebrow. "Where'd *that* come from?"

"Suit shopping, for one."

A twin with an annoying habit of asking the wrong questions at the wrong time.

"She's not *forcing* me." That was the truth. "If it makes her happy, I'm happy to do it."

Before Winter could argue back, Tan shot out the door.

2

Stanford Shopping Mall smelled of pine needles and spiced cider. Beside the Christmas tree, Rebecca watched a juggler on a unicycle. She was festive in a red pantsuit and Santa hat.

Tan slipped up from behind, snatched her hat, and put it on his own head.

"Hey!" She smiled. "You goofball." Rebecca had just a lilt of a Chinese accent. She'd studied English since age five, and her vocabulary was even better than his.

"Only around you."

Tan swept aside the thick black hair framing her soft face and brown eyes. He'd never been good with girls. Never even been on a coffee date . . . but somehow, this princess had picked him.

He kissed her and when they broke apart, she rubbed his nose. "You have flour there."

"Must be sugar." He smiled, sheepish. "Winter and my sister are building a gingerbread house."

"So American. Like this whole mall." She gestured at the tree. "I love it."

"I brought *cong you bing*." He handed her the package.

"I *adore* your mom's *cong you bing*." She tucked it away and threaded her hand through his elbow. "Let's go in. I wish the selection here wasn't so limited. If we lived in Manhattan, we'd shop Fifth Avenue." They headed inside. "Winter's really worked her way into your family, hasn't she?"

There was that edge to her voice. She knew Winter from the yearbook, but it hadn't exactly brought them closer together.

"She and her mom are good people."

"It's so odd, someone living in your home. One day, I'll turn around and you'll be dating her."

"Winter's a pal! She's sweet to Sana. And *I*"—he kissed her temple—"am with you. Besides, you're staying in *your* friends' apartment. Maybe you're the pot calling the kettle black?" he teased.

Rebecca's frown dissolved into a wry smile. "Another idiom?" They'd met over idioms—his English teacher had suggested he interview her about Chinese ones and she enjoyed parsing English ones. *Beat around the bush. Call it a day. Speak of the devil.* Meanings weren't always clear from the words themselves.

"This one's easy to guess," he said.

"The pot is black, the kettle black. In Chinese we say, 'Fifty steps laughs at one hundred steps.'" As they passed Macy's, she added, "But it's not a fair comparison. My parents' friends are in London. I've met their son once."

"Okay, you win. My favorite Chinese idiom is still 'Nine cows and one strand of hair.' I want to find a way to use that one."

"九牛一毛 (jiǔ niú yì máo)." It rang on her tongue. "Something so small it's like one strand of hair among nine cows."

"Much more colorful than 'a needle in a haystack.'" He'd tried it on Sana last night and made Winter snort so hard she sprayed milk through her nose. "Oh, here's a use: How will we find the one suit among suits that fits my beefy shoulders and doesn't make me look like a penguin?"

"You won't look like a penguin." She didn't laugh this time.

They passed a store window outlined in holiday lights, showcasing scarves covered in interlocked *V*s and *L*s.

"Louis Vui'tton," Tan said. "Like your purse."

"Louis Vui-*TON*." Rebecca accented the second syllable. She released his arm, frowning. "Honestly, Tan . . ."

He bit his lip. He wasn't *afraid* of her—he wished Winter

hadn't planted that idea in his head. But he didn't like disappointing her.

"Sorry."

She shook her head. "Don't worry about it."

3

Tan tried on twelve outfits at four stores before four three-way mirrors. The last blue plaid suit was the only one Rebecca didn't immediately nix. Tan struck a muscleman pose. The jacket stretched tight in the shoulders, but so be it.

"Does the suit suit?"

She laughed. "Yes, that one will do."

He flipped its tag. Brioni. Never heard of it. "Um, is the decimal in the wrong place? This says two thousand dollars."

"That's just the jacket. The pants are more."

He was dismayed. "Sorry, I can't afford—"

"I told you, I'll get it. I don't want meeting my parents to be a burden."

"It's not." He shrugged out of the wooly cage with relief. "But dropping four-thousand-plus on a suit I'll wear once isn't something to sneeze at. Meaning not small." He felt like he was lecturing Sana on wasting money. If Winter saw this tag, she'd be horrified.

"Find another use for it later."

He wanted to argue, but if this was what it took to meet her parents and make them official . . .

He followed her to the register. "When are we meeting up? Tomorrow sometime?"

"They're pretty busy. Meeting the dean of Stanford, Facebook C suite. Honestly, Tan, I want them to meet you, but not sure they'll have time this trip . . ."

"What parents *wouldn't* want to meet their daughter's boyfriend? I'm taking you to prom. They should make sure I'm okay."

She bit her lip. "You know, most guys would jump at a pass on meeting the parents. But you . . . are fanatical—"

"It could be another year before they're back." He squeezed her hand. "Don't worry. Asian parents like me. I've got straight As in *Palo Alto*."

She didn't smile. "My parents would rather I date someone at Eton."

"What's Eton?"

"Private boys' school where the British royal family attend."

He scoffed. "Only someone trying to be as white as whole milk would go there."

"So Tan Lee!" She swatted him, smiling. "Come on. Shoes next . . ."

4

All Saturday, Tan waited for Rebecca to text the time to Meet Her Parents. But Saturday night passed. Nada. Winter came home, smelling of buttery theater popcorn. The lights of their Christmas tree glowed against her skin.

"Don't you have something better to do?" she asked.

Tan had just refreshed his phone for the umpteenth time. He

tucked it away, embarrassed. Winter knew how to get under his skin. Why Rebecca considered her a threat, Tan would never understand.

"I'm waiting for Rebecca to schedule her parents."

"It took *forever* to get that suit."

"She wanted to find the right one."

"Maybe it's better to keep it casual?"

"She's trying for the perfect intro."

Winter sniffed. "It smells like skunk in here. Sorry, literally— not the idiom."

"Hah."

Winter had actually inspired him to study idioms in the first place. Her dad had been an English professor. "I got a new one from Rebecca." He shared the one about fifty steps.

"I like 'pot calling the kettle black' better. You pot, you!" Winter skewered him with an imaginary sword and he doubled over and died.

They laughed and he rose for bed. "Thanks for getting me off my ass."

In the morning, he pinged Rebecca: We on for project Meet the Parents today?

Her text buzzed: Working up to it. They're jet-lagged. Next week's safer.

So she hadn't even asked yet?

Sure, he texted. Sounds good.

5

Rebecca tried for a dinner slot, an afternoon coffee. Her parents kept making plans, one dignitary after another. They were flying out the following Monday—Tan was running out of time. Maybe Winter was right. Better to keep it casual, take the pressure off. So Saturday evening, Tan headed down University Avenue, hoping to catch them at Rebecca's.

Luck was on his side—down the block, Rebecca was opening the door to Tamarine, a modern Asian restaurant. An older couple followed: a trim man with salt-and-pepper hair and a woman with a soft face like Rebecca's.

"Rebecca!" Tan caught the door before it shut. "Hey!"

Rebecca's eyes widened. "Tan! What are you doing here?"

"I swung by." He hugged her. "These your parents?"

Her mother looked so young: like Rebecca five years from now. Her dad was shorter than he'd imagined, shorter than him. They smiled in a way that put him instantly at ease.

Rebecca twisted her fingers nervously. "Mom. Dad. This is Tan. He's a junior, too. My parents, Mr. and Mrs. Shin."

"So nice to meet one of Rebecca's schoolmates," Mrs. Shin said.

"My uncle was a Tan." Her dad shook his hand. Their British accents gave them a sophisticated air. "You a Giants fan?" Mr. Shin noted his shirt.

"A *fanatic*."

"Me too. I'm a Californian at heart. I watched their games instead of studying." He smiled the same warm smile Rebecca used to win over everyone at school, Tan included. "We're grabbing dinner. Would you like to join us?"

"Oh, um," Rebecca said at the same time Tan said, "That would be great. I've heard so much about you from Rebecca."

"All good, I hope." Her mom smiled.

"Yes," Tan answered truthfully. "But this place is expensive for the tiny portions you get. My dad says it's not worth the money. There's a good place just off University, if you want bigger portions."

Rebecca gave him a stricken look. "My parents got a recommendation here."

Tan had committed a faux pax, clearly.

Rebecca's dad just laughed. "Let's make it an evening? It's not every day we get to have dinner with our daughter and her playmate."

"Dad, I'm *sixteen*. I don't have *playmates*."

Her dad's eyes chilled, but then the ice was gone. Maybe Tan had imagined it.

"We've been worried about her," her mom said. "Across the globe—"

"She's our only child. We've let her run wild." Her dad turned back to the maître d'. "Make that four."

As they followed the maître d', Rebecca whispered, "You were supposed to meet them in your *suit*."

He didn't want to waste the money either.

"I can wear it next time," he reassured her.

6

The hostess seated them in a private room, at a table covered with two white tablecloths draped in a diamond, and fancy square dishes. Tan hadn't even known Tamarine had a private room. Mr. Dad ordered wine . . . he was even more Westernized than Tan's parents.

Tan peeked at the price of the bottle on the menu and choked on a sip of water.

"Costs more than my shoes," he whispered to Rebecca.

She frowned. "Special occasion. Don't mention it."

The waiter brought fried calamari and tea leaf beef on a bed of lettuce.

Her mother motioned him to help himself. "What are your favorite subjects, Tan?"

"I've been programming since I was five. Making an algorithm to match idioms across different languages."

"How nice. Rebecca likes computer science, too."

"Tan helps me with homework."

Rebecca's mother smiled. "Rebecca is a good student."

"Studies harder than everyone." Tan grinned at Rebecca; it wasn't quite true, but he had her back. She fiddled with her bracelet.

"We're worried about her being here on her own."

"*Please*, Mom. I've got Priscilla hawking after me." Priscilla was Rebecca's education consultant. They checked in weekly on homework, grades, and exams. *Hawking* was pretty accurate.

"I wish she were more attentive. She didn't seem in tune with your activities." Her mom turned to Tan. "And what brought your family to Palo Alto?"

"Schools. Like Rebecca." He smiled. "My parents were able to buy a house by renting out a room to help with costs."

Her mother's brow rose. "How enterprising."

"Yeah—"

A sharp pinch on his thigh broke him off. Rebecca's eyes cut at him.

What?

"Crab?" Her mother tried to serve her a spoonful, but Rebecca pushed her hand away, spilling crab onto the tablecloth.

"I can get it myself." It sounded like an ongoing argument.

"Very well." Tan's mother got up to use the restroom but Tan caught the flush of anger on her face. Tan's father got into a conversation with the waiter about the shaking beef dish, but his knuckles were white.

"Everything okay?" Tan murmured.

"You shouldn't have mentioned renting out your room," she whispered. "My parents don't know anyone who has to do that."

Tan frowned. Between the suit and rent, Rebecca was doing her best to make him look like a rich kid to her parents. But he wasn't *poor*—his scrappy parents had pulled off impossibly expensive Palo Alto housing. Now they had an asset, not to mention Winter and her mom as a bonus. But they'd have to talk about this later, not now, when Rebecca didn't seem to be getting along with her parents.

"I'll be more careful," he said. "Are you going to tell them about us?" Maybe now wasn't a good time after all.

"I'm working up to it."

"It might have been easier to say it upfront," he said doubt-fully.

"I told you!" She calmed with an effort. "They're compli-cated." She exhaled. "I can never tell with them. Okay. Just . . . I'll do it at dessert."

He opened his mouth to say *Never mind*, but if they didn't talk about it now, when would they?

"Okay," he said.

7

Rebecca gazed with dread at the coconut tapioca pudding her mother spooned onto her plate. Tan caught her eye and she reached for her glass of red wine, took a large swallow, and announced, "So actually, Tan's my boyfriend!"

The air froze. Her mother set down her spoon. Her father's stopped halfway to his mouth.

Rebecca laughed a high-pitched, very un-Rebecca laugh.

"What's gotten into you?" her mother cried.

Then slapped Rebecca's face.

It wasn't terribly hard. Or loud. But what the hell?

Rebecca's face flamed red and Tan flew to his feet. "Leave her alone!"

Her father's phone was at his ear. "Peng-Lai, bring the car. Now!"

Rebecca's mother grabbed her wrist.

"Ow!" Rebecca cried.

"Don't touch her!" Tan sprang at them, but a man in plain

black clothes blocked his way. Where had he come from? Who the hell had bodyguards in Palo Alto?

And all this because she'd said he was her boyfriend? Or was something else going on?

"Please just get away from her." Rebecca's mother yanked Rebecca out as her father dropped a few hundred-dollar bills on the table. The guard shoved Tan aside and followed.

Tan raced after them, charging out the front door as a black car pulled to the curb.

"Rebecca, what's going on?" Tan shoved at the guard blocking him, trying to break through to her. But she didn't answer. Her eyes were downcast. "Rebecca!"

Her father opened the back door. "Get in."

"Rebecca, what do you want me to do?" Tan cried.

Her mother put her hand on her head and pressed her inside. She climbed in after her and shut the door.

"You leave my daughter alone." Her father took the front seat beside the driver.

"Wait!" Tan threw himself against her window, but the glass slid from under him as the car pulled away. He ran to keep up. The tinted glass hid them, but he imagined Rebecca pressed against its insides, watching him. The car picked up speed.

"Rebecca!" Tan's lungs ached for breath. His shoes pounded on the brick sidewalk as the car vanished down the road. "Rebecca!"

Where were they taking her?

He slowed at last, panting. He called her. Texted. What's happening? Should I call the police?

No answer. They must have taken her phone. That would

have been the first thing his parents would have done . . . except they'd never have told him who to date.

Was it boyfriends in general? His crooked teeth? That their daughter had gone rogue away from their watchful eyes? But they'd acted as though everything was awesome . . . until it wasn't. It was harder to parse than an idiom in another language.

Rebecca had been right not to introduce him, and he, over-confident fool, had insisted.

He ran to her apartment and rapped on the door, but there was no answer. He sat on the stoop and waited until the sun set and the outdoor lights came on. He stayed until long past midnight, leaning against the wall, refreshing his phone.

8

From his desk, Tan watched his classmates streaming into second-period biology. Rebecca never missed class unless she was deathly ill. As the bell rang, their teacher shut the door.

No Rebecca.

Tan bolted to his feet.

"Tan!" Winter said as he passed her desk.

"Where are you going?" asked his teacher.

But he headed out the door without another word.

Tan sprinted the entire mile and a half to her apartment. Her door was ajar. His heart leaped into his throat as he slammed into it.

"Rebecca!" he shouted.

Silence greeted him. The apartment was emptied of all its

Pottery Barn furniture. No more lace doilies, no more table of Christmas ornaments for the tree he was helping her pick out.

He pulled out his phone to try to reach her on her Facebook page. He expected the cute photo of her turned to the side, her black hair covering her face. Her fifty friends—followers—from school.

But her Facebook page was gone.

Frantic, Tan searched all of Facebook, then the internet, but none of the Rebecca Shins who came up were her.

He sent her a final desperate text: Rebecca, please call me.

The text spun and returned a message: This number is no longer in service.

It was as though she'd never existed.

"Oh, who are you?" A gray-haired woman in a white apron and plastic gloves had stepped from the bedroom and was staring at him.

"Where's Rebecca?" he cried.

The woman looked puzzled. "The family has left for the airport."

9

Tan's cousin drove Tan to San Francisco International Airport.

"Kidnapping is a very serious offense, but these are her *parents*, Tan." Shaun was a policeman with the San Mateo County Sheriff's Office.

"Her mom hit her. They have a *guard*." Tan's heart pounded. The next direct flight to Shanghai was leaving in just over an hour. If they were on it, if he didn't reach Rebecca before she passed security—

"If we catch up to her—" Shaun began.

"When."

"You'll need to ask if she's leaving with her parents of her own free will."

"She's not."

As Shaun pulled up to China Air, Tan bolted out the door.

"I'll meet you inside!" Shaun called.

Tan raced by holiday wreaths and travelers carting suitcases and children. His breath rasped in and out of his lungs. He scanned the China Air counters to a girl with a pink clip in her black hair.

"Rebecca!" he yelled, but the girl turned—it wasn't her.

He ran on toward security. A prayer sobbed in his heart. If she'd passed the checkpoint . . .

There!

At the front of the winding aisle of cables. Her Louis Vuitton purse was slung over her shoulder and her favorite black suede jacket hung over her clasped hands. Her father handed passports to an officer behind a plexiglass shield.

"Rebecca!"

He leaped the cables toward her, ignoring a cry behind him. He didn't care if security arrested him. Or if the Shins' bodyguard tried to take him out. He shoved past travelers. His foot snagged on a cable. Behind him, metal poles clattered to the floor.

"Rebecca, wait! It's Tan!"

"You can't go in there without a ticket!" someone said.

Rebecca's eyes widened with terror. Her lips moved with words he couldn't hear.

Rough hands seized his shoulders, yanking him back an aisle's width away. The bodyguard.

"It's that boy," her mother said.

"Wait," he shouted. "She's being kidnapped!"

Everyone was gawking at them, but Tan had to save her. Shaun raced up beside him, breathing heavily. Shaun. Shaun had the power to stop this.

"What's this?" The officer holding their passports looked at Rebecca. To everyone else, she must have looked poised, but Tan caught the tremor in her hands.

"Rebecca," he pleaded. "Tell them. Are you leaving of your own free will?"

Her eyes brimmed with tears. She glanced away, refusing to look at him.

"This is ridiculous," said her father. "He's stalking my daughter."

"Rebecca!" Tan pleaded.

"Miss." Shaun pulled out his badge. "I'm a police officer. Are you leaving the country of your own free will?"

Rebecca lifted her chin. "Yes."

10

Winter found him in his old treehouse, lying on his back beside the wooden crate that had served as his table when he was a kid. He gazed unseeingly at a dark patchwork of leaves obscuring the starry sky. She handed him an apple.

"Not hungry."

She sat cross-legged beside him while he picked the old blanket to shreds.

"Want to talk about it?"

He rolled onto his side to look at her. Winter always said it like she saw it, no holds barred, but her expression in the moonlight now was only kind. He found himself pouring out the story.

"She was under duress," Tan concluded, sitting up.

"She said yes. You asked her point-blank."

"They had a gun to her head."

"Wouldn't security—"

"Not a *literal* gun!" His fist splintered the crate. "Of course she had to say yes!"

"Her mom slaps her because she's dating you and they fly out," she said. "Did a teenager in their family get pregnant?"

He imagined her parents demanding to know exactly what he and Rebecca had done, but they'd never gone further than kissing.

"Maybe."

"You're not *that* bad."

"Thanks." His voice dripped sarcasm.

"So what are you going to do?"

He got to his feet. "I need to find her."

11

Tan ran image searches through the internet, but came up empty. She'd always been camera shy, turning her head as their friends took selfies and candid shots. Now he realized how subtly and completely she'd dodged them all. On purpose?

As for her parents, they could be one of a million Shins among Shanghai's population of twenty-five million.

He searched the online groups of clubs she'd been a part of—Honor Society, Yearbook—no photos, and there, just last night, Yearbook had posted:

Searching for a hair among nine cows.

He read it three times before it sank in. It had to be Rebecca. A coded message for him. As he stared at those seven words, they vanished.

A knock on his door made him jump.

"Your dad made breakfast." Winter set a bagel with lox on his desk. Tan's favorite. "How are you going to find her?"

To Tan, there were no unsolvable problems, only problems he hadn't solved yet.

He took a big bite and drew his laptop close. "I'm going to build an algorithm."

12

His algorithm for the science fair had focused on matching idioms across languages. Now, he retooled it to match *her*. He went through their text messages and put in everything he had—her turns of phrases, their back-and-forth with Chinese and English idioms. It wasn't enough data. He needed tens of thousands. He re-created what he could from memory. If her pattern of speech was out there, an interview, a blog, an anonymous social media profile, he would find it. He had to.

13

"She's gone, Tan." Winter stood in his doorway, holding a plate. Nearly two weeks had passed since Rebecca disappeared. Maybe she'd only existed in his imagination.

"No!" His voice bounced off the window panes. He was still fine-tuning his algorithm. It either returned one hundred million useless matches, or zero. At least he could sort by date of publication, but it needed more inputs. "I'll find her."

She handed him an egg sandwich. "Here, eat."

He bit into the softness, surprised by how hungry he was. "If you didn't remind me to eat . . ."

"Your dad or my mom would." She folded her arms. "You haven't been to school in a week. Ms. Blimpton's asked twice about you and I said you were sick—which is true, I see—but I can't keep covering up for you." Her frown deepened. "*And* you look like a madman."

He rubbed the stubble on his chin impatiently. "I'm close. She's waiting for me to make contact."

"She could call."

"Her parents have probably locked her up. You weren't there, Winter!"

"Yeah, but I've been classmates with both of you for a year." He frowned. "And?"

"I just never got the feeling she was as excited about you guys as you were. Like Valentine's Day, you got her roses, she was all smug . . . but she didn't get you anything."

"Maybe it's not as big a holiday in Shanghai."

"You're always making cultural excuses."

He looked at her. "You got me chocolate mooncakes, but I didn't get you anything. Doesn't mean I don't care." He cared. A lot.

"I just figured you'd like them." Winter sighed. "So how does your algorithm work?"

"It's trying to match her speech patterns. If she's written anything on the internet—a social media post, column, essay, I hope it will find her." It was a long shot, but he refused to give up.

"Would some of her writings help?"

He turned in his chair. Winter slouched against the door, hands wrapped around her elbows. She was more athletic than Rebecca, with toned muscles on her arms and legs.

Her face reddened, and she straightened—why was he even noticing?

"You have things she's written?"

"She wrote a few essays the yearbook editor decided not to use. I'll dig them up."

Winter brought him an unused page housing Rebecca's essay on Chinese and English idioms. At the bottom, a sketch of a striped book spilling out fantastical creatures was captioned *Winter Woo*.

"'Can't judge a book by its cover,'" Tan said. "Your picture's better than the idiom."

She shrugged, but looked pleased. "It's what I do."

"You should still publish your sketch."

"I'm trying to write a memorial for my dad," she says. "So maybe I'll find a way."

"I'd love to read it." He smiled at her, then uploaded Rebecca's essay for his algorithm. "Thanks for this, Winter. I think I might actually love you."

"Because I'm saving your ass as always," she said briskly.

But her hand, squeezing his shoulder, was gentle.

14

Christmas passed in a distracted blur of roasted duck and wrapping paper. Winter got him an album from his favorite band. He got her that year's Printz Award–winning novel, which she'd been ogling. But his gift for Rebecca, a mix of ten songs he'd picked out, stayed unsent on his laptop.

Returning to school in January tore the scab off again. Her seat was empty. He walked by her apartment as a strange man with a cat came out. Rebecca wouldn't have wanted a cat there, making her sneeze and her eyes water. What was happening to her now? Were her parents letting her see friends? Had her mother slapped her again for trying to text him?

Tan doubled down on his search. He built a reverse-image search tool to continuously scroll the web for her photo. He hacked records and security cameras in Shanghai malls, parks, museums—places he thought she'd like to go . . . but he wasn't sure. Maybe he didn't know her so well after all. He didn't have enough data for his algorithm, but maybe the reason it didn't work ran even deeper.

Winter dropped by, tying her black hair back with a red hairband. "If your life were a movie, this is where I'd put in a montage."

He was glad to see her. "What's a montage?"

"Sequences of video without words, just music. It would be this."

She read aloud, from an imaginary script:

- *Tan at his computer*
- *Tan at his computer*
- *Tan collapses at his computer*
- *Tan throws his computer out the window and falls to the floor*

"This supposed to make me feel better?"

"Yep."

He laughed ruefully and closed his laptop. "Let's go for a walk. I need to get out of here."

15

Sana skipped hand-in-hand between them. Winter steered them onto Hamilton Avenue, probably to avoid Tamarine—she was thoughtful like that. They stopped for sipping chocolate. Winter tried to pay, but Tan won.

Crowded together into a warm booth, stirring the cocoa with tiny spoons, Tan almost felt normal again.

16

After dinner, he joined Winter for homework at the kitchen table. She was working on her science fair project.

"What are you doing yours on?"

"Refugee migration patterns using satellite imagery."

"Really? How'd you get into that?"

"My dad read a lot of refugee literature. Before he passed away, he took me to a virtual reality tech demo. We got to see life in refugee camps in Kenya: crowds, public bathrooms, people waiting for food. There are more refugees now than any time since World War Two."

"I had no idea you were working on all that." He'd never asked.

Winter laid her head down on the table.

"What's wrong?"

"I'm wiped out," she admitted. "Just got a part-time job."

"You did? Where?"

She flushed. "Nothing big. Washing dishes at Chocolatier. To help my mom finish night school."

How could he not have noticed how weary Winter had been? She'd been such a friend to him—but what kind of friend was he?

"How much is she short?"

"Five thousand dollars."

Tan wished he had a few thousand to give her. But he did—sort of.

"Wait a sec." He raced to his room and came back with his blue plaid suit. Winter had fallen asleep on the table. He waited patiently, working on homework, until she woke.

She sat up as he shoved the jacket and pants at her.

"It's brand-new. I should have returned it before the period expired. But we can resell it on Craigslist. Plus the shoes."

Her expression was wondering. "I can't take your suit! It's all you have left of her."

True. Rebecca wouldn't like him selling it for Winter, but that was nothing compared to what Winter was going through.

"You need it more than I do."

Winter's fingers tightened on the wool. "Guess her billionaire parents won't mind?"

His throat tickled; he was surprised when a laugh came out. "I'm sure they won't."

A few days later, he put an envelope with five thousand dollars into her hands. She did something he never thought the mighty Winter Woo would do.

She burst into tears.

17

Tan was reviewing his algorithm's results when the thought struck.

"Winter, when you said they were billionaires, did you mean that? Or just that they're rich?"

"They're billionaires. Esther told me."

Billionaires! Yeah, there were billionaires in Silicon Valley—people who founded Facebooks and Amazons. But Tan didn't *know* any. Rebecca had mentioned trunk shows and didn't blink an eye at his suit price, but . . .

"She never told me."

"That's her. She never told you she was allergic to *cong you bing*, either, did she?"

"What?" He was dismayed. "She adored my mom's *cong you bing*."

"Well, maybe . . . but she couldn't eat it. I'm sure she just didn't want you to feel bad."

Tan's head spun. Rebecca never ate the *cong you bing*. She was practically royalty. It was too much to take in.

But one thought came through: being a billionaire made it harder to hide.

Tan found a list of ninety billionaires in Shanghai. He ran his finger down the names and businesses—glass, shipping, electronics—

Tan's algorithm on his laptop began to buzz: MATCH.

18

Tan's algorithm had directly matched a Chinese-language essay by Shin Chien-Li, a student at Shanghai International School: "*Rén BùKě MàoXiàng*—Can't Judge a Book by Its Cover." It was her unpublished essay for the yearbook.

And on the list of billionaires, number twelve was Shin Chu-Bing, CEO of Shin Yun Tech Ltd. Chairman of Shanghai Metropolitan Hospital. On the board of Shanghai International School. The photo of the man in a suit was Rebecca's father.

"Shin Chien-Li." Her Chinese name was strange on his tongue. He'd never known it. It felt like a stranger's.

Tan found Shin Chien-Li on Facebook, an account started the day she was born. Her profile was the pink Pearl Tower. Her last post, of a new Louis Vuitton purse, was just yesterday.

"Why didn't she friend you? Or any of us?" Winter asked.

"Her parents must've forbade her."

"Chien-Li seems pretty active. Not a girl in prison."

"I need to reach her." Tan created a new account under a gender-neutral name, Alex. His birthday was next week. Would she even remember? He messaged her: "Hi Chien-Li, it's an old friend from Palo Alto. I've been searching for a hair among nine cows. Can we do a video call?"

In the morning, he opened his account to a reply:

"Tomorrow evening?"

19

"It's weird." Winter said the next afternoon. She lay on her stomach on his bed, heels kicked up. "Was her Rebecca Shin life just a blip in her real one?"

"Of course not. Her life here was real." He was cleaning his room in preparation for the video call with Rebecca; he needed to keep moving to keep from panicking. After all this time, he was going to see her face-to-face. Was she safe? Frightened?

"Maybe they keep such a low profile because they're billionaires." Winter shivered in her purple blouse.

"You cold?" Their house was often chilly during the rainy season.

"A bit."

"Here . . ." He shrugged out of his gray fleece and she shrugged it over her shirt and zipped it to her neck. He liked seeing her cocooned in its folds, with her legs in jeans crossed under her.

"Why did her parents disapprove of you? Because she's rich and you're not?"

"She got upset when I mentioned you lived in the back of our house," he admitted.

"That shows you're poor."

"We're not poor. This house cost over two million dollars!"

"Rich people don't have to rent out part of their house to pay the mortgage."

"So we're not billionaires. Most people aren't!"

"My mom and I are the ones renting. We're worse."

"Whatever. We're all people. But yeah. Her parents want her to date Eton guys. I just want to build things that work."

"You're a great guy, Tan." Winter's face was fierce. "Loyal, smart, open-minded . . ."

"Handsome." He jutted out his jaw, displaying his crooked lower teeth.

"Narcissistic!" She sobered. "Tan, you deserve better than this."

"She does, too! She's been trying to reach me! I'm sure of it."

Winter bit her lip. "So you meet up, then what? You're back together? She's in Shanghai and you're here. It's hard to connect online."

"I know . . . most of the time, we were more . . . physical."

Winter's ears flamed red. "I don't want to know."

His own ears burned. "Not what I meant! But I can't afford a ticket. We'll have to make do with Zoom for starters."

"You'll need to woo her extra hard."

"I know." He despaired. "How?"

"Serenade her?" Winter pretended to play violin.

"I'm tone-deaf."

"Okay, she never struck me as someone who'd think off-key singing was adorable . . . What if you gave her flowers?"

Winter swooped onto her knees and handed Tan a bouquet, so goofy and sincere he busted out laughing.

"You really *should* go into acting."

"Working on it. Okay, so no flowers. I don't know. A strip-tease?"

"Ha! Make like Sana's gingerbread girl and lose my gumdrops."

"Yeah, why not? But like this." She swayed to imaginary music, as goofy as the gingerbread. "Unzip slowly and suggestively." She lowered the zipper on his fleece and peeled off one shoulder and then the other, still swaying. "Take your time. Make her want to jump your bones."

"You're ruining my innocence!" he scoffed, but couldn't take his eyes off her . . . But this was wrong! He was supposed to be Rebecca's boyfriend. How could he be enjoying watching Winter pretend to strip? Not to mention Winter *lived in his house*. She was family.

"Shrug off your . . ." She raised her shirt hem, flashing her belly button and pale stomach.

"STOP!" Tan yelled. "I get the idea."

Winter dropped her shirt and smirked. "I wasn't really going to do it." She flopped back on his bed. "See? Easy."

"You!" He shoved her and she fell back on his pillow, laughing. He pounced—and found himself braced over her, staring down into her face.

Their eyes locked, hers dark brown, lined by thick lashes.

Her face grew still and serious.

A blush infused her cheeks.

He came to himself and pushed himself off. "Sorry," he mumbled. He couldn't meet her eyes. "Got carried away."

"Don't be." Winter sat up on her elbows. "I did, too."

"I shouldn't be like this. I'm with Rebecca."

She was silent a moment. "She could have sent a note saying she was safe."

"If you're trying to say something, just say it."

"I just wonder if she . . . really wants to get back together. With you."

"Of course she does!" he exploded. "She wrote a whole piece about idioms—that was our thing! And on the yearbook page, the night she vanished, someone wrote, 'Searching for a hair among nine cows.' But that got taken down, too. She's been trying to reach me, and once we talk, we can work out a plan."

Winter's mouth dropped. "*I* wrote that nine cows note. I didn't think you'd see it. You're not even on Yearbook."

"What? Why would you post that?"

"You said it yourself—it was your thing. I hoped Rebecca would see it and know we were looking for her and make contact. But the editor removed it."

The blood drained from his face. Those words—all this time he'd believed Rebecca was trying to reach him . . . but it was Winter. He'd shared way too much with her.

Winter's face had fallen. "Tan, I'm sorry."

All those months. He drew himself up, so angry he could barely speak. "Just because you live in my house doesn't make my business yours. So . . . mind your own, for once!"

Her face flamed gumdrop-red. He was instantly sorry. He'd screwed up with Rebecca, and now Winter—he couldn't face her.

So he fled, leaving her alone in his room.

20

Rebecca's name appeared first on his Zoom screen. Tan's hands shook.

Her face was next. Her chin-length bob framed her heart-shaped face. Her soft blue blouse matched an abstract painting on the wall behind her.

"Rebecca!" She was alive! Safe! Real! After these weeks of searching, here she was at last.

But she wasn't smiling. "What do you want?"

"Want?" Tan blinked. "I've been trying to reach you. For months."

Her gaze was wary. "I had to come home."

"Why didn't you contact me?"

"*Why?*" she exploded. "Isn't that obvious? You ruined my life!"

"What?" This meeting wasn't going at all as Tan had imagined. "Your parents *kidnapped* you and you vanished off the earth! I've been so worried!"

Her eyes blazed. "All I wanted was to study in the States. I even begged my parents to let me go to public school so I could see what it was like! And then you kept pushing me to *introduce* you, and tell them we were dating, and now . . . I'm stuck back in Shanghai!"

The footing he'd found turned out to be a board floating on water.

"Were you never going to tell them about me?"

"On my own time! Maybe. Maybe not."

All her excuses suddenly became clear. The impossible-to-find suit. The never-ending working up to a get-together. If he hadn't crashed her dinner, they might never have met.

"Was I just part of your great American experience?" He was bitter.

"Rebecca, your mom asked me to call you for dinner," said a boy's English-accented voice. Rebecca jumped as a boy their age appeared behind her. His shoulders were full of hard muscle, his face square-jawed. He put a hand on Rebecca's shoulder and glared at Tan. "This him?"

Rebecca frowned. "This is Tan."

Tan stared at the boy's fingers, curved intimately into Rebecca's blouse.

"How dare you harass her? She doesn't want anything to do with you."

"Who the hell are you?" Tan snarled.

"John Young. I'm visiting from London, staying with her family."

Tan looked at Rebecca. "Like Winter?"

Rebecca had the decency to flush. "I stayed in their place in Palo Alto."

"Pot," Tan said.

"John"—she patted his hand—"tell them I'll be there in five minutes."

Five minutes. Months of tracking her down and that was all he was worth?

Tan glowered at her. "Does he go to Eton?"

She pressed her lips together. "He goes to my school here. His parents run a pharmaceutical conglomerate that does business with our hospitals."

"And you're dating him."

A reluctant nod.

"Americans don't let their parents think for them."

"That's the most *ethnocentric* thing I've ever heard!" she cried. "I think for myself."

"You've been brainwashed!"

She took a deep breath. "Look, I've had a lot of time to process what happened."

"Me too. You announce you're dating a guy. Big deal. Your mom smacks you—"

"No, I mean *us*. The truth is, I was lonely in Palo Alto. You're a great guy, Tan. We could have been great friends. But somehow, we slid into more."

He'd asked if he could kiss her. She'd said yes.

"I was crazy about you!"

"You were so sweet I thought it worth taking the plunge. The reason I had so many excuses not to introduce you to my parents was it didn't feel like the right step, but I didn't *know* I felt that way. But when I had a chance to consider, *dating* you wasn't what I wanted."

"What does the drug lord have that I don't?"

"*John* would never call my parents snobs for wanting me to date someone from Eton."

He was stung. He'd made that Eton comment off-the-cuff. "I thought you agreed. You acted like you did."

"How else was I supposed to act?"

Wasn't that their entire problem? When had she ever said what she really thought?

"It's okay," she continued. "It's because you're anti-elitist, salt of the earth. I love that about you and the kids in Palo Alto."

Warm, kind words. Like her parents. *Let's make it a night.* She was good at saying what he wanted to hear. Maybe that was the Shins.

But why did he feel like a science fair project?

"Truth is," Rebecca continued, "boys who go to Eton learn to navigate the world I live in. Government, business leaders. To be honest, I'm considering schools like Eton myself. Wanting to be prepared for my life doesn't make me a *snob.*"

"I didn't say *you* were." But Tan *had* judged her parents. He'd assumed she did, too. That they stood on the same righteous side of the aisle.

But Rebecca didn't sound brainwashed at all. She sounded like a girl who knew what she wanted. And where Tan Lee stood in the pecking order of her world.

"You're right." Winter had left his fleece on his desk. He balled it in his lap for comfort. "I *didn't* listen to you. I don't agree with what your parents did, but I put you in a hard position and I'm sorry."

"I'm sorry I wasn't brave enough to tell you how I felt." A rueful smile. "Be well, okay, Tan?"

So farewell, then. It wasn't as painful as he'd have expected. Those months searching . . . he was more glad to know she was safe than anything else. And oddly relieved. He had no interest in going to Eton. He was making his own path.

And along the way, he wouldn't be cramped inside a suit that didn't fit.

"Be well, Rebecca."

21

"Have you seen Winter?" Tan asked her mom in the kitchen. She was layering a lasagna with Tan's parents.

"She took Sana to the park," she answered.

"Everything okay?" Tan's mom asked.

"Almost," Tan answered.

He put a cupcake from their favorite shop on Winter's desk with a note: *Happy birthday. I'm sorry. Come by?*

At his desk, Tan updated his idiom algorithm for the science fair. He was training it on a data set culled from his favorite authors' works when Winter knocked. Her blue yoga outfit hugged her toned body. Her black hair flopped in a knot on her head, showing off her cheekbones. She brought the scents of grass and wind . . . and a decorated gingerbread man from Chocolatier.

"Happy birthday," she said.

He pushed his laptop aside. "Thanks."

"Call went well?"

"She has a new boyfriend."

Winter crossed her arms. "I always thought there was a code against going after someone dating someone else."

"Me, too." Tan and Rebecca came from different values. Rebecca had realized that sooner than he had.

She sat on his bed. "How do you feel about it?"

"Mostly relieved she's okay. I wish she'd been more honest upfront, but that's her family. So the joke's on me. I'm not the open-minded hero. I'm the villain."

"I never thought you were the hero, so your peon status remains safe with me."

"Phew." Unlike Rebecca, Winter always said what she thought. It bugged him at times, but he appreciated that more than ever now. He bit into her cookie. "Yum."

"Humans are complicated," she said. "You're open-minded, and you're getting better. That's all we can ask of ourselves."

"When did you get so wise?"

"My dad always told me life is short, and he was right. So here goes. I like you—a lot. I thought it was wrong to go after a guy with a girlfriend . . . but you're not that guy anymore."

He was astonished. "You never let on."

"I'm a good actor, remember?" She swallowed hard. "So now I've told you, and we can go to prom together, or we can pretend I never said a word—"

He silenced her with a kiss.

After a century, two, they broke apart for air. He was braced over her, lying on his pillow. Trembling with the electricity of their connection.

"*Wow,*" she said. "Did you want me to finish that, um . . . striptease?"

"*What?!*"

"Just kidding!"

He laughed. "How about after prom if you decide it's still a good idea?"

"Hmm . . ."

His laptop dinged. His algorithm was churning to life with a list of articles. At the top was a piece from the yearbook: *Peas in a Pod: My Palo Alto Family.* With a sketch of a pod loaded with six fat peas representing . . . Tan's and Winter's families.

"That's my article." Winter sat up, confused. "It came out today."

Tan frowned. "What does my algorithm know that I don't?"

For an answer, it flashed: MATCH.

AULD ACQUAINTANCE
(The Best Friend Love Epiphany)

CALEB ROEHRIG

*T*he banner over the school's trophy case normally reads
GO, SCREAMING EAGLES! Tonight, however, partly
obscured by a clutch of festive balloons, it reads simply, *GO,
SCREAMING.*

I'm trying not to see it as an omen.

Just for the record, had I any other choice? I would not be
where I am right now: standing in the middle of Linwood High,
holding a sleeping bag. But the Linwood Lock-Up is an annual
tradition—a New Year's Eve party-slash-sleepover, with refreshments, alcohol-free beverages, and a hired DJ to make it . . . a
little less embarrassing than it sounds. For twelve hours, from
8:00 p.m. to 8:00 a.m., the doors are bolted and students are
encouraged to eat, drink, and be "responsibly merry, with adult
supervision!"

Maybe there's no way to make that sound less embarrassing.

I've told everyone I know that I'm only here ironically, but the truth of the matter is that my plan B for tonight—*New Year's Actual Eve*—was hanging out all alone with my best friend Garrett, pretending to get drunk off sparkling grape juice in his basement. I'm not sure what it says about me that "spending the night at school" is the *least* pathetic of my options, but . . . it's obviously not good.

"Well, we're here," I announce, when Garrett and I rendezvous outside the gym. There are cheap streamers everywhere, and a bunch of teachers in paper hats chug past us, doing a truly awkward conga line to Lou Bega's "Mambo No. 5." With a dark sigh, I add, "The third ring of hell."

"Don't say that, Ollie." Garrett furrows his brow with paternal disapproval. "You're talking yourself out of having fun tonight, and I won't allow it."

"I know, I know," I grumble. "Everybody's having fun, *or else*."

"That's the spirit." He gives me a hug, and I have to admit it does lighten my mood a bit. He's the best hugger I know. If I have to be trapped here, at least it's with him.

"We might as well get moving." Squinting into the blue darkness of the gym, I estimate it to be about half full. Or half empty. "There's only four hours left until midnight."

Garrett clears his throat. "So . . . the Pact is still on, right?"

"Definitely." I'm surprised he's even asking. "If we can't find boyfriends by the time the ball drops, we're each other's New Year's kiss—we shook on it!"

Some people might think it's weird to make a handshake agreement about kissing your best friend, but those people don't know Garrett and me. We've practically shared a brain since freshman year, and we both turn seventeen in March; we're tired of waiting for Mr. Right—and, if anything, we're even *more* tired of waiting for Mr. Right Now.

Neither of us has ever had a boyfriend, and neither of us has ever been kissed, so at this point? We're basically desperate to know what it feels like. Hence, the Pact. Even if we can't find Prince Charming, at least we can still cross this important frontier with someone we already love and trust. What's weird about that?

Anyway, it makes sense to me. But when I explained it to my second-best friend, Layla, she frowned until I was afraid her chin would cramp, declaring, "This is a really bad idea. You're messing with forces you don't understand."

"Okay, Layla, we're just *kissing*—not reading from the Necronomicon," I'd retorted, trying not to roll my eyes. "Can we keep things in perspective a little?"

"I am keeping things in perspective, *Oliver*." Her expression was flat and unamused. "There's no such thing as 'just' a kiss, and I don't want you doing something you'll regret."

She was so serious that I didn't dare laugh, but the whole thing was kind of silly. Garrett and I have been best friends for two and a half years, and we are definitely mature enough to mash our lips together for a few seconds without getting weird about it.

Pushing it all to the back of my mind, I follow him through the crowded gym, until we find a corner with enough space to move around. The DJ starts a string of danceable pop hits, and we quickly lose all track of time—having some actual, non-ironic fun after all.

It's when Harry Styles's "Adore You" comes on an hour or more later, everything slowing down again, that I realize we've also lost track of our whole boyfriend-finding mission. And that, in turn, makes me recall my second-best friend's dire prediction.

"Why do you think Layla has such a problem with the Pact?" I blurt at last, unable to keep my thoughts to myself. "She can't seriously believe we'll mess up our friendship with a stupid kiss—right? It's not like it means anything."

"Forget about her," Garrett returns, shaking his head. "The only time Layla's happy is when something goes wrong and she can tell everyone she saw it coming." Then, leaving no time for a rebuttal, he grabs my hand. "Come on, let me dip you!"

Garrett took ballroom dancing in middle school, and he's taught me a few of the flashier tricks—stuff we can do at parties for fun and attention (but I repeat myself)—so this isn't a totally unexpected request. Smiling a little, I nod, taking a step out.

With a few deft moves, he spins me in a tight circle, grabbing my waist and bending me so far backward that for a few breathless moments I have an upside-down view of the room. It's a huge rush, and when he swings me upright again, my heart is racing.

Some girls who were watching break into applause, and one of them tucks her fists under her chin. "You guys are so adorable!"

"And lucky," her friend adds, sighing. "I wish my boyfriend liked to dance."

Garrett and I accept the praise, and let the misunderstanding go uncorrected. People always assume we're a couple, and I guess it's not hard to see why: We're both gay, we're always together, we hold hands in the hallway, and sometimes we maybe even snuggle a little. Not in a romantic way, but just because . . . I don't know, we like being close?

Okay, if I have to be honest, I *was* smitten with Garrett when we first met freshman year. *Temporarily.* But back then, he was crushing hard on some guy named Jackson—a friend of his from middle school, who'd moved away over the summer. They kept in touch via text and social media, and I admit that I burned with envy every time I had to hear a recap of their latest flirty-adjacent conversation.

Ultimately, though, Jackson broke Garrett's heart, ghosting him after getting a girlfriend; and in the meantime, I'd fallen head over heels for Seth Rylance—a painfully beautiful junior, who was sweet and smart and just . . . unbelievably hot.

Honestly, if Seth had one flaw, it was that he didn't know I existed.

At this point, Garrett is way more than just my best friend; he's my favorite person. I've told him things I haven't told anybody—things I can't even believe I told *him*. We get each other in a way that no one gets either of us.

But sometimes I worry we might be . . . holding each other back?

When the girls are out of earshot again, I hazard, "Maybe step one of our plan to find boyfriends should be, I don't know . . . trying not to look like we *are* boyfriends?"

"Whatever." Garrett keeps dancing, but his body language turns angular. "Who cares? I mean, we're not gonna meet any-one *new* tonight. We've spent two and a half years checking out the merchandise, and all the guys here suck." Then, "Except for Kieran Dugan."

"I guess." My tone is as neutral as I can make it . . . but I'm no fan of Kieran—an arrogant senior who, unfortunately, is just as gorgeous as he thinks he is—and Garrett knows it. "Too bad he's a stuck-up douche."

My best friend just shakes his head. "You don't even actually know him, Ollie. And besides, it's not like I want Kieran to marry me. I just want him to compromise my virtue."

With a devious little smirk, he throws himself back into the music, his moves clean and fluid. Ordinarily, I love to watch Garrett dance, but I've lost the good feeling I had earlier. "I'm going to get something to drink. You thirsty?"

I have to repeat myself before he finally offers a frustratingly indifferent response, and then I'm pushing through the crowd toward the distant corner where the snacks live. For some reason, this has been happening a lot lately, us disagreeing over boys—Kieran in particular—and I'm more bothered than I care to admit.

Under a banner proclaiming REFRESHMENTS there are two tables covered in cheap plastic and even cheaper foodstuffs. None of it is appetizing, but the punch is a glorious, neon red—a dentist's worst nightmare—and my mouth waters as I grab a plastic cup.

"I can't believe there are this many people here," someone says into my ear, and I yelp, my cup jumping immediately to the floor and rolling under the table. "I may have grossly overestimated Linwood's average coolness factor."

"Layla?" Startled, I gawp at her. "I thought you weren't coming to this!"

"I didn't want to." She sulks. "My parents changed my mind on my behalf. At the last minute, too, thanks very much."

"Why didn't you text me or something?"

"I was going to make it a surprise." She shrugs, looking elsewhere. "But you and Garrett have totally been in your bubble since I got here, so I figured I'd leave you alone."

Her tone is lightly barbed, and personal, and my skin prickles. Like any two people who've been friends for years, Garrett and I have a shared frequency—common references, familiar gestures, inside jokes—a way of being together that's just easy, just *us*. Layla calls it our "bubble," as if the whole point of it is simply to exclude others.

"You wouldn't have been, like, intruding or whatever," I finally say, reaching for another cup. The music is a little quieter on this side of the gym, so at least I don't have to shout it in her face. "We were just dancing—you could have joined us."

Layla narrows her eyes. I'm expecting a smart remark, but what she says is, "You're not seriously going to drop a cup on the floor and then leave it there, are you?"

"I wouldn't have dropped it if you hadn't scared me," I point out snippily, "and, anyway, I was just about to pick it up!"

This is a lie. I was absolutely going to leave my cup on the floor—but now I'll feel like a bad citizen if I do, so instead, I make a big show of getting down on the ground and crawling under the edge of the table. Luckily, it turns out the floor is not the sticky, textured nightmare I expected; *un*luckily, my cup rolled about two freaking miles, and I have to shuffle the whole way to it on my hands and knees.

Just as I reach my destination, though, I hear Garrett's name—spoken by someone standing on the other side of the thin tablecloth—and I go still.

"Garrett Loring? Which one is he?"

"He's a junior this year . . . tall, dark hair, dimples? He's in the marching band, he used to wear glasses with clear frames—"

"*That* guy?" The speaker sounds doubtful. "I thought he was too nerdy for you."

"I never said that!"

"Kieran, you said he looked like he still uses bedsheets with cartoons on them."

When I realize that I'm listening to *Kieran freaking Dugan* trash-talk my best friend, I am immediately furious. I want to tie his shoelaces together. I want to jump out and confront him, and announce that Garrett got rid of his Pokémon sheets freshman year, *so there*. But an instant later, he says something that makes my heart crash-land in my stomach.

"Okay, well, whatever—maybe I changed my mind." Kieran gives an easy laugh. "He's nerdy, but it's a cute nerdy, you know? Good enough for the Lock-Up, anyway. I still need to figure out my midnight kiss."

"Oh, that's what this is about. Don't tell me: The guy you were planning on canceled at the last minute, and now you're desperate for a replacement?"

"'Desperate' is a really strong word, okay?" Kieran protests. Then, after a brief pause, he continues, "It's also accurate. But

I am *not* going to ring in the new year with dry lips. Not after getting ditched by a six-out-of-ten who's lucky I even noticed him in the first place!"

"Okay, so, what's the plan, exactly? You just walk up to some dude you barely know all, 'Hey, I'm Kieran, and I'm six foot two—wanna make out?'"

"Come on, gimme some credit." Kieran sniffs. "Josh copied the key to the pool behind Coach's back and hid it in one of the gym lockers; all I have to do is convince one cute little nerd to take a romantic, late-night swim with me—bathing suits optional—and the rest is nature taking its course." He shifts his weight. "And, just for the record? I'm six-three."

If there's more to their exchange, I don't hear it. Blood is roaring in my ears as I scramble backward, knocking into table legs and crossbars, moving as fast as I can.

When I lurch out from under the table again and get to my feet, my heart is beating so hard I feel it in my forehead. Horror must be writ large across my face, because Layla takes one look at me and her eyes bulge. "Ollie? What is it, what's happened?"

"Kieran." My mouth is dry enough to store matches. "We have to save Garrett!"

"Save Garrett. From Kieran . . . who? Dugan?" Layla shakes her head. "You're gonna have to fill in some more blanks here. What the hell are you talking about?"

Swallowing, I do my best to describe the nefarious plot I've overheard—and quickly. Who knows how much time we've got before Kieran puts his scheme in motion? But even when I tell her the part about the "optional bathing suits," Layla still barely reacts.

"Just so I've got this right," she begins with a peevish frown, "you're having a panic attack because the boy Garrett likes wants to make all his dreams come true?"

"*Yes!*" I exclaim, tossing my hands up. "Wait—no. Why are you saying it like that?"

"Because that's how it is?"

"That's not how it is!" Several people glance over, and I realize I'm shrieking. "Were you even listening to the part about how Kieran is only looking for a last-minute plan B, and Garrett means nothing to him but a notch in his bedpost?"

"Yeah, I got all that." She's still scowling like *I'm* the one who's done something wrong. "Did it occur to you that maybe Garrett *wants* to be a notch in Kieran's bedpost?"

"*Yes!*" I'm shrieking again. *"That's the whole problem!"* We are totally fighting the clock here, and I don't know why she's acting this way. "Garrett deserves better than some knuckle-dragging senior who . . . who makes fun of his sheets, and calls him a nerd!"

"*You* call Garrett a nerd."

"*Affectionately!*" It is absurd that I even have to point out the difference. "Kieran is only interested in himself. He's a player, and he goes through boys like, like . . . I don't know, something people go through really fast! I won't let him do it to my best friend."

Layla folds her arms across her chest, her gimlet eye turning suddenly philosophical. "You know what I think? I think you're jealous."

The snort that comes out of me is surprised and ugly. "I'm sorry . . . 'jealous'?"

"Yeah. Garrett's himbo fantasy finally coming true means he'll be doing tongue sports with Kieran at midnight, while you have to stand there alone and watch."

"Oh, and I'm so childish that I can't handle it if he gets to kiss someone and I don't?" My patience has reached the end of its tether. "That could literally not be further from the truth. I *want* him to find somebody. In fact, I would be thrilled to make sure he finds *anybody*, as long as it isn't Kieran!"

"Oh, okay." Layla bobs her head. "So if I know someone else who's here tonight, who has a huge crush on Garrett, you'd be fine with me hooking them up? You're absolutely cool with Garrett getting his first hickey while we just watch?"

Something in her tone makes it clear that the scenario she's describing is not purely hypothetical, and for an instant, my throat closes. *Layla knows another guy who wants to get with Garrett?* The image unfurls in my mind, and my hands go tight, panic rocketing inexplicably up my spine. Maybe I lied to her a second ago, because the fact is that I really hate what I'm picturing . . . and I'm not sure I fully understand why.

I unstick my tongue to say something—anything—but it's too late; my silence has already incriminated me.

"*I knew it!*" Her eyes light up. "You *are* jealous."

"I am not! I would rather kiss a bug zapper than Kieran Dugan."

"You're not jealous of *Garrett*," she declares, stepping closer. "You're jealous of Kieran. When that clock hits midnight, the only person you want kissing Garrett is *you*."

"What?" I splutter, sucking in some air. "What are you talking about?"

"You know what I mean."

"No, I don't!" Now I'm annoyed. People love to tell Garrett and me that we "need to date already," like we're a reality show they get to vote on, and not real people; but Layla ought to know better. "We are *just friends*, okay? How am I having to explain this to you! All I want is to keep him from making a really big mistake."

Another moment passes, and Layla's shoulders slump. "I don't want either of you to make a mistake," she says with a sigh. "And that's why I won't let you keep this from him. If you don't want Garrett to kiss Kieran, then you have to convince him not to—because he deserves to know the truth."

"Fine," I say, because I can't say anything else, my stomach going all crampy. Layla's threat is a bullet bouncing around in my skull—and now there's two people I need to keep away from my best friend tonight.

Without another word, I turn away from her and plunge into the crowd, adrenaline shaking all my thoughts to pieces. Garrett won't listen to reason when it comes to Kieran Dugan—I know that from experience—and Layla has apparently taken full leave of her senses, so it's all on me to prevent imminent disaster.

And I have no idea what to do.

When I get back to where I left Garrett, I'm relieved to find him still there, dancing alone. Twirling disco balls scatter light across his cheekbones, freckling his face with stars, and something twinges in my chest. Involuntarily, my memory dredges forth the day we met in Spanish One, freshman year.

If a class doesn't have assigned seating, I always choose the back row; but I hesitated that day, when I walked in and saw

Garrett at the front of the room. Tall and angular, with a sulky mouth and puppy-dog eyes, he was exactly My Type; and when I sat down next to him, he smiled at me, and my heart had a freaking orgasm.

I was crushed when he told me about his thing for that Jackson guy, and by the time their whole saga was over, I'd moved on to Seth, and Garrett and I had officially decided we were Best Friends for Life.

Was there a time I would have dated Garrett? Sure. Was there a time I was sick with jealousy, because all he cared about was some guy from his middle school who didn't even live here anymore? Absolutely. But all of that was in the past. We'd been through so much, and the way I felt about him was completely different now.

Wasn't it?

"Earth to Ollie!" Garrett waves his hands in front of my face, and I snap back into the present, realizing that I've been staring. "Are you okay?"

I go to say something, but words don't come out. Suddenly, all I can think of is the stars on his face, and the shape of his mouth, and the fact that I'm supposed to kiss him later. The back of my neck films with a cold sweat. *This is all Layla's fault.* She stuffed these thoughts in my head like a curse, and now I can't get rid of them!

"Ollie?" Garrett's smile falters, and he looks like he might reach out to touch me; and before I can think twice, I'm speaking.

"We need to get out of here." I glance around, nervously, but Kieran is still nowhere to be seen, and Layla is giving me a head start so I can "be honest"—which is really just a colossal mistake, and she's got no one to blame but herself for what I'm about to do.

"Get out?" He scrunches his nose up. "Ollie, we're literally locked in."

"I know, I just . . . I need to get out of *here*." Swallowing hard, feeling every muscle in my throat, I hold out my hand. "Trust me?"

Garrett doesn't answer. He just threads his fingers through mine, and lets me tow him across the crowded dance floor for the exit.

To his credit, he raises a brow but no objections when I lead him to the men's room outside the gym; but when I drag him all the way past the stalls, to the door at the back that connects through to the boys' locker room, he finally lets out an awkward laugh. "I'm kind of afraid to ask, but . . . what the hell are we doing here?"

Mustering a sly look, I answer, "We're going swimming."

Fresh on my mind, this idea was the lightest brick at hand when I was struggling to think of ways to hide Garrett from Layla and Kieran long enough to . . . you know, think of other ways to hide him. If it doesn't work, my backup plan is to set something on fire and force an evacuation of the building.

Not aware of the depths to which I'm prepared to sink, Garrett balks. "*Swimming?* Ollie, what are you talking about?"

"I'm talking about the pool, duh," I whisper through my teeth. "I might know how to get us in there." My hope is that it sounds too exciting and forbidden to resist . . . but he still looks doubtful. "Please? It's New Year's Eve, and I want to be spontaneous and risky! I want to have fun—just the two of us."

Something in his expression softens, and he finally nods, ducking apprehensively through the door. I follow behind, relieved and . . . a little grossed out. Even empty, the locker room reeks faintly of sweat and dirty hair, malevolent testosterone lingering in the atmosphere. Flicking on the lights, we make our way to the deadbolted pass-through that guards the pool, trying to be quiet.

Garrett coughs. "I don't suppose it occurred to you that we didn't bring swimsuits."

"The whole point of doing spontaneous stuff is not preparing first," I answer importantly—ignoring a petty voice inside that says he wouldn't be complaining about the "bathing suits optional" part if Kieran were asking. "We can swim in our underwear."

Demonstrating my commitment to this foolishness, I yank off my shirt and throw it across a low bench between the rows of lockers. Garrett still hesitates a little, but then he steps out of his shoes, and I begin my hunt for the key Kieran mentioned. Without any guidance, it takes me a while—but that makes victory all the sweeter when I hit paydirt.

"Aha!" I declare, spinning around . . . and then I freeze, the key slipping through my fingers. Garrett stands there in nothing but his briefs and a Wonder Woman T-shirt that's so small he's practically Hulking out of it. Seeing my expression, he turns a bright pink.

"I know—I look ridiculous." He folds his arms awkwardly.

"But you can't make fun of me! This is my lucky shirt, and I've worn it every New Year's Eve since eighth grade."

In reply, I only make an audible gulping sound. The shirt is comically small, but mockery is *not* what's on my mind. The fabric clings to him like a second skin, accentuating the width of his shoulders and the gentle swell of his chest; and six inches of flat stomach are visible between the bottom edge and the waistband of his underwear. The air thickens, and I . . . feel something. *Down there.*

Garrett's smile goes sideways. "Ollie?"

"Sorry—" My voice cracks, *literally cracks*, like some cheap gag from an old sitcom. "I just . . . I spaced out!"

My heart pounding like the DJ's subwoofers in the gym, I dive after the key. In my peripheral vision, Garrett peels off that stupid shirt, but I refuse to take another look. I can't. *This is not acceptable.* He's my best friend, and I'm on a mission to save him from himself; I cannot afford to become *further confused* by his underwear!

Self-consciously, I struggle out of my pants, looking resolutely at the floor—trying my best not to think about what I can't stop thinking about. But it's only by the skin of my teeth that I unlock the pass-through before Little Ollie becomes an unconcealable problem.

"'Last one in' and all that stuff," I call in a shaky voice, hurrying for the pool. We can't afford to turn on any lights, so the only illumination comes from moonglow that shimmers through a wall of glass-block windows. The water is dark and bottomless, more than capable of hiding my sins, and I cannonball into it.

Turns out it's also freezing, and I gasp as I surface, my skin drawn tight; I'm spluttering again an instant later when Garrett slams down beside me like the asteroid that killed the dinosaurs, sending up a tidal wave. We splash-fight for a while, and then, because he's winning, I try to escape. He's got longer legs than me, though, so that doesn't go in my favor, either, and we wrestle in the shallow end until I finally concede defeat.

After swimming a bit longer, we eventually grow bored, and end up sitting on the edge of the pool—side by side—shivering a little in the damp air.

Garrett cuddles up to me for warmth, his arms around my waist and his head tucked in the curve of my neck . . . and I go tense. I've been trying to forget all my issues, but now that it's quiet—now that it's just us *in our underwear*—a feeling not unlike terror settles in.

I have to fight the urge to fuss with Garrett's hair, which is sticking up as it dries. I can't stop thinking about how smooth his skin is, how sleek he looked climbing out of the water—how much I don't want to be anywhere but right here, right now.

"You know what I just remembered?" he asks suddenly, his voice soft, but the words echoing. "The Forbidden Zone."

This is so unexpected, I laugh in spite of myself. The summer after freshman year, a chain restaurant on the edge of town went belly-up, the building boarded over and abandoned—left pretty much to the elements. In July, Garrett and I discovered that there was a way inside, thanks to a loose sheet of plywood and a missing window.

The interior was stripped to its sparest parts—built-in booths, dulled fixtures, rotting carpet—but filled with the memory of life, like a lost civilization. We spent days exploring it, existing in it, turning it into our private universe. We told ghost stories, snuck a wine cooler, and even said "Bloody Mary" into a bathroom mirror.

We called it the Forbidden Zone.

"I can't believe they tore it down," I lament now, thinking of those last few days, when the bulldozers finally showed up. It was the end of an era—a tragedy.

"It was probably full of rat feces and black mold and radon." Garrett shudders, speaking at the same time. "I hated that place."

"Wait, what?" I try to look down at him, but he won't meet my eyes. "What are you talking about? You always wanted to go to the Forbidden Zone!"

"Well, yeah." He says it softly, his hand shifting on my waist. "Because I knew you loved being there. Honestly, that place scared the crap out of me—it was one-hundred-percent haunted, and I was sure we were gonna get caught—but . . ." Garrett shrugs. "I wanted to make you happy. I . . . always want that."

He basically whispers this last part, and guilty heat stings my face. I had no idea he didn't actually like the Zone. That whole summer, I thought we were on the same page—and now I don't know if that's because he's really good at faking enthusiasm, or if I'm so self-centered that I can't see the truth when it's right in front of me.

Just like that, it occurs to me where we are—and how I coaxed and wheedled and begged until he agreed to break into the pool, despite his clear misgivings.

"Garrett . . ." These words are the hardest to get out yet, because I'm afraid he'll be honest. "Am I . . . a bad friend?"

"Ollie, no." He squeezes me tighter. "You didn't know how much it creeped me out—I didn't want you to." Laughing, he adds, "That's kind of the whole point of lying."

I should feel better . . . but somehow his answer makes me feel worse. Because I'm starting to worry that it's true, whether he realizes it or not. What other lies have I let myself believe? "But you deserved to be happy, too."

"I was," Garrett insists. "I mean, I was usually only about a microsecond away from peeing myself at any given moment, but the Forbidden Zone *was* kinda cool, and I liked having a secret lair." After a moment, he adds, "Plus, I always let you go ahead of me, so the killer would see you first and I'd have a chance to escape."

"Okay, that part sounds honest, at least." I roll my eyes.

"You're not a bad friend," he says firmly. "Ollie . . . you're my favorite person."

He hugs me a little tighter, his fingers grazing the waistband of my underwear—and when electric sparks shoot through my body in all directions, the truth hits me like a sucker punch. My chest goes tight, and I begin to silently freak out as I confront something I should have realized for at least the last two years:

I'm in love with Garrett.

Old memories rush back, with new colors and sharper dimensions, tearing a web of delicate self-deceptions out by the roots. I'd bullied my feelings into a corner when I learned Garrett was pining for that Jackson guy, and then I turned my back—convinced anything could be that simple. But I always had a ready excuse to hold his hand, to fix the tag on his T-shirt, to smooth his hair if it threatened to dry funny.

I'm in love with Garrett.

I remember the first time he hugged me, and how it felt like I'd leveled up; my guilty satisfaction when I was the only person he wanted to see after the Jackson thing ended for good; my skin buzzing when he taught me those ballroom dance moves, his hands on my hips or the curve in my lower back. Those hot, dusty days at the Forbidden Zone, when I could only talk about Seth Rylance . . . even though my best friend, Garrett, was the first person I thought of in the morning, and the last person I thought of before bed.

Abruptly, I'm aware of his breath, his grip, his thigh pressed up to mine; and I know that Layla was right after all: I can't stand the thought of Garrett being with anyone else. And I start to tremble as I realize I can't keep this from him—I can't kiss him at midnight with a lie on my tongue.

"Garrett . . ." I turn my head just as he begins to sit up. It's pure luck that we move at the same moment, that our cheeks touch and then our lips brush together—the fleeting imitation of a kiss as we draw apart.

But in that instant, I taste the soft promise of what I've been anticipating all night long, and my nerve endings start to fizz like that sparkling grape juice we're not drinking tonight. Moonlight dances on the water, and I just stare at him, speechless and terrified.

Something is supposed to happen right now. One of us is obligated to laugh it off, to ignore it—or maybe even to lean back in. But I'm too much of a coward to choose the one I really want, and I can't seem to find my voice, so the moment just keeps . . . stretching . . . out.

Garrett licks his perfect bottom lip. "Ollie—"

Then:

"I'm telling you, I heard people in there!"

The voice comes from outside in the snow—muffled, but sharp with urgency—and two flashlight beams cut suddenly through the wall of glass blocks. Garrett and I look up, going rigid, and he hisses, *"The resource officers!"*

We might be locked down, but Linwood High's security team remains on duty, and they've been circling the school grounds all night.

Lunging to his feet, Garrett makes a break for the pass-through, and I stumble after him. My blood is cold and bristling, visions of expulsion dancing in my head, and I'm a nervous wreck by the time we regain the locker room. If we get caught, we're dead meat. *What was I thinking, stealing ideas from Kieran Dugan?*

Garrett starts pulling on his clothes immediately, but my mind is spinning out of control. I can't stop thinking about what just happened—and I'd give anything to know what's going through his head. My lips still tingle from that accidental contact, and I can't believe it took me this long to realize what I really want.

I can't believe I have to tell him something I've only just managed to tell myself.

I'm so agitated I put my shirt on inside out—and then backward, and then backward *again*—before I even start forcing my wet legs into my dry pants. It's got to be nearing midnight, and unless I come up with an even better distraction, Garrett will insist on going back to the gym, and the second Kieran sets eyes on him . . .

The truth strikes home, just like that, and I drop onto the bench between the lockers.

The second Kieran sees Garrett, *they'll hook up*. Because that's what they both want.

All this time, I thought I was protecting Garrett from Kieran, when I was only acting in my own self-interest. At last, Layla's warning makes sense: She could tell how I felt even when I couldn't, and she knew that one taste of forbidden fruit could cost me everything.

The air in the locker room rings with an accusatory silence, and when I turn around, I realize that Garrett has already finished getting dressed. His phone in his hand, he's staring at me, and he looks . . . bewildered. And hurt.

"Why does Layla say that I should ask you about Kieran wanting to kiss me?"

I freeze, the floor dropping away as I meet the bullet that's had my name on it all night long. It's a testament to my lack of organizational skill that I knew this moment would have to come—and yet I've got nothing to say for myself. "I . . . I can explain—"

"Wait, it's *true*?" Garrett blinks. "Kieran wants to kiss me, and you . . . you knew, and you didn't tell me?"

"I . . ." Words speed around in my head, a crowded highway with no exits, and the look on his face makes me feel worse than I thought possible. "I overheard him saying something like that, but—"

"Something like he wanted to kiss me?" He reiterates, his tone taking on an edge.

When I can't deny it, he shakes his head, turning away; and my heart gives a painful twist. Heat behind my eyes, I stammer, "He—he said other things, too. He made fun of your sheets!"

"My *sheets*?" His cheeks flush. "I don't even understand what that means. All I know is that a guy I've been fantasizing about for years finally wants to be with me, and you . . ." He trails off with widening eyes. "Was *that* what this was all about? Breaking into the pool, and all that 'spontaneous fun, just the two of us' crap? You were . . . hiding me?"

He ends in a trembling question mark, sounding so utterly betrayed that I wish the earth would swallow me whole. I don't want to cry, because I'm afraid of being even that honest right now . . . but I hate myself. For what I've done, for what I haven't said, for making him feel this way. "Garrett . . . it's not . . . It's more complicated than—"

"Why would you do this?" His eyes glimmer in the overhead light. "How could you?"

"Because Kieran *sucks*, okay?" I'm too loud, too shrill, my voice bouncing off the lockers. "He's a stuck-up narcissist, and . . . he's not good enough for you!"

"Then who is, Ollie?" Garrett challenges, staring me down. "Who *is* good enough for me—and what makes you think you get to decide that?"

"I . . ." What can I possibly tell him? He's right. And yet, he's not seeing the whole picture. "Look, I know you're all obsessed with Kieran, but you didn't hear the things he was saying!" My voice is raw, my safeguards falling apart. "He doesn't care about you, okay? He's shallow and self-centered, and *average*. He doesn't get how cool you are, or how lucky he is that you'd even let him hang out with you! He's just bored. You deserve someone who respects you, and who wants your first kiss to be special."

"Like who?" He counters again, insistent. "Who do I deserve, Ollie?"

But I can't say it out loud. I just keep seeing my life flash before my eyes, an old-timey filmstrip with big red letters spelling *REJECTION* across the final frame. If I admit how I feel, it changes our relationship forever. What if it makes things so awkward that he starts avoiding me? I'd rather eat my heart out in the friend zone than be someone he doesn't know how to talk to anymore.

In the end, my silence only seals my fate. Garrett's face goes from pink to red, and he finally shouts, "So the answer is nobody?" Tears slipping down his cheeks, he thrusts a finger at the pass-through. "What *was* that in there, Ollie? If we hadn't been interrupted, what were you about to do?"

My vision tunnels, the room closing in as he reads my secrets out loud. Somehow, he's seen through me as easily as Layla did; somehow, I've left myself unbearably exposed, and all I can do is backpedal. "I didn't . . . I don't know! It wasn't anything, okay? I swear. Please—"

"I'm such an idiot." He presses his hands to his face. "I thought . . . when you said we should kiss tonight, I was so sure it *meant* something." He lets out a bitter laugh, full of self-loathing. "I thought it was finally going to happen. I'm so stupid."

"Wait . . . you thought *what* was going to happen?" I can't catch up. "What are you talking about?"

"I'm in love with you, Ollie!" he finally blurts—and it's a

good thing I'm sitting, because the whole room turns upside down. "I don't know how you don't see it, but you don't, and tonight I thought . . ." Garrett's voice catches and breaks. "I thought maybe you felt something, too. But you were just trying to keep me away from Kieran. You don't want me, and you don't want me to be with someone who does, and . . . I can't do this anymore!"

Ending in a sob, he rushes for the connecting door to the bathroom, disappearing from sight before I can even process what he's said. My skin throbs with it, though, every cell repeating, *I'm in love with you, Ollie.*

I'm on my feet in an instant, yanking my pants up, giving chase. I can't let him go—not now, not like this. Barreling into the hallway, I call out, "Garrett, wait!"

"I'm going home," he yells back. He's crying, and the sound of it cuts through me like a knife. "I don't want to be here anymore, so just . . . leave me alone."

"Wait a minute!" I snap, my confusion and shock snowballing out of control. "You can't just say all that stuff and then run away—it's not fair!"

"Oh, *that's* not fair?" He whirls to face me. Our voices carry up and down the empty corridor, competing with the music coming from the gym. "I don't want to listen to you feel sorry for me, not after asking me to go swimming in my underwear, and, and—"

"How was I supposed to 'see' that you were in love with me?" I demand. "You've been obsessed with stupid Kieran for two whole years! It's all you—"

"I don't care about stupid Kieran!" he shouts back, even

louder. "He's just a *guy*. I only made a big deal out of it because I wanted you to be jealous." Giving a snort, Garrett adds, "Like it mattered. You couldn't care about anyone but that pompous douchebag, Seth."

"I only got interested in Seth because *you* couldn't let go of that boring poseur, Jackson!" I'm fuming. How dare he try to put this on me! "*You* were the one who only wanted to be friends. How is it my fault that I stopped waiting for you to like me back?"

"Wait." Garrett stares at me for a long moment. "What?"

"Look, I'm sorry I didn't tell you about Kieran, but I panicked, okay?" My emotions spill over at last, tears making hot tracks down my face. "I thought I was stopping you from making a mistake, but you were right: I was jealous." Swiping at my eyes, I continue, "I hate the thought of someone else kissing you, Garrett. I didn't realize how much I hated it until tonight, and I . . . I wish I'd done this better. I wish I'd figured it out earlier. I'm . . . I'm sorry."

"Wait." Garrett steps closer, his eyes shiny. "What was all that stuff about you waiting for me to 'like you back'?" He looks at me like he sees more than my outsides—and it makes my skin go tight again. "Why do you hate the thought of someone else kissing me?"

"Because I love you, too." I'm a complete wreck, my whole body shaking. "I guess I have for a while, but I was so sure you didn't feel the same way, that I tried not to. But tonight . . . I can't lie anymore, Garrett. I love you, and I want to be with you . . . and I don't know what to do about it."

Inside the gym, a boisterous countdown suddenly begins: *"Ten! Nine! Eight!"*

"Ollie . . ." Garrett shakes his head—but he takes another step closer, his voice dropping to a whisper. "Please don't say this stuff unless you really mean it. Because I've been in love with you for a long time. Maybe even since Spanish One."

"Seven! Six! Five!"

"I do mean it, though." I blink away more tears, fighting a smile onto my face. "You're my favorite person, Garrett. I wouldn't hang out in a haunted restaurant with anyone else."

He laughs at this, the voices in the gym getting louder. *"Four! Three! Two!"*

"And you're the only person I want to kiss—tonight, or any other time," I continue, feeling bold. He's close enough to touch, now, and I reach for him. "If you'll let me?"

His fingers link with mine, our palms touching, sparks everywhere.

"One! Happy New Year!"

Cheers erupt, and a horrific, dubstep remix of "Auld Lang Syne" starts to play, filling the hallway like carbon monoxide. It's so bad that we both start to giggle, in spite of everything, and Garrett brushes a tear off my cheek with his thumb.

"I've been waiting two and a half years to know what kissing you feels like, Ollie," he says in a tender voice, his hair sticking up adorably in the back. "And I really want a happy new year."

I can only nod, more tears falling, because I don't trust my voice at this point.

And then I fit my lips to his, a circuit connecting, and those electric sparks go live again in every atom of my body. There's magic in the way his mouth first presses and then pulls against mine; in the way he tastes, the way it tingles in the pit of my stomach when his hand finds a familiar spot on my waist.

It's even better than I imagined—soft and warm, hungry but careful, filled with memories . . . and yet totally surprising. It's strange how someone so familiar can still make me so weak in the knees.

But I guess it's a new beginning for both of us.

SHOOTING STARS
(One Bed)

MARISSA MEYER

*T*he train lurches as I'm brushing my teeth and I jab the inside of my mouth with the toothbrush, right behind my molar. "Ow," I groan, rubbing my cheek as I spit into the tiny metal sink. I rinse my mouth with the bottled water I bought at the train station and it isn't until I'm drying my face with a paper towel that I spy the trail of toothpaste dribbled down the front of my T-shirt.

With a sigh, I wet the paper towel and try my best to dab it off, but all I manage to do is leave a wet spot on my chest.

"Smooth, Misty," I whisper. "Cue the totally awkward run-in with Roman, and the cycle will be complete."

This is the story of my life:

Ketchup splattered on my dress during lunch? Roman will want to compare notes in math class.

There's spinach stuck in my teeth? Figures, since Roman and I were paired up for discussion all last period.

Baby sister got cotton candy in my hair at the ball game? Oh, here comes Roman with his entire family, and they just happen to be sitting right behind us.

I'm a bit of a mess on the best of days, but when Roman Spencer is around, I turn into a full-on Jackson Pollock painting. Which might not be so bad, if I wasn't hopelessly in love with him.

I comfort myself now with the fact that everyone is asleep. Beka and I stayed up later than we should have—her playing *Trial of Thieves* on her phone, me sketching out some ideas for a graphic novel I've been working on. I've never slept well when I'm away from home, which is just one reason why I regretted signing up for our senior trip to Yellowstone from the moment my parents paid the deposit, but Beka has been insisting for months that it's going to be amazing. Fresh air! Meteor showers! Freedom from adults! (Because the chaperones don't count?) And—most important—*almost five whole days with Roman.*

A prospect that made me more nervous than excited. So many more opportunities to embarrass myself.

Stuffing my toothpaste and brush back into my bag, I pull open the door to the tiny bathroom just as the train hits a curve. I stumble into the corridor, tripping over the knee of the boy sitting right outside. I yelp and start to fall forward, barely catching myself on the wall.

"Crap! I'm sorry!" Roman kips to his feet. Because *of course* it's Roman. "Are you okay?"

"Yeah, I'm fine." I straighten myself and cross my arms to cover the damp spot on my shirt. I don't even know why I'm surprised. "Why are you sitting in the hallway?"

"Was waiting for the bathroom," he says, jutting a thumb at the vacated room. Which would be perfectly believable, except . . .

"Why do you have a blanket and pillow?"

He glances down at the sleep accoutrements bunched at his feet. "Um . . . I might have been looking for a new place to crash."

"What's wrong with your room?"

"The room? Nothing." He slumps against the windows, which are pitch-black. I think we might be going through a tunnel, and my stomach swoops with this strange sensation, like Roman and I are the only two humans awake in the Rocky Mountains. "The roommates? Eh."

"Aren't you with Tyler and Manuel?"

Part of the so-called adventure of the class trip was taking a train to get to the park, and even getting to choose our own roommates. The trip is supposed to give us the sense of being on an old steam train during westward expansion, even though we're traveling north from California. Plus, Beka showed me photos of what sleeper cars used to look like, and they were about a thousand times more luxurious than Amtrak's modern sleepers. I'm not complaining, though. At least we each have a bed. We won't be saying that during our three-day hike through the wilderness.

"Yeah, and Jeremy," says Roman. "And it was great, until everyone fell asleep. Turns out, Tyler snores like a band saw. I can't believe he hasn't woken up half the train by now. Listen." He lifts a finger in the air and for a moment we both stand there, holding our breath. At first, all I hear are the sounds of the train speeding along the tracks, but then . . .

"Oh," I say, picking up on the distant rise and fall of *really* loud snores.

"Oh," he agrees.

"So . . . you were going to sleep in the bathroom?" I glance back through the door. The bathroom is about the size of a coat closet.

He follows the look, a little sheepish. "I hoped maybe there'd be a tub or something? I don't know. I've never been on a train before, much less a sleeper car."

"Me either."

We stay looking at each other a moment longer, sleepy and awkward, but then he straightens and drags a hand through his dark hair, making it look even fluffier than usual. Despite his name, Roman is not particularly *godlike*. He's taller than most boys in our class, but skinny and pale, with a goofy smile and acne scars and the sort of hair that is always sticking up in random directions.

And yet, whenever he turns that goofy smile on *me*, my heart very nearly implodes.

"Anyway. You should probably go to bed," he says. "I'll figure something out."

I nod, because he's right. I really need to get some sleep.

I get halfway to the room I'm sharing with Beka, Janine, and Montgomery (who is one of five Emmas in our graduating class, so at some point everyone started calling them by last name), before I pause and look back.

Roman is still standing against the window, staring at his phone, the pillow and blanket at his feet.

Where is he going to sleep? The hallway?

I swallow. What I'm contemplating is 100 percent against the very clear, oft-repeated rule of *no coed sharing in the rooms/ sleepers/tents* that has been stressed to us a dozen times. And I am a rule-follower through and through.

But it's almost three in the morning.

And he looks so lost, a little forlorn.

Besides, it isn't like anything's going to *happen*.

This is Roman Spencer.

This is me.

Nothing is ever going to happen.

"Hey, Roman?"

His head snaps up.

"You can have my bed. I'll share with Beka."

"What? No, I can't do that." The hope that flashes in his eyes gives him away, though.

"And I can't let you sleep in the hall. Come on."

He wavers for a moment, before smiling gratefully. "Thanks, Misty."

His lips. My name.

Is it melodramatic to say it kind of makes me want to swoon?

We trudge back to the room, and yeah, my heart is doing little flips. *Don't get too excited*, I tell it as I slide open the door. We step inside, where it is startlingly dark. When I'd left, the room had still been lit by the blue screen of Beka's phone, but now there's just the tiny orange nightlight by our feet.

"Beka?" I whisper. "You awake?"

The only sound that greets me is steady breathing from my three roommates.

Roman turns on the flashlight on his phone, facing it toward the floor so we don't shine it in anyone's face and accidentally wake them up. And yep, they're all passed out. Only my bed remains empty, my sketchbook lying open and facedown on the pillow.

I'm suddenly aware of how tiny the beds are. More like cushioned benches, really. Beka is lying on her back on the bunk above mine, one arm dangling over the edge.

This isn't going to work.

Not that two people *couldn't* share one of the beds. But it would be more of a big-spoon, little-spoon situation.

Warmth rushes through me, pooling in the pit of my stomach.

"I can sleep on the floor?"

I glance up. Roman's got a bit of a deer-in-headlights look about him.

"If you're sure it's okay for me to stay in here?" he adds.

"Oh. Yeah. Of course. Here." I grab the extra blanket—Montgomery had opted to use her sleeping bag instead—and hand it to him. Then, before this can get any more uncomfortable, I slip into my bed.

For a long time I listen to him shuffling around, straightening the blankets. I try to determine when his breathing steadies, when he finally drifts off, but I never do.

He's gone when I wake up, the extra blanket folded on top of the luggage rack.

My roommates don't say anything, so either he left before anyone woke up, or it was all a dream. That seems unlikely, though. I've had plenty of dreams featuring Roman, and if my ever-optimistic subconscious had been involved, he definitely would not have slept on the floor.

I don't see him again until we're on the platform in Salt Lake City. As the chaperones gather us in a big group for a mandatory head count, I catch his eye. He's standing with his friends. The look is fleeting, but it's electrified with our shared secret.

We broke a cardinal rule together.

I try to will away my blush while we're shuffled toward the bus waiting outside the train station. It's a five-hour drive before we get to the park, and I spend most of it staring out the window, reminiscing about last night, storing it away in my mental scrapbook of all the moments that have made me fall deeper and deeper in love with Roman Spencer, all the way back to Day One.

Seventh grade.

I tried to audition for our school's production of *Hamlet*, but got such terrible stage fright that I ran behind the curtains, crying. Roman was backstage, having just reinterpreted the "to be or not to be" monologue as slapstick comedy, which was equal parts hilarious and bizarre.

As soon as he saw me, he walked over and, without saying a word, wrapped me up in the sweetest hug I've ever received, even though I was at least two inches taller than him back then and we barely knew each other.

After rehearsals, Roman was cast as Guildenstern, one of the foolish courtiers, and also the first gravedigger, who is arguably the funniest character in the play. I got put on stage crew, building and painting the sets. It was an open invitation to watch him from behind the scenes for four straight months. To marvel at how he put everyone around him at ease, whether he was feeding lines to Rosencrantz, or dropping into a completely unrehearsed cartwheel on opening night because Hamlet missed his cue to come onstage. Mostly I was in awe at how Roman never seemed to doubt himself, whereas I'd pretty much made a full-time career out of doubting myself by then.

So, yeah. That play is what started it all, and I guess not a whole lot has changed since then, except that Roman definitely isn't shorter than me anymore.

Once we finally get to the park, we spend the day being carted around to some of the big tourist draws—Old Faithful, the Midway Geyser Basin, Lamar Valley. We gawk at steaming rainbow-colored pools that make it feel like we're on a different planet, and ogle at the herd of bison that won't get off the road and end up putting us forty minutes behind schedule, sending Ms. Zapata into a bit of a tizzy.

By the time we arrive at the lodge, we're all pretty exhausted. We grab our bags and linger in the lobby while the chaperones check us in. The vibe is stereotypical hunting lodge—all the pillows covered in cowhide, all the décor covered in antlers.

"For a place that encourages people to come admire the wildlife," mutters Beka, "they sure do romanticize the idea of killing them off." She glances at the check-in desk, then leans in toward me, whispering. "Hey, I have a huge favor to ask, but you can totally say no. Although . . . I don't think you're going to want to."

I'm immediately anxious. "What is it?"

Her voice gets even quieter. "Would you mind if I switched rooms with Roman?"

I stare at her, confused. "Why would we want their room? Does it have a better view?"

"Not *we*. Just me."

My confusion does not improve. "You want to switch with Roman? So, like, you would stay with—"

She hushes me.

"—Manuel?" I finish, whispering.

"And you"—she nudges me with her shoulder—"would stay with Roman."

My mouth opens, and she must accurately interpret my expression as absolute horror, because she rolls her eyes. "Not for *that*. I mean, unless you want to." She wiggles her eyebrows suggestively.

I smack her on the shoulder.

She laughs. "No, listen. I was talking to Manuel when we were waiting for Old Faithful to blow, and it turns out he plays *Trial of Thieves*, too. We wanted to have a mini tournament tonight. But Roman said he wasn't interested, something about not getting much sleep last night and wanting to crash early, and I just thought . . ."

"Beka! That is *so* against the rules."

"You only get one senior class trip, Misty. We're *supposed* to break some rules. And you can't tell me you haven't fantasized about some random happenstance in which you and Mr. Spencer just happen to find yourselves trapped in the same room together. He'll probably need to take a shower, and next thing you know, his hair is dripping wet and he's wearing nothing but a towel and—"

"Stop! It!" I punch her two times for emphasis. "Someone will hear you!"

She laughs again. "Okay, sorry. But come on. We're all getting rooms with two queens *and* a sofa sleeper. And we're all practically adults. But!" Her face becomes serious. "If you're not comfortable with this, then no problem, the party's off. Just say the word."

I'm definitely *not* comfortable with this, and I know I should tell her so. And yet . . . the picture she painted *was* enticing . . .

"Misty? Beka?" calls Mr. Shephard, waving a plastic key card in the air.

Beka's eyes get all big and pleady.

I groan. "Fine."

She beams. "Thanks, Misty! You get the key, I'll get our bags?"

I make my way through the lobby. Roman is sitting with his friends beside a gigantic fireplace made of river stones, and while I'm hyper-attuned to his presence, I force myself not to look in his direction. Has he heard the change of plans yet? Is he okay with it?

"Misty, there you are." Mr. Shephard hands me two key cards, the number *216* handwritten on little envelopes. "Just so you know, the hotel was out of queen rooms, but they had one king available. I figured you and Beka would be fine sharing?"

I take the keys before his words fully register. "Wait. What?"

"That's not a problem, is it?"

My mouth goes dry. "Uh . . . no. No, that's fine."

He grins, having expected this response. I am a rule-follower. I am a people-pleaser. I am a bit of a teacher's pet.

It would be very out of character for me to complain.

"Don't stay up too late," he says. "We've got a big day ahead of us."

I smile weakly and head toward the elevators, where the group is waiting with our bags. I have tunnel vision as I approach. All I see is Roman. His carefree smile, like a lighthouse drawing me closer . . . or warning me to stay away before I crash on the rocks.

I want to open my mouth and explain that there's been a mix-up with the rooms. We don't have two beds, and I can't possibly share with . . . with . . .

Roman looks over and our eyes lock and all the words evaporate from my head.

Which is just as well, because everyone except Roman and me are chatting about *Trial of Thieves*, and I don't have a chance to get a word in anyway.

I decide to pretend not to know about the king bed. Surely, when Roman enters the room and sees it, he'll immediately march off to the other room and tell everyone that it isn't going to work. Beka has to go back to her room, *our* room.

The group parts ways on the second floor. My heart is in my throat, and the hiking backpack I borrowed from my outdoorsy aunt feels like it's gained fifty pounds since that morning.

"You all right?" asks Roman. "You seem quiet. I mean, you're always quiet. But . . . if you're not comfortable with this, I can go to tell Manuel—"

"No, I'm fine," I say hastily. I'm not sure why I say it, and I know it can't be all that believable given the squeak in my voice. But he cannot *ever* know how much I secretly want this. How much I secretly want *him*. "Besides, each bed has two rooms. I mean—each room has two beds. So. It's fine."

We reach the room before he can say anything more. I scan the key card and push open the door. A lamp has been left on, drawing us forward.

When we see the bed, we both freeze. Somehow, even knowing it would be there, in all its California king–size glory, did not prepare me for actually *seeing* it. A quilted duvet sports a pattern of pine branches. Six enormous pillows are propped up against a headboard.

I refuse to speak first. Because any minute now he's going to turn around and leave and go find Beka and return this trip to its regularly scheduled programming—the one in which I sneak glances at Roman while we snack on turkey sandwiches at separate picnic tables. Not the one in which we share a hotel room.

This programming is filling my head with possibilities that are anything but possible.

This programming is just plain mean.

Finally, Roman speaks.

"I'll take the floor."

I whip my head around to look at him, but he is already crossing to the other side of the room. He shrugs off his backpack and starts unrolling his sleeping bag.

"No, Roman," I say. "You slept on the floor last night, on the train."

He shrugs. "I'll be fine."

"But . . ." I look at the bed. The *huge* bed.

Unlike the train, there is definitely room for us both.

"We could . . . like, make a wall?"

He pauses.

"Of pillows," I explain. "We'll just line them up down the middle and . . . you know. You don't have to sleep on the floor."

Roman looks at the bed and all those pillows. He's thinking about it. He's tempted.

I can't help being tempted, too, even though I know I'll never fall asleep if he's lying mere feet away from me. Close enough that I could reach out and touch him. Close enough that I'll probably be able to smell him. Close enough that, if one just happened to accidentally knock off a couple of pillows while they were sleeping, and roll over into the middle of the bed, and someone on the opposite side just happened to roll over at the same time, then they would be—

"That's okay."

Roman turns away from the bed. Away from me. "I think it's best if I sleep on the floor."

Midnight.

He clearly doesn't like me. If he liked me, he'd have shown at least *some* interest in being in this bed with me. Right?

Unless he's trying to hide the fact that he likes me by taking the floor. Like, maybe he finds me so irresistible he's afraid that if we were in the same bed, he wouldn't be able to control the urge to pull me into his arms and kiss me senseless.

I mean. I know that's *probably* not the case, but . . . it could be.

Couldn't it?

No. That's only my imagination running wild. Wishing, always wishing.

Roman doesn't like me. Not like that.

I'm sure.

Well. I'm pretty sure.

1:16 a.m.

I can't stop thinking about being kissed senseless.

My whole body is tingling. I kicked off the blankets ages ago because I was too warm thinking about it.

I've spent the last hour wondering what would happen if I climbed down off this bed and lay down on the floor. If I went to him, instead of silently wishing he would come to me.

I won't do it. There's no way I would ever have that sort of courage.

But I can't stop wondering. *What if I did?*

1:49 a.m.

Why does he keep rustling around?

Is he awake?

Should I say something?

2:04 a.m.

"Misty? Are you still awake?"

2:15 a.m.

I should have answered.

I've been dreading the hike ever since the itinerary for the trip was announced, even though the coordinators assured us that it is a hike intended for every experience and fitness level.

It's not my fitness level I'm worried about. It's just that if anyone is going to stumble into a patch of poison ivy or step in a pile of bear scat, it will be me.

Given that the only hikes I've ever been on are the kind with paved trails and bike paths, I may have overprepared. I took the internet's recommended packing lists very seriously and have everything from bug spray to a bear horn, a water bottle with built-in purifier, a first-aid kit, and four extra pairs of moisture-wicking socks. And that's just the first pocket.

As the bus drops us off and we begin our jaunt through America's first national park, I realize that maybe I should have worried less about bears and more about carrying around an extra twenty pounds in miscellanea.

I spend the morning at the back of the group. Beka sticks

with me, and pretends not to notice or care that we're dragging behind. She spends most of the time telling me how she slayed in the makeshift competition last night, and asking what I think about Manuel, because she'd never really noticed how cute he is, but . . . he's kind of cute, isn't he?

I agree, happy for the distraction from my huffing. Manuel is super cute, and has been making super googly eyes at my friend all year.

The group pauses to admire the Yellowstone River, which gives us a chance to catch up. Roman is sitting on a boulder, but his eyes aren't on the river. They're on me.

"There you are," says Manuel. "We were taking bets on which one of you got eaten by the bear and which one got away."

I shrug off my pack, dropping it with a heavy thud. "If there was a bear, I'd throw this bag at it. Would easily knock it unconscious."

Roman leans over and grabs one of the straps. He grunts as he does a couple bicep curls with it. "What do you have in here?"

"Only the necessities," I say. "According to XtremeWildernessHiking.com, at least."

"Come on," says Beka, slinging an arm around my shoulder. "Let's check out this marvel of Mother Nature."

I'm not sure whether the river is a marvel, but there is a pretty cool-looking suspension bridge up ahead. Plus, the guides hand out snacks. Trail mix and oranges never tasted so good.

"All right, let's get this show on the road!" cries Mr. Shephard once we've all rested. "We've got another hour to go before we reach the campsite."

I roll out my shoulders as I head back to the rock. But my

pack is no longer leaning against the stone. I freeze and look around.

"I thought we could switch for a bit?"

Roman stands a few feet off, stringing his arms through the straps of my backpack. "Mine's a lot lighter," he adds.

"You don't have to do that."

"I know. But . . . I want to. If that's okay?" He picks up his bag and holds it out for me. "I'm thinking about trying out for track when I get to CalArts, and this will help build my endurance."

I blink. Roman is many things, but athletic has never been one of them. Even that onstage cartwheel all those years ago was pretty sketchy.

"Really?" I ask.

He hesitates, then cringes. "No. I just didn't know if offering to carry your bag might be, like, annoyingly misogynistic or something. I just . . . thought maybe you could use a break."

It takes me a second to realize he's *blushing*.

I swallow hard, trying not to let my knees get all weak.

"Thanks," I say. "I would actually really appreciate that."

We start off after the group. I see Beka up ahead with Manuel and I expect Roman to catch up with them, but he doesn't. He stays back.

With me.

"So . . . I'm going to CalArts, too," I say.

For the record, I had already applied before I heard that Roman was thinking of going there, too. They have an excellent graphic design program. But I won't lie and say I wasn't really, really thrilled when I heard he'd be at the same school. Though, it's a bittersweet sort of thrilled. I'm already bracing myself for four more years of unrequited yearning.

"Really?" he says, legitimately surprised, but . . . happy? "Do you know what you want to major in?"

And thus begins the most amazing hour of my life.

It isn't the natural beauty of the park. It isn't the wildlife. It's an actual conversation with Roman Spencer. After a while, I even forget to be nervous.

We jump from graphic design to graphic novels to Japan to our travel bucket lists to mutual wonderment that we both want to see Machu Picchu more than any other site in the world. We talk about how this experience is sort of preparing us for hiking the Inca Trail one day, and then he says that maybe we can go together during summer break next year and proceeds to tease me about packing lighter next time. It requires some severe mental gymnastics for me not to blurt out all my feelings right then and there.

Thankfully, we reach the campsite before I can.

I try not to look sad that it's over, and I try not to read into what appears to be a tinge of regret in Roman's face, too, as he returns my backpack.

I'd been worried that our food options would consist of hot dogs, beef jerky, and scavenged berries, so I'm pleasantly surprised when dinner turns out to be delicious. The guides prepare foil packets full of sausages, potatoes, and peppers over the fire, followed by s'mores for dessert, because #camping. Then one of the guides pulls out a ukulele and the choir kids impress us with the prettiest version of "Kumbaya" you've ever heard, and yeah, I know how cheesy that sounds, but I'm having a surprisingly good time.

It doesn't hurt that my gaze keeps landing on Roman, the orange sparks from the fire like little bits of magic dancing around us. It's not so unusual, this magnetic pull my eyes have. I can always find him in a room, no matter the size of the crowd or how dim the lighting.

But the funny thing is, tonight, I swear, his eyes keep finding mine, too.

I don't want to give myself false hope. I don't want to believe that maybe he's actually noticed me. *Finally.*

But it's impossible not to wish.

Even after all these years of unanswered wishes.

Suddenly, someone gasps and points up. We all crane our necks as a dozen shooting stars zip across the heavens. I laugh in delight, mesmerized.

I wish I may, I wish I might, have this wish—

Something drips onto my thigh.

I look down. The marshmallow has oozed free of the graham crackers and landed in a sticky splodge on my favorite jeans.

Typical.

Roman's tent is next to mine. I didn't plan it that way, and I can't tell if *he* might have, or if Beka did a bit of clever maneuvering to put us in such close proximity. It hardly matters.

It was a good reminder, the marshmallow thing. I am awkward and shy and incapable of going more than twenty-four hours without embarrassing myself.

While Roman is confident and relaxed and *nice*. So flipping nice. Nice enough that he would take pity on me, with my toothpaste stains and too-heavy pack.

Climbing into my one-person tent, I try to get comfortable, but I haven't slept on the ground since I was nine, and that was in our backyard, knowing the security of my bed was mere steps away if I needed it. But two straight nights of less-than-stellar sleep, coupled with a full day of adventuring, has me feeling completely wiped out. I just have to close my eyes . . .

I hear footsteps. Someone pulling the zipper of the tent next to mine. Roman's tent.

And I'm wide-awake again. I hold still, laser-focused on every sound. The shuffle of shoes and clothes and canvas. I think about how, if there weren't two tent walls between us, we would be sleeping right next to each other.

But then I remember that we *were* sleeping right next to each other the past two nights and nothing happened. No hand-holding. No cuddling.

But I can't keep the daydreams from seeping in. I picture him and me in a one-person tent. My head on his chest, listening to the drum of his heartbeat. His arms around me, tracing designs onto my back.

A cry startles me from the fantasy. Roman is cursing and scrambling out of his tent.

I sit up and pull down my tent's zipper to poke my head out. Roman is spinning in circles, swatting at his hair and clothes.

"What's wrong?"

"Bugs," he says, kicking his legs. "Ants, maybe?"

I cringe.

With a shudder, Roman leans down closer to me. "Can you see any on me?"

I grab my phone and climb out. Turning on the flashlight, I have him turn around while I inspect him. "I don't see anything."

He pulls back the tent flap. An infestation of small black ants is crawling along the bottom of his tent.

"Gross," he says, swiping at his arms again.

"You're good," I say, checking him with the flashlight again. "I'm pretty sure."

He sighs, and starts clearing out his stuff from the tent before the ants can get into his pack. "There must be a hole in the tent lining somewhere."

Once the tent is clear, we both stand back, staring at it like it's the enemy and we're debating our war strategy.

Then I yawn.

And Roman yawns.

We both start to laugh.

"I'm going to sleep for a week when I get home," he says.

I glance over at him, only to see that he's eyeing *my* tent.

My pulse skips.

I know it's only because he's tired. We're both so tired. And clearly, no one's going to be sleeping in his tent tonight.

Then his gaze darts up to the stars that blanket the sky, his brow furrowing with suspicion.

The meteor shower is over, but something about the look makes me wonder if he believes in wishes. If he made one tonight.

I shake the thought away and try to keep my voice even. "We can share my tent?"

He doesn't answer.

I can't bring myself to look at him. "It'll be snug. But I think we'll fit." It takes all my nerve to add, with a hint of laughter, "I trust you not to take advantage of me."

He chuckles, but it sounds forced. Our eyes meet and there's a long moment where I'm sure he's considering it. Where I'm sure he wants to.

Share the tent, I mean.

Not take advantage of me.

Oh gosh, I'm blushing again. Thank heavens it's so dark out here.

Then Roman's gaze flickers to my mouth, before he takes a step back and drags a hand through his hair, messing it up in that frustratingly adorable way he does.

"Thanks," he says. "Um. But—I think the guides said they have extra hammocks if anyone needs one, so . . . I'm just . . . I'll just check with them." He inhales deeply and nods, as if congratulating himself on a fine decision. "Good night, Misty."

I wake up mortified.

What was I *thinking*?

Did I really invite Roman to sleep in my tent with me?

I bet my feelings were written all over my face and now he probably thinks I've been pining for him for years and I don't even care if it's the truth. What did I think? That he would say yes? That we would keep each other warm all night long and by the time the sun rose he would realize that he's been in love with me all this time?

As I'm crawling out of my tent, I notice Roman's tent has been relocated closer to the firepit, and one of the chaperones is helping him get rid of the ants while the guides make breakfast.

Roman looks . . . honestly? Kind of awful. His bloodshot eyes are accented by dark splotches underneath and he looks wobbly on his feet.

Still nursing my wounded pride at his rejection, and my embarrassment for having suggested such a thing in the first place, I decide it's best to avoid him. I wait to see which log he claims to devour his berry-cinnamon French toast (again with the foil packets . . . who knew?), then choose the one farthest away.

I attach myself to Beka as we set off on the trail. We follow the river for a while, and are dutifully impressed when we cross paths with deer, elk, and even one mangy-looking coyote who dashes away before any of us can get our phones out to take a picture. Whenever I catch sight of Roman, I turn the other way.

I try to enjoy being in the Great Outdoors, rather than agonizing over what did or did not happen. I take long breaths and see how many scents I can name, but all I can pick out are pine trees and my own sweat. I listen to the birds and allow myself to be charmed by the wilderness, at least for a little while.

This is our last full day in the park. Tomorrow, another bus will be waiting to take us to the airport. Then I'll be home, getting ready for finals and graduation and picking out a prom dress—Beka and I decided to be each other's dates a long time ago, and I hope this business with Manuel hasn't changed that. Soon, these past few days will be nothing but a memory, one that I can already tell I'll be analyzing and inspecting from every angle until the end of time.

"Group photo!" shouts Ms. Zapata when we reach the shore of Crevice Lake. Everyone crowds together. Jeremy and Lillian crouch down in front with jazz hands, while Casey grumbles something about hating photos and tries to hide in the back. I go along with it all, letting myself be jostled in toward the middle of the group, when I crash shoulder-to-shoulder with Roman.

He looks at me, a little startled.

"Cheese!" shout the teachers.

Roman smiles and loops his arm around my waist. I tense for a second, my heart racing, but then he turns to face the camera and I know it would be weird to just stand there, so I gather my courage and slide my arm around him, too.

The photo takes forever. There's a lot of yelling at us to squeeze in tighter, crouch down in front. My cheeks hurt from gripping the smile. My nerves are fluttering to have Roman's arm around me for so long.

We're finally given permission to break apart, but Roman doesn't immediately pull away. He looks at me, that smile lingering around his lips, and I can't be imagining this. This cannot be all in my head. The question in his gaze. The way his fingers press into my shirt, right above my hip, sending electrical currents surging through me.

"Here we go! Back on the trail!" calls Mr. Shephard.

Even though no one is paying us any attention, Roman and I leap apart.

Then we both start to laugh, and I'm not entirely sure what we're laughing about, but it leaves a warm spot in my chest for the rest of the day.

"The wolves circled the group of hunters, who sat oblivious around the campfire," says Greenfield—another Emma. Her voice is low and confident as she spins the story, and I wonder if she's making it up on the spot or if it's one she's heard before. I'm trying hard not to look shaken up, but the story is downright creepy. "The genetic tampering didn't just make them stronger and faster than average wolves. It also made them thirstier . . . thirsty for human blood. Now—the hunters had become the hunted." She paused, her eyes scanning the group. "Jeremy was the first to be taken!"

Grinning, Roman shoves Jeremy on the shoulder.

"The wolves waited until he got up to use the bathroom . . . waited until his pants were around his ankles . . ."

Some of my classmates hoot with laughter, including Jeremy himself, who winks at Greenfield. "You know you don't need an excuse to picture me with my clothes off."

"Jeremy!" warns one of the chaperones, eavesdropping from the next fire over.

"The wolf lunged from the shadows, swiping its massive claws across the hunter's abdomen, spilling intestines and organs across the urine-soaked ferns at his feet—"

"Greenfield!"

The laughter turns into grimaces and feigned retching. Despite the teacher's warnings, Greenfield goes on in endlessly gruesome detail as the rest of the hunters, all named after people in our class, meet their brutal ends. By the time she's describing how Roman gets the bones of his legs smashed into bits between the wolf's jaws just so he can't run while the wolf devours him alive, I'm thinking I might be sick for real.

When Greenfield finishes, to overwhelming applause, I am so ready to leave. That is, until I actually start heading toward my tent and realize just how dark it is. Beyond that protective circle of light, there is nothing but shadows.

I use a flashlight to find my way. My phone battery is dead, and since the guides and Manuel are the only ones who thought to bring portable chargers (thanks for nothing, XtremeWildernessHiking.com), we've all been suffering as we wait our turn to get our devices turned back on. Judging by the smirks on the teachers' faces, I think they might have planned it that way.

Something moves in the forest.

My adrenaline spikes. I aim the flashlight toward the trees, but don't see anything.

"I heard it, too."

I scream and whip the flashlight toward the voice. Roman jumps back in time to keep from getting clobbered.

"Sorry!" I gasp.

"No, it's okay," he says, a little breathless. "I didn't mean to sneak up on you."

We both turn back to the forest, but are greeted only by crickets. Our attention eventually shifts to the two tents before us. Two perfectly good tents, after one of the guides helped Roman patch up the hole where the ants were getting in. She told Roman they were probably attracted to something that smelled good inside his tent, and I couldn't help but relate.

"That was some story," he says. "Greenfield. Who knew?"

"Yeah." My laughter is strained.

Neither of us make a move toward our separate tents.

"Well," says Roman.

"We should probably try to get some sleep," I say.

"Yeah. Definitely." He glances at me. "Night, Misty."

"Good night, Roman."

Our eyes linger a second longer, then I suck in a deep breath and move to unzip my tent. A few feet away, he does the same.

When we hear it.

Howling.

There are wolves in Yellowstone, along with bears and mountain lions. So there could be an actual wolf, or even a pack of them, somewhere out in the dark.

"It's gotta be Jeremy," says Roman. "He's just trying to scare people."

As one, we both look back toward the fire, where Jeremy is still sitting with the others.

"Or not," he says.

I swallow.

Roman makes a miserable sound, something between a groan and a sigh. "I've really got to get some sleep. I've barely gotten any on this whole trip."

I look at him sympathetically. The train, the hotel room, the bug-infested tent . . . "It has been rough for you, hasn't it?"

His smile is weary. "I probably should have taken you up on your offer last night. People say hammocks are really comfortable, but I beg to differ."

Another howl sends shivers down my spine. I can't tell if it was closer or farther away.

"Maybe it's Andy?" I say.

We both look back at the fire. Andy is nowhere to be seen.

"Maybe," Roman agrees, half-heartedly. Then he clears his throat. "All right, well, I'm going to pass out on my feet pretty soon, so . . . see you in the morning?"

"Yeah. Last day. Tomorrow you'll have your own bed again."

"I'll never take it for granted again." He disappears into his tent. I start to crawl into mine, too, when more rustling in the woods stops me. I pause and send the flashlight beam over the tree boughs, hoping to spot a mouse, a deer, an owl . . . anything that could be making those noises and not getting ready to devour me.

"Hey, Misty?" Roman's head and shoulders appear again. "I know there's nothing wrong with your tent or anything . . . and maybe this is weird, but—"

"Yes."

He stills.

I've surprised myself, too.

But there is definitely something *out there*, so . . .

"Yes," I say again, more firmly.

His smile is nervous and relieved as he holds open the flap on his tent.

It only takes a few seconds for me to grab my sleeping bag and lay it out next to his. For once, I don't let myself think or doubt or question as we zip the flaps closed and snuggle into our separate pouches. It is tight. It is cozy. We barely fit, side by side in the dark, the lengths of our bodies pressed together, my arms on top of the sleeping bag because I'm suddenly very warm. I lie with my eyes open for a while, trying not to overthink what's happening. I'm *in his tent*. Just him and me. Me and Roman. Alone. *Sleeping.*

Well, not sleeping. Not yet. I watch as flashlight beams dance across the canvas. I listen to the crackle of the bonfire. I try to discern when Roman's breaths deepen, but they never seem to.

Another howl makes me gasp. My hand shoots toward him before I can stop it.

His hand meets mine in the middle. Our fingers lace together, squeezing.

We both start to laugh at the absurdity of it. Here we are, going off to college in a few months, and we're both suddenly afraid of the dark?

Absurd or not, embarrassing or not . . . we don't let go.

I wake up first. I'm on my side facing Roman and he's on his side facing me, his arm draped over my hip in a way that makes my insides go all shivery. I allow myself a few minutes of staring at him. His lips are a little chapped, his cheeks a little sunburned.

I never want to move.

But if he wakes up and finds me gawking at him, I'll die of mortification, so I gently shift his arm off of me and inch my way out of the sleeping bag. I'm halfway to freedom when he groans unhappily and wraps his arm around my waist, pulling me close again, my back now against his chest.

"Not yet," he mumbles.

I freeze, unable to tell if he's talking in his sleep. Even with the sleeping bags between us, I can feel his heat pouring into me.

"Roman?" I whisper.

"Mm?"

"If the chaperones catch us . . ."

He's silent for a minute, and I think maybe he's fallen back asleep. But then he mutters, "What're they gonna do? Send us home?"

I consider this for a second. It *is* a fair point.

My body starts to relax. This might be the only time I ever get to experience this, after all. Would be a shame to waste it. When he wakes up—*really* wakes up—he'll realize what he's doing and that will be the end of it.

The end of utter bliss.

"Finally got a good night's sleep," he says through a yawn. "I really needed that."

My eyes snap open.

Hold on. He *is* awake?

And he's still holding me?

On purpose?

There's another long silence, and I've just convinced myself that it was a fluke and he's still fast asleep when he asks, "Do you remember that time we ran into each other at the Badgers game?"

My mind trips over the question and it takes me a moment to respond. "Yeah. Your family was seated right behind mine."

He falls silent again, and I wonder if that was it. He was just wondering if I'd remembered.

But then—

"When I saw you, I thought . . . 'Okay. This is my chance. The first opening I get, I'll ask her to go get some popcorn, or . . . go try to catch foul balls on the lawn, or something.' I psyched myself up for seven straight innings. Then . . . your sister started to cry, and you left."

I want to roll over and look at him, but his arm is weighing me down, not unpleasantly, and I'm a little afraid to move.

He adds sleepily, "You never turned around. Not once."

That game has been burned into my memory for years. I don't recall anything about the actual game—who we were playing against, who won. But I remember sitting so still, feeling his presence behind me, listening when he and his family cheered, self-conscious about every move I made, debating, constantly debating if I should turn around and say hi, until it got to be too late. Until I was convinced that if I turned around, it would just be weird.

Besides . . .

"I had cotton candy in my hair."

"Hm?"

"My sister had cotton candy, and some got in my hair. I was embarrassed. I'm always such a clod when you're around. Always spilling things and . . . making a mess of things . . ."

We fall silent.

"If that's true," Roman finally says, so quiet I barely hear him, "I haven't noticed."

I snort. "Right."

"Misty . . ."

He props himself up onto his elbow. I hesitate, hypersensitive to every move of his body, every move of *mine*, but then I force myself to roll onto my back so I can meet his gaze.

He takes in a deep breath, his face a mix of terror and nerves and hope. "Misty . . . I like you. I pretty much always have."

I stare at him.

My brain is dissolving.

I'm fairly sure I'm still asleep.

And because I can't ever just accept a good thing, what comes out of my mouth is: "No you don't."

His eyebrows shoot upward. Surprised. Maybe even a little amused. "Um, yeah." He makes a gesture, indicating the fact that we are sharing a one-person tent. "I do."

"But—but you wouldn't share the bed," I stammer, embarrassed to even be bringing it up. "Or my tent the other night."

"Not because I didn't want to," he says with a small chuckle. "I definitely wanted to. But . . . it seemed like you were panicking a little bit? And I didn't want to make it worse."

My lips part.

It's finally starting to crystallize. His words becoming clear to my sleep-addled, desire-muddled brain.

"So . . ." he starts, uncertainly. "Do you . . . ?"

He doesn't finish, just lets the question hang between us, engulfing us.

"I do," I finally manage. "I like you back. Like . . ." I swallow hard. "Like, a lot. Really a lot."

It's probably the most un-smooth confession of all time.

But Roman's grin widens. "Okay, good, because I was only about ninety-seven percent sure that you did, and that other three percent has been killing me all week."

For a second I think I should be embarrassed, to know that I was so obvious, that of course he could tell I liked him.

But—what does it matter?

He likes me.

Roman likes *me*.

I raise my hand to his face, tentative at first, daring to brush aside a lock of hair that's done nothing but taunt me since seventh grade.

He takes it for the invitation it is. Leaning down, he touches his lips against mine. Still hesitant, like maybe that last 3 percent isn't entirely convinced yet.

Until I wrap my arms around his neck and kiss him back. His hands slip beneath me, pulling me closer.

"Breakfast, sleepyheads!" someone shouts. "Rise and shine!"

We break the kiss, but we don't release each other. I'm sure my smile is every bit as goofy as his.

"Think there's any chance we could convince them to let us stay one more night?" Roman asks.

I bite my lower lip, pretending to think about it. "Maybe we could lie and say there's supposed to be another can't-miss meteor shower tonight."

He brushes his lips against mine again, murmuring, "Maybe it wouldn't be a lie."

He's right. As he kisses me again, my body fills with shooting stars.

KEAGAN'S HEAVEN ON EARTH

(The Secret Admirer)

Sarah Winifred Searle

Hello, Mr. Kelvin.

Mickey. You were going to skip Chemistry again, weren't you?

N-no?

Detention obviously isn't working, and when you do show up, your mind's lost somewhere up in the atmosphere. Perhaps if you're so determined to disengage with school, it's my job to help you *re*-engage.

I'm staff advisor for the Valentine's events this year, and I could use some extra help.

I hereby appoint you for Flower Day and dance duty.

Please, just give me another detention! I'm so *good* at sitting and doing nothing!

That's precisely why I can't do that anymore, and you know it. Come on, we're late for class.

Yeah, in middle school my friends had this group where we all pretended to be characters from that Hattrick High series. It was a lotta fun. I played the gnarly underdog hockey player from the wrong side of the tracks.

That's amazing. I can see it.

He had the best-worst mullet.

What about you?

I–I don't roleplay. I write fan fiction.

Ooh! What about?

Mostly about *Hoshi's Heaven on Earth*.

What's the story?

It's a light novel series about these...well, they call them angels, but not the religious kind. It's about these ethereal, genderless aliens that fall to Earth and the humans who help them.

It's a little embarrassing, but they sort of represent this idealized form of my identity in a really fun way? In that they're these gossamer-clad beings made of light and trying to assign any worldly sense of gender to them feels absurd.

Hey, Mickey!

Everyone loves the theme. You look cute.

Keagan, c'mere, you gotta see Max's costume!

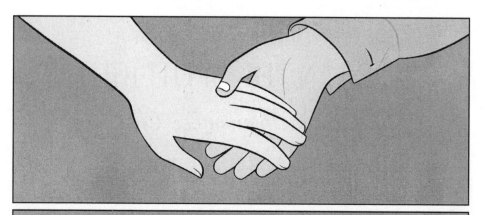

ZORA IN THE SPOTLIGHT
(The Grand Romantic Gesture)

ELISE BRYANT

I'm beginning to realize we're not walking into Bixby High's winter formal with good intentions.

See, Astrid's ex-girlfriend, Alannah, is supposed to be here with her brand-new girlfriend. And while I argued that we could witness everything we needed through Alannah's exhausting Insta stories (she's an oversharer—I'm talking periods, not underscores), Astrid *insisted* that she needed to see her in person.

And, like, I get that. The wound is still fresh, and maybe she just needs this last moment to accept that Alannah has really moved on, you know? To finally get closure and then hopefully we can stop listening to that depressing lady singing "Both Sides Now" on repeat every time Astrid drives us somewhere.

So we—Jorge and I—agreed to accompany her, scrambled together some outfits real quick and paid for the tickets with Astrid's mom's credit card.

But now we're walking up to the gym, and Astrid has this look on her face—right eye all squinty with her left eyebrow arched unnaturally high. I know this look. It's the look that's accompanied almost every bad decision I've been the sidekick for since I was three years old.

"So . . ." I start, tentatively, trotting along to keep up with Astrid's long strides. "Are you just going to say hi real fast or . . ." I trail off, not wanting to speak the other, way more likely alternative aloud.

"Oh Zora, don't you worry about it," Astrid says, hitching up the front of her impossibly tight strapless black dress and throwing her shoulders back. Her eye gets even more squinty, and her eyebrow is practically touching her hairline now.

Just like it did before she, newly vegan at ten years old, hijacked the cafeteria's shipment of frozen chicken nuggets and tossed them into the school parking lot, like tea into the harbor. Or when she threatened her lawyer parents would take legal action against Mr. Thurston after he wouldn't let us audition for the male parts in Billie Jean King Middle School's production of *Hamilton*. (Astrid ended up playing Aaron Burr. I was the girl who flirts with Philip Hamilton right before he dies. And *perfectly fine with it*.)

I side-eye Jorge, who's flanking her other side. He's wearing a faded T-shirt with a tuxedo printed on the front and black jeans so skinny I'm consistently surprised he can walk normal, even though they're part of his daily uniform. His wavy black hair, shaved on the sides and long on top, is twisted into a somewhat formal knot.

I send him a look that says, *Are we really going to let this happen?* Which he can understand because he's been around since we were three, too. This unholy trinity was forged in Ms. Bernadette's preschool—though back then the alliance hinged more on keeping the sunny spot in the sandbox.

He shrugs and sends me a look back that says, *Well, what are we going to do?*

Okay, so we're letting this happen.

"What? Are you worried about poor little Emily?" Astrid continues, adjusting the front of her dress again. Emily is Alannah's new, probably-in-danger girlfriend. "Oh, she'll be *just* fine . . ."

Those last words are barely a whisper, but her tone is so menacing that a couple in formal gear making out on the curb springs apart, ogling her instead. Astrid is oblivious to this, though, as she determinedly climbs the stairs to the gym, taking two at a time.

"Emily," Astrid says, her lip curling over the word like it tastes bad. "What kind of name is that, anyway?"

"The worst name," I say, though Astrid's rant is way past the point of needing a response.

Jorge falls in step next to me. "We can still stop her," I whisper.

"You're saying that like you actually believe it," he snorts, rolling his eyes.

"We could," I insist, though with admittedly less confidence. "Both of us . . . together."

He waves that away. "What's the worst she'll do? It's not as if she's going to, like, fight her or whatever."

I can tell by his face that we're both thinking of the squinty-eyed stare that eventually progressed to her shoving a red-hat-wearing guy who was taunting her at a protest we went to our freshman year. Astrid didn't get the "peaceful" memo.

"Okay, maybe she's going to fight her," Jorge concedes. "But—" He waves one finger in front of my face like he has one of those *Men in Black* memory-eraser tools. "I never said that. If we don't speak of it beforehand, then we have plausible deniability when Astrid pulls . . . an Astrid."

Jorge and I basically have PhDs in Astrid-pulling-an-Astrid at this point. And we've got our roles down to a science, each of us moving perfectly in tandem to ensure that nothing too catastrophic happens. Jorge is always ready with a joke, a charming smile, to distract and dazzle. And then I swoop in to smooth things over, clean up any big messes, and call Mr. and Mrs. Keller if it looks like we're in over our heads. Sometimes I wonder what it would feel like to be Astrid: to express emotions with abandon, to say what I want and not worry about the consequences. To have everyone take care of *me*.

But, of course, there's no room for that in our trio. One Astrid is controlled chaos. Two Astrids would be like Armageddon.

So, I do what's expected of me. I know my role, and I'm fine with it. *Really.*

We sprint up the last steps to catch up with Astrid who is already presenting our tickets at the entrance. It's a bigger to-do than I realized, with some stuck-up ASB girl checking for our names on a list and another guy in a pinstripe suit inspecting our tickets like they might be fake. As if this is some exclusive club rather than the gym where Jorge came this close to failing

PE and where the janitor threw those magic wood chip thingies over Joshua Sonora's neon-orange vomit after the physical fitness test in ninth grade.

"Get over yourselves," Astrid scoffs, speaking the words that I wish I had the nerve to say, like she always does. She grabs back her beaded clutch from the flustered sophomore who was attempting to inspect it. I flash my signature apologetic smile, and then follow after Astrid as she sashays through the mustard-colored double doors, all confidence and fury.

I have gone to exactly zero dances in my 3.5 years at Bixby High, and as we enter the gym, I'm reminded of why. I mean first, I don't recognize half of these people, which I guess is probably more of a *me* problem than a *them* problem. But also, I don't want to recognize these people. There's a mass of sweaty bodies in the middle of the gym—half unironically doing some old-ass TikTok dance moves and the other half throwing all pretense to the wind and grinding their parts against someone else's. The air feels moist (which, it turns out, I hate as much as the actual word), and it smells like a mix of Axe Body Spray, sweat, and the sickly-sweet mass of corsages. The blue and white twinkle lights and painted butcher paper Eiffel Tower are a nice touch (Paris theme, very original), but do nothing to cover up the hot mess that's actually going on here.

"You know, in moments like these, I understand Thanos," Jorge says. "*Alllllll* of this can get dusted as far as I'm concerned." He gestures to the crowd like he's waxing on and off. Astrid snorts out a laugh as she looks around the gym.

I take the opening. "Well, if we're in agreement here at the lameness of our current environment, we could just leave, you know. I think Hole Mole is still open. Astrid, I know how you love their potato tacos—"

"No," Astrid cuts me off, her eyes continuing to survey the room. Her bleach-blond hair and pale, milky skin, which she has to work really hard to maintain in Southern California, practically glow in the blue light, making her look like an angel. Or, with the vibes she's giving off, the angel of death. "I have something I need to do, and I'm not leaving until I do it."

"I just don't want you to . . . make a choice you'll maybe wish you could take back later," I say softly, reaching my hand up to touch her shoulder.

"Do I ever do things I regret?"

I just stare at her, and her icy demeanor finally cracks.

"Okay, yeah, all the time," she says with a red-lipsticked smile. "But you guys love me anyway."

I take an exaggerated breath. "We do."

"Speak for yourself!" Jorge calls, and Astrid play-shoves him.

"Give me an hour, tops," she says, clasping her hands together like she's begging us. "Help me win back my girl, maybe run interference on Emily if she gets in the way, and then potato tacos are on me."

Jorge starts, "What exactly do you mean by run inter—"

"We're in!" I interrupt. Jorge rolls his eyes at me, and I roll mine right back. We both already know how this is going to go, so why drag it out? The path of least resistance is always the better option.

Astrid lets out a little squeal of delight before hooking her arms around both of our necks and then kissing our cheeks.

"Okay," Astrid says, clapping her hands together. The squinty eye, arched eyebrow combo is back. "I need to take care of phase one. Be back soon."

She stalks off to the right of the gym, and I frantically look around for Alannah and Emily, hoping phase one isn't ripping out someone's hair extensions. I've got her back, yeah, but I've gotta psych myself up for that. I sigh in relief, though, when I see she's just headed for Bryan Bronson, who's serving as the DJ with his iPhone. We're safe for now . . . I think.

Jorge and I make our way over to the bleachers. He stretches out his long legs and leans back, basking in this temporary reprieve from high alert. I smooth out the peach dress I borrowed from Astrid's older sister, a castoff from one of her many sorority events, and gingerly sit down, careful not to snag any of the intricate beading. It's the most beautiful (and *definitely* most expensive) thing I've ever worn. I wish I was wearing it for a more special occasion.

Jorge sighs next to me. "Zora, we can say no to her, you know." I turn to look at him, and his playful eyes have turned serious. "We don't always have to be her savior sidekicks, like . . . caping for her after every bad decision."

I shrug. "If we don't, then who will?"

"I don't know. Maybe Astrid would figure it out herself?" he says with a laugh, and I hate it. It feels like he's laughing at me.

"She needs us."

"Yeah, but . . ." He reaches out to squeeze my hand. "There's no shame in just being what you need."

I squeeze his hand back and try to smile, but I can feel it coming out all wrong. I know he's right, but what good does that do us? If I let thoughts like that take root, well . . . it will only mess up what the three of us have. There's no room for resentment or change.

I can't have this conversation. I stand up. "I'm going to get a drink."

I walk over to the punch table, but of course there's no punch. Years ago, Mrs. Bronson, the PTA president and Bryan's mom, argued against the typical beverage offerings with fervor, as if saving Long Beach's youth from the dangers of processed sugar was the cause of her lifetime. So instead, like at every Bixby High school-sanctioned event, there are bottles of coconut water (which tastes like licking the top of a glue stick) and LaCroix (which tastes like someone got a *real* soda and then burped in my mouth). Great.

I look up to commiserate with Jorge. Maybe laughing about this will smooth out the wrinkle that his words, and my inability to accept those words, caused. But as I try to catch his eye, I'm distracted by something else. *Someone* else.

Standing in the corner of the gym is a boy I've never seen before. I know I've never seen him before because if I had, I would have remembered. This boy is *memorable*.

He has tan skin and shiny black hair that's slicked back from his face. His dark eyes catch all of the flashing lights in the room and reflect them back even brighter. And he's wearing a black velvet tuxedo with a crisp white shirt and bow tie. But it doesn't look cheesy. It just looks like he cares.

And I think . . . yes, he is. He's looking right at me.

My heart jolts, and my gaze shoots to the ground. The leopard-print faux-fur bolero I'm wearing suddenly becomes really warm, too warm. I feel like every inch of my skin is burning up.

I've seen *that look* before. I know what *that look* means. It means: *Wow, you're beautiful.* It means: *Out of everyone in this room, you stand out to me. You are someone special.*

But I've never seen *that look* directed at me.

It's usually beaming from some girl or boy to Astrid like a spotlight. And then it's my job as wing-woman to help Astrid go from *that look* to something bigger. It's what I did for her and Alannah.

Except this time, Astrid is nowhere in sight, and this gorgeous boy is looking at me like I'm the one who shines.

I take a deep breath, shake away my worries, and force myself to look up.

He smiles. And it explodes across his entire face like a firework. A sunburst of lines appear at the corners of his eyes, and his nose wrinkles and I can see every one of his sparkling white teeth. He holds his right hand up and waves, tentatively. It's such a perfect, gentle movement, that it makes my chest ache.

And so I do the only thing I can do. I smile back.

But . . .

His sunshine smile clouds over. His eyebrows press together, and the sides of his mouth turn down.

I don't know what I expected to happen, but it definitely wasn't that.

I suddenly become very interested in my black sequined mules. I push down the scratchy feeling at the back of my throat, and close my eyes tightly so my mascara doesn't run. Just like that, this moment—this perfect moment where I was in the spotlight for once—is gone.

I leave the gross beverage table behind, and make my way back over to Jorge. I keep my eyes on the ground so the stupid, beautiful boy can't see the effect he's had on me. And Astrid reappears at the bleachers at the same time. Her eye is still squinty, but now it's paired with an almost manic smile.

I'm grateful for the distraction. I'm grateful to slip back onto the sidelines of someone else's moment.

"You good?" Jorge asks. I'm pretty sure he's talking to me, but luckily Astrid answers.

"Magnificent," she says, and it sounds only a little bit scary so I'm going to count that as a win. "Now we wait."

Waiting involves drinking room-temperature coconut water while we rank our classmates' dances from full-body cringe to meh.

Waiting also involves listening to Astrid list all the things she misses about Alannah. Even though Alannah's the type of person that keeps her read receipts on, then *still* doesn't respond to you. And, like, how can you miss a monster like that?

Waiting does not involve making awkward eye contact with the boy from earlier. He, thankfully, disappeared, when I got the nerve to look around for him. And I don't even mention the terrible, mortifying moment where he visibly regretted giving me *that look* to Astrid and Jorge. I don't need them trying to explain it away to make me feel better—or worse, feel sorry for me.

"Zora Giovanni Jones!" Astrid hollers, digging her pointy purple nails into my arm.

My full name is her favorite exclamation, like, *Goddamn!*

Or *Boom shackalacka!* As in "Zora Giovanni Jones, I got a B-minus on my AP Lit paper!" Or, "Zora Giovanni Jones, look at that hot-pink minivan!"

I follow her other pointy nail to what has her attention now, and, wow, it's actually deserving of the excitement.

Walking past us is Lulu Richardson, a senior like us. She's Instagram famous because of her waist-length dark hair, ridiculously overlined lips, and unlimited designer wardrobe funded by her loaded dads. She actually listed "influencer" as her career when we were researching future jobs in Econ, and she argued with Mr. Gonzalez, citing her engagement numbers and sponsorship income when he told her to pick something else. She's the literal worst.

And right now, she's wearing an outfit that's almost identical to mine: a leopard-print fur bolero (hers is probably real fur, though) and a beaded blush midi-length dress. Her stuff looks like an elevated version of my own, though. Like, she definitely didn't piece it together with items that were borrowed or picked up from the thrift store on Ten Percent Off Tuesday. Our hair is even in the same low buns, but mine is held in place by a hard layer of Eco gel and hers looks a lot more effortless.

"Yo, is there a tear in the multiverse?" Jorge laughs.

"Lulu is definitely the evil twin in this situation," Astrid says, shaking her head and cackling.

I try to laugh along, but it sounds hollow. I know I shouldn't care. Wearing the same outfit as someone else isn't a world-ending, tragic scenario. But it's like, even when I try to stand out, when I think I look really good—there's still nothing special about me.

I feel my throat get tight and scratchy again.

So, I'm grateful when I spot Alannah to the left of Lulu. Alannah's taking a selfie with Emily, both of them cheesin' in a way that's going to make Astrid see red. But I'm ready to get this over with, whatever antics Astrid has planned. At least then this terrible night will finally end, and I can go home and watch *Sister, Sister* episodes on Netflix until I fall asleep.

"Astrid, heads-up—"

"I AM AWARE!"

She springs off the bleachers and starts to do some weird blinky thing at Bryan standing at his card table DJ booth. Suddenly the music, which I was pleasantly unaware of before, is eardrum-bursting loud, and after a few beats I realize what song this is.

Jorge and I make eye contact and the same words come out of our mouths. "Oh no."

But before we can grab Astrid or talk some sense into her, she's running past us into the middle of the gym and begins to do a very obviously rehearsed dance to Ariana Grande's "Break Up with Your Girlfriend, I'm Bored."

"We said we were going to let this happen," Jorge says, covering his mouth to hold in his giggles.

"Yeah, but I didn't know it was going to be this!" A fight would have made sense, but a choreographed dance to declare her love? This isn't the plan to get Alannah back I was expecting.

Most of the crowd has stepped back now to clear room for Astrid, maybe out of awe but definitely out of necessity. She's jumping and kicking, twerking and flinging her hair around. She snaps and swings her arms in circular motions around her face and does a surprisingly impressive pirouette. It's a mix of Misty Copeland meets Beyoncé—but, like, way, *way* white.

And it's not that she looks bad. The stretchy black fabric of her dress clings tightly to the rolling, curvy landscape of her body in just the right way. I can even say that she's, objectively, a good dancer. But her fiercely determined, squinty-eyed gaze, targeted like a laser right on Alannah, makes it look like she's participating in one of those dance battles that only happens in movies—except it's very much one-sided. And also slightly aggressive.

I can see the blush on Alannah's cheeks from here. And Emily just looks pissed, like she's about ready to jump into the ring and do the worm to protect her woman. People in the crowd are whooping and taking their phones out to record this beautiful train wreck.

Astrid is in the process of lowering herself into the splits, and I'm praying for the stretchiness of her dress and her hopeful forethought of booty shorts, when all of a sudden the music stops.

"WHAT THE FUCK, BRYAN!" Astrid bellows from her place on the floor. But it's not Bryan at the card table anymore. It's some guy I don't recognize with floppy brown hair and a skinny tie. "This one goes out to a special lady," he says into a microphone, queueing up something on his phone. I swear he's looking at me, but that makes no sense, right? And now "Call Me Maybe" by Carly Rae Jepsen is blaring from the speakers.

Astrid eases herself up, booty shorts thankfully in place. And before she can even exit the dance floor, there's twenty dancers taking over, perfectly spaced and doing synchronized moves like we're in a music video. It's mesmerizing.

"Is . . . is this part of your plan?" I ask when Astrid makes her way over to us, but it's clear from her stormy expression that it's not.

"God, no." She's trying to catch a look at Alannah across the gym, but it's impossible to see her through the dancers doing spins and shimmies. Jorge is bobbing his head to the beat, and I can't blame him. This song is catchy as hell.

I thought flash mobs were over. Antiquated relics of social media past, like the mannequin challenge. Just about as old and played out as this song. And yet . . . here it is, happening. It's as if we popped into some adult's idea of what high school is like, the stuff of movies and TV shows where the teens are played by thirtysomethings and still use weirdo abbreviations in their texts. Two consecutive dance-based declarations of love—how is this reality?

And the even more bizarre thing is, they seem to be performing toward my general direction. Like, I'm making prolonged eye contact with multiple dancers. I move to the right to test it, and I swear their stares move with me.

But no. That's ridiculous. No one is dancing *for me.*

I look around for who this grand gesture is really meant for, but no one seems to be sure. There's just a sea of recording phones and wide-eyed, delighted faces—and of course the pure rage radiating off Astrid. That'll be *my* job to deal with later.

The song winds down and it gets to that ridiculous and genius line at the end—the one it just repeats over and over again into infinity. And perfectly timed to the beat, a giant pink cell phone is wheeled into the room. No joke. Everyone gasps and claps. It looks like it's made out of papier-mâché, a fourth grader's really intense arts-and-crafts project. The phone keeps moving until it's right in front of me.

I spin around, searching for who the lucky recipient is. But there's no one there. Everyone has stepped back, except for Jorge and Astrid, who both have their eyebrows pressed together in confusion.

And when I turn back around, I can't even explain it away now: The dancers are definitely pointing at me like I'm the "you" in *I missed you so bad.*

And I realize, with horror, that the phone is just about human-size.

Like there could be an actual human inside of it.

Please don't let someone pop out of there, please don't let someone pop out of there, I chant in my head like a prayer.

But of course that's what happens.

The side of the phone bursts open, metallic gold confetti raining down around me, and a blurry figure jumps out. Right onto my foot.

"Ow!"

"Wait . . . what?" The gorgeous guy from earlier, with the perfect velvet suit and the sparkling eyes, is standing in front of me. The gorgeous guy, who I thought I was having a moment with until it was painfully clear it wasn't a moment, just exploded out of a papier-mâché phone and probably broke my toe.

For what feels like an hour but is probably just a few seconds, we stare at each other, and there's a flash of hope. Did I get it all wrong? Did he see me earlier and then immediately fall in love, and scramble to put together this over-the-top grand gesture? But then his perfect, full lips form the words that burn all those stupid, stupid hopes to the ground. "Who are you?"

Of course it didn't go like that. Of course this wasn't meant for me.

I harden my face, praying he couldn't see any of the thoughts that just flickered across my mind. "What the fuck?"

"You're not Lulu."

Of course. *Lulu.* Lulu is the kind of girl who guys organize flash mobs for, not me.

"What in the actual fuck?"

"What happened to Lulu?"

"I think my question is a little more important right now."

"This . . . this isn't how this was supposed to go . . ." His dark brown eyes are looking past me, scanning the room. Looking for Lulu, no doubt.

I snort. "Yeah, I'm aware."

That brings his attention back to me. "Look, I'm sorry, okay?" he says. He runs his hand through his hair, messing up his perfectly slicked-back style.

"Thanks. That feels really genuine." I bend down to inspect my throbbing right foot. The sequins in the front of my right shoe look all busted, and I feel the fury rising in my chest, pushing out all the sadness. *This asshole* . . . I just got these. I slide the shoe off, and my right toe is an even worse sight. It's already swelling and turning an alarming shade of maroon.

I spring up, ready to tell this guy off, but . . . he's not there. I'm standing in the middle of the gym alone.

Is this really happening? Did I fall asleep waiting for Astrid on the bleachers? Because this is a nightmare.

"Ow!" I hear a garbled scream come from my right, followed by a spattering of giggles. I turn to see a cluster of girls in sparkling dresses staring at a phone, watching a replay of my mortifying moment. One of them, a blond girl with her hair in a too-tight chignon, makes eye contact with me and then returns her gaze to the screen. No shame. Probably already planning her caption for when she posts it to her stories.

I'm suddenly aware just how quiet it is in this space that was vibrating with music just minutes earlier. And I'm also aware that everyone in the gym is staring at me. The hired dancers are creeping back, almost comically. The guy at the makeshift DJ booth is squinting in my direction, probably trying to figure out where he went wrong. At least a couple hundred other pairs of eyes are all on me. Mouths open, phones out, watching me get rejected by a guy I didn't even want in the first place.

I want to cry. And punch someone. And then cry some more.

I'm in the spotlight for once in my life, but in the very worst way.

I feel Astrid and Jorge next to me, their comforting hands on my waist and shoulders.

"What just happened?"

"I'll tell you what just happened. That jerk ruined my attempt to bare my soul to Alannah through dance."

"Astrid, Zora just accidentally received someone else's proposal. This is officially not about you anymore."

"Proposal? We are in high school. Slow your roll. Though,

you know, I wouldn't put it past Lulu. Wedding shit gets likes, and that whole production was practically made for the 'gram—"

"You guys?" I cut her off, my voice scratchier than I want it to be. I swallow down the lump in my throat. I will not give these people watching us any more content. "Can we talk about this in the car?"

"Oh yeah." Jorge gives me a quick nod and starts walking toward the exit, eyes straight ahead.

"We're getting you outta here, baby girl!" Astrid calls, waving her finger in the air as she strides forward, like a general going to battle. "Out of our way!"

I start to follow after them, but my toe screams and the pain shoots up my leg. It takes all my strength not to fall over.

"Uh? A little help here?" I call after them feebly, wincing.

"Of course, of course. I'm so sorry," Jorge says, smacking his forehead and trotting back to me. On his way, he kicks something that goes sliding over to my feet. Reaching down, I realize that it's my phone, the screen a spiderweb of broken glass.

My stomach drops. *Great.*

"I want that asshole's insurance information!" Astrid declares to no one in particular. "Call Me Maybe" Guy is long gone. "We have your assault documented on film! You will be hearing from my lawyers!"

She takes one of my arms around her neck, and Jorge does the same, tucking my busted phone in his pocket. Bryan's back at the card table, playing some mumbly rap song, as the three of us hobble outside.

I envision being whisked away into a waiting car, my face hidden by an aggressively wielded umbrella, like a celebrity running from the paparazzi. But Astrid can't parallel park, so her car is a couple of blocks away in the neighborhood—she needed to find a spot that could actually fit four cars. And Jorge went with her to make sure she didn't have a change of heart and double back to find Alannah. So, instead of being where I'd prefer to be (i.e., literally anywhere else), I'm sitting on the curb alone, mere feet from the scene of the crime, all the feelings bubbling up in my stomach like a pot about to boil over.

I'm embarrassed. Pretty much the whole school saw me get dissed by some guy I don't even know, and at least half of them caught it all on their phones.

And I'm mad. Fist clenching, eye-laser-shooting mad. Because who even is this guy to put me in this position in the first place? Lulu and I don't look alike at all. I mean, I'm light-skinned, but not *that* light-skinned. Can't this jerk tell me apart from some girl that he's supposedly into enough to do some dated flash mob for? Then he ruins my shoes, shatters my phone screen, and maybe breaks my toe, and instead of making things right he just, like, takes off? Leaves me there to endure the giggles and inevitable meme-making alone?

And *then* there was that flicker of hope. When I thought maybe this all was for me. When I thought maybe I was singled out, special in someone's eyes. For once.

My jaw hurts and I realize I'm grinding my teeth. The edges of my eyes burn, too. I squeeze them tight and wipe away the tears that managed to escape. I hate, hate, HATE that I always end up crying when I'm angry. It makes me feel weak and delicate. And it just makes me even more mad at "Call Me Maybe" Guy—no, "Call Me Maybe" *Asshole*. There are so many things I should have said to him.

A faint sniffle interrupts my mounting fury. It takes me a second to realize it's not mine.

I whip my head around, and there's no one. I'm over near the loading zone behind the cafeteria, and it's pretty isolated, which is why I chose it in the first place to wait for Jorge and Astrid. I didn't want to risk running into anyone who witnessed the incident in the gym.

Sniffle-sniffle again. Followed by a loud, unmistakable nose honking into some tissues. Someone is definitely there. And they're crying.

"Hello?"

There's some rustling, and, squinting in the darkness, I can see a figure sitting on the edge of the planter next to the ramp, half-hidden behind a bush with pink flowers. It's a boy, definitely, tall with broad shoulders. And he's wiping his face with a sleeve of his suit jacket, obviously trying to get himself together now that he's been caught.

"Sorry, I didn't, um, see anything," I say, trying to help him save face—though there's nothing wrong with a guy crying, for the record. It's endearing, even. A guy showing normal human emotions. "I'm just waiting for my friends. Didn't mean to intrude."

"It's . . . m'okay," he mumbles, so quiet I can barely hear him. He shifts to the right, closer to one of the dim orange lights, and I'm able to make out more details. A velvet tuxedo and a bow tie, undone, hanging around his neck. Dark hair that's sticking up in all directions, like he's been running his hands through it.

And . . . oh. I know him. Well, I mean, I don't *actually* know him. But how else do I describe my relationship with this person that just humiliated me in front of the entire school?

It's "Call Me Maybe" Asshole.

But okay, he's crying, so maybe he can be upgraded to just "Call Me Maybe" Guy again. I take back that endearing comment, though. There is nothing endearing about his tears.

His eyes widen as I lean into the light. "It's you."

"It is," I say, giving him my best side-eye. "But as we've already established, not the 'you' you're looking for."

"Listen, I'm really sorry about that. It's just that . . . I was surprised." He blushes. For real blushes—so deeply that I can see it even from this far away. I actually feel something in me softening toward him because it makes him look so vulnerable and sweet, and I guess maybe this was all embarrassing for him too . . . but no. *No.* I harden myself right back up. This guy doesn't deserve my sympathy. He destroyed my shoes!

I purse my lips and cock my head to the side. "*You* were surprised?"

"Yeah, I mean, what are the odds that you and Lulu would be wearing exactly the same outfit?" he says, and for some reason he's up and walking over to me now. "I feel like such an idiot. I made a fool of myself in front of everyone." His voice catches. He shakes his head and sits down next to me on the curb. "And I mean . . . all that planning, all that work, for nothing."

"Nothing, huh?" I suck my teeth and feel something hot building in my chest. I mean, I know objectively that he's not calling me "nothing," but that's what it feels like. And Lulu is *something*—a girl that guys do "all that work" for.

"What exactly were you hoping would happen?" I continue, making sure to keep my voice cold. "That you would woo her with that weak, outdated mess? Like, a flash mob? Really? You're about a decade too late with that."

"Whoa, tell me how you really feel." He clutches his chest. I think he's trying to be playful, to cover up his embarrassment over being caught crying. But it just makes me even more irritated.

"Okay, I will. 'Call Me Maybe' is a corny-ass song choice. No girl would fall for that. Well, I guess maybe Lulu would, because she's corny too."

He laughs quietly and runs his fingers through his hair. It's annoying how good it looks, even as a mess. "Shit . . . well, what should I have done, then?"

I look him right in the eye. "Step one: Approach the right girl."

He points at me and nods, one of those firework smiles breaking across his face, and it takes me by surprise. His long eyelashes still glisten from the tears that were just there, but this smile doesn't feel put-on. It's like sunshine cutting through the clouds. It makes me feel good that I've inspired a smile like that. But also . . . I hate how it's affecting me the same way it did when I saw him the first time tonight.

"And after that?" he asks.

"Hey, I'm not here to fix your poor attempts at romance, man." I give him my best hard stare, and then cross my arms and look out onto the street for Astrid and Jorge. Why are they taking so long?

"Fair," he says. "But don't you want to help protect other women from any future horrible flash mob attacks? Really, you'd be doing a community service."

Against my better judgment, I turn back to him. The smile is still there, and it makes me want to rage. But there's also something about it that's so genuine, so vulnerable—an extended olive branch. I just can't make myself walk away and ignore him. Plus, with my foot, I probably wouldn't get very far.

"Okay, if a guy was going to do a flash mob for me," I start, "he better come with some good music. Stevie Wonder, Marvin Gaye, something classic. Timeless."

"Yeah, but—"

"You want my advice or not?"

He nods quickly.

"But a flash mob was just the wrong move, full stop. And all those dancers, that big scene . . ." I shake my head. "It distracted from what should have been the focus. Your feelings for Lulu. You should have done something with just the two of you. A big spectacle isn't necessary, and who really is all that for, anyway? Deep down, I think most girls want that connection with their person. To feel special."

He nods again, thoughtfully. And not in that fake way some people do, when you know they're just putting together their next response, tuning you out in the process. He seems to be really listening.

Not that he deserves an award for it, or anything. He should be. I'm doing him a favor.

Finally, he says, "You're right. I'll keep that in mind for next time."

"Next time? Not giving up on Lulu?"

"No, I'm definitely giving up on Lulu." He smiles again, but it's not the bright firework one. This one looks forced. "She came to find me after and made it very clear that it wasn't going to happen."

I want to know more, but I also don't want to show that I'm interested at all. Luckily, he keeps going without prompting.

"It's probably for the best, though, because we didn't really know each other. I thought there could be something, but you're right that it was all too much . . . considering."

"You two met recently?" The question escapes, despite my intentions to appear aloof and uninterested. So much for that.

"No, I actually *just* met her. Tonight."

"Wait . . . like, in person?" I ask, firmly ruining any illusion that I don't care. "But you talked online?"

"Well . . ." He blushes again. I thought only white people could get that red. "We actually haven't talked. I just follow her on Instagram."

My eyes go wide, and his cheeks flame even more. I swear I can feel the heat of them from where I'm sitting.

"I mean, she follows me, too," he rushes to explain himself. "Or she did. Doubt she does anymore. And she always liked and responded to my comments on her pictures."

I lean away from him, so I can fix him with a side-eye. "Like, actual responses, or emojis?"

His face is scarlet now. Like it should have been when he embarrassed me in the gym. I can't say I hate it.

"Emojis, but the kissy-winky face. And even those two pink hearts one time." He holds up his hands in defense. "Not just, like, the standard smiley face."

I press my lips together to hold in the cackles trying to escape and start to look around us.

"What?" he asks.

"Oh, just checking to make sure there are security cameras here. So if I'm really going to be taken out by some creepy stalker bro right now, at least I'll get some prime screen time during the *Dateline* special."

He reels back, his face horrified. But that's all it takes for my laugh to come tumbling out. And then he starts laughing too, hesitant at first, and eventually big and loud in relief.

"Oh god. You're so right and just—oh no." He sputters out and then snorts, which sets me off even more. I like that he can laugh at himself. That he can admit how ridiculous this all is without putting on airs.

"For real, though. This is all pretty sus. Like, do I need to alert the authorities?" My cheeks hurt, and I wipe away a tear. "And man . . . Lulu! Where's Lulu? What proof do you have that she's not being held back at your lair? Should I check her socials for proof of life?"

I pick up my phone and see the cracked screen, and that stops the next giggle that's bubbling up in my throat. It's nice—really nice—to laugh with him, but I remember why I'm here sitting with him in the first place.

"You know, saying it all out loud . . . I guess I kind of get your point," he says. He pulls at his collar and winces. And wow—it's so adorable that I look down. "Uh, I'm Dean, by the way. Dean Bayani."

"I'll write that down. For when I'm interviewed for the inevitable true-crime podcast." My voice is off, cold again. And I've got to keep it there. I can't forget that this cute boy is only next to me, laughing at my jokes, because I wore the same outfit as the girl he *really* wanted. That I interrupted the romantic grand gesture, no matter how misguided, he had planned for someone else.

I sigh. "I'm Zora."

Dean reaches out to shake my hand, and I take it for some reason. His palm is smooth, and his grip is strong.

"Nice to meet you, Zora," Dean says in a low voice, leaning in closer so his shoulder brushes mine. My stomach does this weird flippy thing, and my whole body warms up, like I just stepped into the sun.

What the hell is going on?

Jorge and Astrid better get here now.

I pull my hand away, studying my shattered phone to keep me tethered to reality, and an awkward silence falls between the two of us. I know it's my turn to talk, but I'm also scared to let anything out.

So, we sit there listening to the muffled sounds coming from the gym, as every molecule in my body is hyperaware of how close his knee is to mine.

"You know," he says, finally. "This probably doesn't help to disprove my characterization as, uh, *not* a reclusive and disturbed stalker." I turn to look at him, and there's a different smile there. Not the firework one, not the fake one—this one is small, unsure. "But I've actually never been good with girls. They kind of just . . . look right through me. They always have."

I don't see how that can be true when he looks the way he does, but I keep that to myself. I just nod, prompting him to go on. "So, I guess that's why I did this tonight. This whole big show? And I'm not totally clueless—I know it was, uh, over-the-top. I spent weeks making that stupid phone . . . and I used all my savings to pay my school's dance team. But, I don't know . . . I felt like I needed to go big in order to stand out to Lulu. To make her even, like . . . consider me in that way. I know I'm nothing special compared to other guys she talks to. That I had to do a freaking flash mob to even be on their level. And you know, maybe it wasn't even Lulu, but the idea of her. Because, like I said, we really didn't know each other." He exhales loudly and looks down. "I think I just wanted someone to finally see me. Does that make sense?"

I feel whatever anger I was harboring melt away because, yes, it makes total sense. I know exactly what it feels like to never stand out, to be overlooked. I just didn't think someone like him would feel the same way.

But do I tell him that? Is he going to laugh and say "just kidding"? Or even worse, wrinkle his nose and make it clear that it's *definitely* not the same as with me?

I decide to play it safe. "You're right. That doesn't help prove your case as *not* a reclusive and disturbed stalker."

He looks down at the ground and lets out a little fake laugh. And I realize I got it all wrong.

"I know what you mean, though," I continue, and his gaze meets mine. "My best friend, Astrid—she has a pretty big personality. She loves to be in the spotlight. She's always shining. You probably saw her tonight doing a grand gesture of her own, to try to get her ex-girlfriend back. The dance right before yours?"

"Oh, is *that* what that was?"

"Yeah." I shake my head. "I wish I could say it was an out-lying event, but it's pretty on-brand for her. So, yeah, always chasing after Astrid . . . I feel pretty overlooked too. Like, I'm a supporting character in all of her big moments, instead of my own."

He brushes his shoulder against mine. "I don't see how someone could overlook you."

I turn over the words in my head, searching for a different meaning, a slight that I'm missing. It must be all over my face, because he quickly clarifies. "I mean because you're beautiful."

"Because I look like Lulu?"

His sparkling dark eyes look right into mine. "No, because you look like you."

I feel those words all over me. My stomach flutters, my skin prickles, my heart thuds all the way up into my throat. I can't speak, and he must take that as offense because he starts talking fast.

"Sorry if that was weird. God, I seem to be incapable of not being weird." His cheeks start to heat up again. "And it's not like I'm trying to hit on you. But uh . . . not that I'm *not* hitting on you. And also your appearance isn't the only thing that matters. I know that we just met—like *really* just met. But I can already tell you're funny, and forgiving, obviously—"

"It's okay," I cut him off, covering the smile taking over my face with my hands.

"Okay." He nods once, then twice. "Okay."

I'm looking down, but I can feel the smile radiating off him, a match to my own. And we both sit there in the darkness, beaming, as my mind races to catch up with what's happening. Not *not* hitting on me . . . so that means . . .

"Anyway," he says, cutting into my thoughts. "It sounds to me like maybe your friend needs to take a back seat to you sometimes. She should let you shine and be at the center, while she cheers you on."

I want to defend Astrid, list all the nice things she's done for me over the years, but instead I just nod. "Maybe you're right."

"And what you were saying about my grand gesture wasn't, uh, totally inaccurate. But also . . . I think I'm glad I still took the risk. Even though I made a fool of myself, I put myself out there and I was seen. You know, I tried. It feels good to have tried."

I scoot a little closer to him, barely a centimeter, and bump my shoulder against his. "Is that just the starch fumes from all that papier-mâché talking?"

He scoots closer too. "It's possible."

I take a deep breath. I could follow up with another joke, bring this conversation back to the surface. But I don't want to.

"I'm not sure I'm as brave as you, though," I admit. Because as silly as his Carly Rae Jepsen tribute was, well . . . it was brave. I can't see myself ever seeking out the spotlight in that extreme of a way.

"Sure, you're brave," he says, and he sounds so confident that I think he might be messing with me. But his face is genuine. "You're not afraid to say what you think, to be real with a stranger, whatever the consequences. That seems pretty brave to me. And, look, I know we've just met. And I don't know you yet. But Zora . . . I really want to know more."

The tips of his fingers touch mine, and when our eyes meet, too, it feels like he really sees me, even if just for this one moment. And that may not be a flash mob or choreographed dance to Ariana Grande or any of the grand gestures I've seen in the movies, but it feels pretty grand all on its own.

Tires screech in the parking lot, and I look up to see Astrid's car rolling up to the curb. The doors are vibrating with the newest Chloe x Halle song instead of "Both Sides Now."

The window rolls down, and Jorge throws his elbow out.

"Get in, loser," Astrid calls from behind him. "We're getting tacos!"

Dean looks at me, confused.

"These are my friends for some reason," I say, shaking my head. I try to stand up, wince at the pain, and then Dean's arm is at my waist, easing me up. I miss his touch as soon as he pulls away.

Jorge wiggles his eyebrows, and Astrid throws her head back and yelps, "Oh, okay! You go, Zora!"

I close my eyes for a second, letting the wave of mortification pass. "Tacos, huh? What happened to Alannah?"

Astrid shrugs, looking surprisingly serene. "Still with her new girlfriend. But, hey, I did what I came to do. And you know, big scenes like that . . . they're really just for the person that's doing them, anyway." I hear Dean let out a small laugh behind me. "Plus," she adds, "I'd rather just hang out with you guys."

"Okay, then." I nod. "Tacos."

I limp over to the back seat. As I open the door, I turn back to look at Dean.

"You coming?"

His firework smile explodes across his face, shining directly at me. I reach for his hand and grab hold of a new beginning.

IN A BLINK OF THE EYE
(Trapped in a Confined Space)

ELIZABETH EULBERG

*W*hen it comes down to it, I blame Disney.

In fairness to me, what little girl doesn't dream of becoming a princess? Most of my impressionable youth was spent watching movies with princesses and their Prince Charmings. So, of course, I believed in fairy tales and true love. In happily-ever-afters.

(Please notice the past tense. *Believed.* Now at seventeen, it's a different story.)

But I still remember watching Prince William and Kate Middleton's wedding on TV while wearing my Cinderella costume from Halloween. I pressed my nose against the screen as a young woman married her real-life prince.

"Mommy, I'm going to be a princess one day," I declared with the utter confidence only a six-year-old could muster. The way I saw it: Kate had brown hair and hazel eyes. I had brown hair and hazel eyes. We were basically the same person. If she could marry a prince, why couldn't I?

"Well, you'll have to live in England, then," my mother commented with a laugh.

Neither of us had any idea that little quip would result in me having a full-blown obsession with the United Kingdom. If a book, movie, or TV show had "royal," "British," or "princess" in the title, I'd devour it. I once spent an entire month speaking in a very poor British accent, thinking it glamorous compared to my bland, boring Midwestern one.

My tea parties as a kid were based off of high teas served at the finest London hotels. I would take white paper plates and try to recreate the blue-and-white stripes from Claridge's china. Which honestly was the highlight as peanut butter and jelly sandwiches were all my limited culinary skills could serve at the time.

I'd watch *Mary Poppins* nearly every day after school, which was when I first set eyes on *him*. The second I noticed his tall, golden frame, I knew it was love. Even if he's a little old for me. And lives thousands of miles away from Wisconsin. Oh, and *is a building*. Of course I'm referring to that handsome devil, Ben.

And here I am, staring up at Big Ben. In all his gorgeous eye-candy glory.

I shake my head, still in shock that this is happening. That the Prairie Glen High School show choir would be competing in our biggest festival to date in *London*. Of all the places in the world, it's here!

Ever since that royal wedding, it's been my dream to visit London. And now I, Morgan Barfield, am in London. *London*. It still hasn't hit me.

I give Ben a deep bow before I make my way over Westminster Bridge.

Not to make Ben jealous, but I've got a very important date with my best friend and the London Eye. We have a reservation on the large Ferris wheel–like structure that towers over four hundred feet on the River Thames. As much as I've been counting down to our performance tomorrow night, this is what I've been looking forward to the most: taking in my favorite city in one of its observation pods with the person who means the world to me. I can't remember a time when Dani wasn't in my life. We grew up sharing secrets, crushes, and heartbreaks. Now we get some precious alone time together *in London*.

There's a spring in my step as I make my way to Dani. She's easy to spot with her signature bright red rain jacket—even though it's a rare April day in London without a cloud in the sky. Her eyes light up when she sees me. I wave like an idiot and even do a little dance, not caring about the tourists around us.

I'm in *London* with my best friend. We have the next thirty minutes together as the Eye slowly rotates above my beloved dream city.

"Hiya, babes," I shout in my worst cockney accent. I always had a suspicion my accent was quite awful and it was confirmed by the angry glares I got from the hotel receptionist when we checked in two days ago.

"Pip-pip, cheerio!" Dani replies in a surprisingly dead-on posh accent as she takes a picture of me with Big Ben and Parliament across the Thames. "You're practically glowing, Morgan! I don't think I've ever seen you so happy."

"I'm in London!" I cry out with glee.

Dani throws her head back in a laugh. "Yes, you certainly are. Now, let's get some more pictures of you and your boy."

"Oh, you mean—" I whip around and point at Ben. *"Him?"*

"Exactly how many selfies have you taken?"

"Not enough," I answer truthfully. I don't think I could ever get bored with London.

"Work it!" Dani calls out as she snaps dozens of pictures. "Supermodel *werk*."

I blow a kiss to her phone, then spin around, and end up in some weird disco pose. Dani laughs hysterically as she starts scrolling through the photos. "Brilliant. It's you in your element. We're going to win tomorrow solely because you are *in the zone*."

"Nothing bad can happen in London," I reply.

Dani shakes her head. "I think Henry the Eighth's wives would disagree with you."

"Touché." I give her a bow like she's the queen of England.

"Oh, I really like this version of you. I think I can get used to this." Then Dani strikes the pose from the beginning of our competition number, her hands framing her face, her hip popped. "Are you ready?"

"You know I'm beyond ready to do this! You and me, babes!" I do a kick-shimmy-jazz-hands combo that proves I belong on the piano bench during our competition and not front-and-center like Dani.

Dani grimaces.

"Oh, come on, I'm not *that* bad." Even though I am. *"Hey, big spender!"* I sing purposely out of tune and do my imitation of a drunken Rockette for added effect.

Dani starts fiddling with her charm bracelet, and then it hits me. The grimace. Her looking uncomfortable. She and I have made fools out of ourselves in public on more than one occasion, which can only mean . . .

Dani gives me a strained, tight smile. It's the one she reserves for bad news.

"Hey there."

No.

My shoulders instantly tense when I hear his voice behind me. This trip was a dream come true, until *he* got invited.

Most of us had to be in show choir—or like me, the pianist in the pit band—for years to get this opportunity. Countless hours of practice and rehearsal. Fundraisers to afford the costumes and travel.

All Tyler Chen had to do was be a boy. He was a warm body to even out our numbers.

So the trip of my dreams with my best friend has turned into the nightmare I've become familiar with during our senior year— one where I play the supporting role of the third wheel.

I spin around and there's Dani's boyfriend with a wide smile on his face and his dimples in full view.

I don't want to come across as desperate or anything, but I feel like asking for thirty minutes alone with my best friend shouldn't be too much.

Yet here he is.

Dani links her arm through mine, which prevents me from running away. "Hey," she says in the soft voice she reserves for her younger siblings when they're about to throw a fit. What can I say? She knows me well. "I thought this could be fun."

No, it won't. Saying something will be fun doesn't automatically make it so. Especially when *he's* involved.

"Hey, Morgan, I got you this." Tyler holds out a KitKat.

Dammit. Tyler's trying to get on my good side with candy.

I begrudgingly take it. Tyler must've overheard me telling a few friends on the bus from the airport that British KitKats are superior to American ones. The chocolate is smoother and richer, and the wafer is thicker.

"Thanks," I mumble before breaking off a piece.

"That's so sweet, Ty!" Dani says as she plants a kiss on his lips while I avert my eyes.

"I wouldn't forget about you, my princess," he says as he tucks a stray braid that's escaped from the massive bun on the top of Dani's head behind her ear. "Sweets for my sweet." Tyler produces an assortment of Cadbury candy bars and Dani claps in delight.

It's all so ridiculously sweet I want to barf.

Tyler looks up at the London Eye. "That's a pretty large Ferris wheel."

"*Technically* it's a cantilevered observation wheel, one of the tallest one in the world," I correct him.

"Great." Tyler swallows and a bead of sweat starts forming on his temple. "I, ah, guess we should get in line."

"It's called a *queue* here. We *queue*."

"Right, yeah . . ." He clears his throat as we walk toward the other tourists.

"Besides, you need a reservation. You can't just crash," I state as I hold up the tickets I bought for my best friend and me. To be alone. Without *him*.

"Oh, I, ah—" Tyler fumbles. He looks at Dani. "I didn't—"

"I've taken care of it," Dani replies softly, with a hint of the guilt she should feel for dragging him along. She then leans in and puts her chin on my shoulder. "Just trust me, okay?"

I follow her, but with a scowl on my face. *Of course* I trust Dani. She has kept every embarrassing secret I've ever told her. And there have been *a lot*. She even got detention last year because she covered for me. My period leaked through my jeans in the middle of school. I was freaking out so Dani had run to her locker to grab her gym leggings and a tampon for me. When she wouldn't give her history teacher a reason for being late, he wrote her up, while I got away with it because all I told my male band teacher was, "I can tell you why I'm late, but believe me, you don't want to hear about it."

But this was something we were supposed to do together. She promised. And now . . .

My throat tightens when I realize I don't want to get on the Eye. That this trip, which I've been fantasizing about as a kid, is being ruined because of Tyler Chen. That my senior year has been painful because of Tyler Chen. That I'm losing my best friend because of Tyler fricken' Chen.

I can't ever escape him. It's not like Dani hasn't had boyfriends before, but Tyler is different. Her other boyfriends didn't need to hang all over Dani twenty-four seven. They gave her time to spend with other people, for instance: her best friend. They weren't insufferable with the fake gestures and showing up uninvited.

Not like I'm not enjoying the KitKat, but still. A chocolate bribe isn't going to erase the last several months.

"I'm so excited to do this with you, Morgan." Tyler's smile is so forced I'm surprised his face doesn't shatter from the effort. "You're like, a walking Wikipedia on London. What are you looking forward to the most?"

You leaving, I want to reply, but instead I just shove the rest of the KitKat in my mouth.

I hate this version of me whenever Tyler's around. I was just dancing and laughing moments ago, then *BAM!* Tyler shows up and I go from Tinkerbell to Cruella in 2.5 seconds.

"And I thought if we have time the three of us could do high tea later? My treat?" He looks at me with his dark eyes.

"You're just the sweetest," Dani coos.

"Impossible when I'm with you."

They kiss and I want to break something.

Tyler wraps his arms around Dani, then turns to me. "So, high tea? Sound good? Morgan?"

Oh, gee, does high tea sound good? I don't know. Do finger sandwiches, scones, and pastries sound absolutely delicious and something I want to eat at every meal? Of course! But with Tyler Chen? Abso-bloody-lutely not!

Tyler's face falls as he clears his throat. "Or, you know, I can go somewhere and you guys can just . . ."

I perk up at this. High tea with just Dani and me sounds heavenly, especially since Tyler crashed our London Eye plans.

"No, it will be so much better with the three of us," Dani says, ever the optimist. But she shifts uncomfortably on her feet, which is a giveaway that she's aware that I would not agree with the statement.

She should know better by now, but when you're best friends

with someone who tries to see the best in everybody, it's hard to be the curmudgeon. Which I only am with one person.

Unfortunately, that person happens to be her boyfriend.

I really wish I could be cool with the three of us together. That we could hang out and have fun. But I can't snap my fingers and shut off my feelings.

"Morgan?" Dani says, and I respond by moving forward in line. We're next to get in an observation pod. It's pretty quiet so we might even get our own, which is why I booked for when the Eye first opens, but now I'm hoping they cram us in with a bunch of other people so I don't have to play tour guide to Tyler and point out everything. Dude thought the iconic bridge near the Tower of London was London Bridge. It's Tower Bridge. *Duh.*

"Ready?" the ticket-taker says as the pod moves for us to board. The Eye rotates so slowly it doesn't stop for people to get on and off.

I step on and Tyler follows me. I turn around to see Dani whisper something to the ticket-taker, who nods in reply. There's a smile between the two that I instantly don't like.

"Let me take a picture!" Dani says as we keep moving and she stays on the platform.

"Dani, you better get on," I reply, my heart beating faster.

She gives a little laugh. "Relax, it's fine." She holds out her phone. "Get closer together."

I tense up as Tyler puts his arm around me. "Say 'British cheddar'!"

"Dani!" I cry as we're getting toward the end of the platform. The door will be closing soon.

Dani takes a step *away* from the pod. "I love you both so

much, but it breaks my heart that you can't stand being around each other. So you've got thirty minutes to figure it out."

"What?" I move toward the door, but it closes with Dani still on the platform.

Locking Tyler and me inside.

"Dani!" I call out and slam my hand against the door.

I can't believe she would do this. I step away and examine the pod. It's fairly big—usually there are over twenty people in here—so it's not like I have to be pressed against Tyler.

Tyler who is currently staring at the door in shock. He looks out the large floor-to-ceiling window as we slowly make our way up.

"Oh God, oh God, oh God." Tyler takes a step away as he puts his hands over his head. "Oh no. This is a disaster."

"Seriously? Is the thought of my company really that awful?" I reply, even though I was thinking the same thing.

"No, it's not . . ." Tyler backs away from the window and sits down on the wooden bench in the middle. His breathing becomes strained.

"Ah, are you going to be okay?"

He groans in response as he curls up in the fetal position on the bench.

"So I take that as a no?"

As concerned as I am about whatever is happening in front of me, it's a little annoying that I have London surrounding me and I can't pay attention to it because of Tyler Chen.

He ruins everything.

"I'll be okay," he replies in a tight voice.

"If you say so." I turn my back on him and watch as we

go higher and higher. I can start to see Trafalgar Square and the National Gallery coming into view. "It's a pretty spectacular sight."

Tyler groans. "I'm scared of heights."

"What?" I spin around. "Then why on earth would you agree to go on the London Eye?" *Especially when you weren't invited*, I want to add, but no point in pouring salt on his acrophobia wounds.

"For Dani. She really wanted me to go with you guys."

"I don't know why she had to—" I start, but then it hits me. "She ambushed us."

I can't believe she thought that locking us in together was going to automatically make me totally cool with Tyler. While, in fact, it makes me loathe him more. Even though, technically, our current situation isn't his fault.

"I'd do anything for her." His voice comes from his armpit, where his face is buried.

"Really? You'd like her to see you in this condition?" I can't help my sarcasm around Tyler, even though I am a little concerned he's going to hurl all over this pod.

At that Tyler uncurls and sits up, but his eyes remain closed. "I'd be fine if she was here."

"I've known Dani my whole life; I wasn't aware that she has some sort of antidote for heights," I reply in the smart-ass tone I reserve for him.

"No, it's just . . . Never mind." Tyler's knee is jittering a million miles a minute.

"Tell me." I don't know why, but I'm curious why with me he's a nervous mess, but somehow Dani would cure his fear.

Tyler takes a deep breath. "Because when I'm with Dani, she's all I see."

Ugh, that's actually really sweet. Like, Disney-fairy-tale-romance-level sweet.

He continues, "She's worth conquering a few fears for. If I panicked, I'd just hold her hand and know I'd be okay if she were by my side. She'd never let anything bad happen to me. If the view freaked me out, I'd look at her and . . . everything else would fade away. I know it sounds corny, but it's true."

A lump forms in my throat. He really does love her.

"But I also want her to be happy, and she's not happy, Morgan. She's pretty miserable."

"What?" This is news to me. Yes, I knew she wanted us to be this great trio who got along and hung out without it being awkward, but I didn't realize it was so bad she would go behind our backs to *lock us in the London Eye.* "You think you know Dani better than me?"

"I'm not saying that. But come on, Morgan. Dani knows you hate me."

"I don't—"

"You can't even look at me. Just . . ." Tyler slowly opens his eyes; his hands brace the side of the bench as he realizes we're about twenty stories up at this point, but he focuses on me. "She loves you. It makes her sad that you don't want to hang out if I'm there, and I respect you need alone time with Dani, I do."

I can't help but snort. "Oh sure, but you still crashed the London Eye."

"I didn't know it was supposed to be the two of you, honest."

I can't help but believe him. Dani clearly had this plan to entrap us. "I didn't want to come because you can't stand being in the same room as me; I knew you'd hate the idea of being in a pod together. So just tell me, what did I do to make you hate me? Please, I need to know so I can apologize. You're really great, Morgan. You are. You're funny and smart and I just want to be your friend. So please, whatever it is, I need to know: Why do you hate me?"

EIGHT MONTHS AGO

Believe it or not, I still believe in love at first sight.

Because it happened to me.

And I'm not referring to that hunky clock tower.

It was the first day of senior year when he walked into World History class.

He was stationed in the middle of the door, unsure where to go. He looked up from his schedule and his dark brown eyes settled on mine. He gave me a hesitant smile and that's when I saw those dimples. My heart actually fluttered.

I'd dated before, but it was just a movie outing here and there. None of the boys I went out with made me feel the way he did before we even exchanged a single word.

"Hey," he said as he sat down next to me. He ran his fingers through his still slightly damp black hair. "I'm Tyler. I'm new here."

"Morgan," I replied, knowing my eyes were wide, taking him in. And the fact that he chose to sit down next to me. "Welcome! Where are you from?"

"Lake Forest, we moved last week, so I don't know a single soul here." He bit his lip and that did it. I was a goner.

"Well, you know me now," I said with a wink. I *actually* winked, desperately channeling the leads in the rom-coms I love so much.

Color rushed to his cheeks. "This day is already looking up."

No kidding.

He handed me his schedule. "Please tell me we have other classes together, since you're my new best friend and all."

"You should know I already have a best friend, but I'm willing to make room for one more . . . as long as you're not a Chicago Bears fan."

"I believe the Welcome to Wisconsin packet stated that Bears fans weren't allowed." He winked back at me. "Would you judge me if I told you that I'm not really into football, I'm more of a comic-book geek?"

I paused, pretending for a moment that I wasn't already a total sucker for this stranger. "I'll allow it."

"Phew!" He dramatically wiped his brow.

"And I have better news for you: We have two more classes together this morning, and lunch."

"Yes!" Tyler did a little fist pump. "I was nervous about walking into a new school, but the idea of standing with my lunch tray, trying to find a place to sit, kept me up all night."

"Well, don't you worry. You can join me and my best friend, Dani. You'll love her, by the way, she's amazing."

"I mean, if she's anything like you . . ."

I was squealing in my head. I couldn't believe this was

happening to me. That a gorgeous, charming guy was flirting with me.

Mr. Knight walked into class. "Good morning, everyone." He scanned the room and his eyes settled on Tyler. "Mr. Chen, welcome to Prairie Glen. Why don't you come up here for a second so I can go over your schedule."

As Tyler headed to the front of class, I snuck my phone out of my bag and texted Dani under my desk. New boy alert! He's joining us at lunch!

I paused, wondering if I should tell her that I'm at crush level a zillion, but decided against it. Dani was still nursing a serious case of heartbreak from her jerk ex who cheated on her over the summer.

Dani replied, !!! Although I'm so over boys.

Understandably, Dani swore off men and looked up nunneries after what we referred to as "the Dirtbag Incident." We also ate pint after pint of Ben & Jerry's Chubby Hubby ice cream while watching all our favorite rom-coms, as was required when one's best friend was recovering from heartbreak.

They are the inferior species, at least this one isn't drenched in cheap cologne to hide his BO, I replied, referring to her ex.

> Dani: And that is why I heart you
> Me: Heart you back

I was counting down to Dani meeting Tyler, to see if she could see the sparks radiating off us. The morning felt excruciatingly long. My only reprieve was walking with Tyler between classes. I noticed how girls—and a few guys—checked him out.

"Let me give you the rundown on one of the most important decisions you'll make at Prairie Glen. I'm, of course, talking about the lunch line," I said to Tyler when it was finally lunch. Where I'd get twenty-five minutes to get to know him better. To continue our banter. To build on the love story I was already writing in my head.

"Food *is* my favorite subject," Tyler replied as he patted his toned stomach.

He gestured for me to go ahead of him in line. "The salads are good, but only with ranch dressing. Pizza is a solid choice, but not sausage because I don't even want to know what kind of meat is used in those lumps. Chicken nuggets are also respectable, and, oddly enough, the veggie sides are pretty delicious. And you can never go wrong with a brownie." I put one on my tray. Tyler followed suit.

"I know we basically just met, Morgan, but you are a wise, wise woman."

My heart started pounding faster and faster; my head was spinning. How did I get so lucky to have this happen to me?

"Here, let me get this as a thank-you," Tyler said as he paid for my lunch.

Oh my God, is this a date? I wondered. When Ian Douglas took me to Pizza Hut after a movie, I had to pay for my personal pizza. And *that* was considered a date. A poor excuse for one, but still.

"Thanks." I gave Tyler my biggest smile and even batted my

eyelashes. I picked up a thing or two watching all those swoony movies.

"Hey, Tyler!" Shawna Banks approached with an extra bounce in her already peppy cheerleader step, Kelvin Olvio right on her heels as always. "We're sitting over there." Instead of pointing like a normal person, she flicked her hip out to the table in the corner where the other ShawnaBots were waving them over.

"Yeah, join us," Kelvin replied, and didn't even subtly hide the fact that he was checking Tyler out from head to toe.

Not that I blamed him.

Shawna and Kelvin stood in front of Tyler, not once acknowledging that I was next to him. A knot formed in my stomach. I couldn't compete with the popular crowd.

"That's so cool of you guys," Tyler replied. "But I'm hanging out with Morgan."

They both blinked at him in reply as if he was speaking a foreign language instead of doing the unthinkable: turning them down.

"I'll catch you later, okay?" Tyler said before walking away. I was so stunned it took me a second to catch up to him. "Now, where were we?"

"Oh yeah . . ." *Did he really choose me over* Shawna Banks? "It's time for you to meet my *other* best friend."

"Ah yes, my competition."

We entered the chaotic lunchroom, and Dani brightened when she saw me. I already knew we'd be spending our walk home after school dissecting everything about Tyler and how he was the perfect guy for me.

As we got closer to Dani, her attention went from me to him. Her eyes went wide as he approached; she smoothed out her braids.

"Tyler, this is Dani. Dani, Tyler," I introduced them.

"Hey, Dani." Tyler's voice was different. He was staring at Dani with his mouth slightly open.

My stomach dropped. I've noticed that look from other guys when they take in Dani. She was beautiful with her dark brown skin, wide brown eyes that she highlighted with shimmery eye shadow, and her elegant posture from years of dance training.

"Hi," Dani replied. She shook her head like she was in a trance and automatically began doodling on the front of her notebook.

"You draw?" Tyler asked as he sat down.

"Dani's one of the most talented artists in school *and* she can sing and dance . . ." Why was I hyping up my best friend to my crush?

"A woman of many talents," Tyler replied as his cheeks reddened about a zillion shades darker than this morning when we were talking.

While I was slowly dying inside.

"Please, Morgan is the amazing woman," Dani said. "She's one of the top students in our grade *and* she gets every solo in band, jazz band, pep band . . . with the piano and clarinet. She's not a double threat, or a triple threat, she's an . . . infinity threat."

Then again, maybe Dani could tell how I felt about Tyler without me saying a word. It wouldn't be the first time. She knew my SAT scores weren't what I wanted by seeing my frown when I looked at my phone. She could tell I was coming down with a cold by how white my already-pale cheeks had gotten. She showed up to my house with ginger shots and chicken noodle soup. Dani just knew things about me. She had to have realized she needed to take the attention off of her and back to me.

That was why she was my best friend.

"And another thing about Morgan: She has excellent taste in friends." Dani flirtatiously flicked her braids behind her shoulder. "Clearly."

"You got that right." Tyler pointed between the two of them. "Clearly."

I felt sick to my stomach.

Dani looked up at Tyler between her long lashes. "So how are you liking Prairie Glen so far?"

"Can't complain."

Of course Tyler didn't have complaints. Half the student body was fawning over the new guy. Why did I think for a second that I was special?

Especially since that charge between Tyler and me had shifted. It was as if actual electricity was radiating between Tyler and Dani as they locked eyes, while I . . . felt like I was intruding. I opened my mouth to try to get their attention off each other, but this was the first time since the Dirtbag Incident that Dani didn't have sadness enveloping her. She looked . . . smitten.

Instead of inserting myself, I picked at my Cobb salad and watched as Tyler and Dani talked about graphic novels. Dani sketched a few characters for Tyler, who handled the scribbled scrap of paper like it was the Holy Grail.

But maybe this was just the kind of guy Tyler was: a flirt. First me, then Dani. He'd probably sit with the ShawnaBots tomorrow.

"Oh wow, I can't believe we gotta go soon," Tyler exclaimed when he looked at his phone. "I need to check in with the front office, but I'll see you around, yeah?" He was looking only at Dani.

"I'd like that. A lot," Dani said as she coiled one of her braids around her fingers.

"Me too." Tyler fumbled with his bag and kept his eyes on Dani before he finally turned around and walked off.

"Oh my God," Dani squealed. "What just happened, Morgan?" She looked as shocked as I felt. "Why didn't you tell me that he was gorgeous and sweet and . . ."

The perfect guy, I almost finished for her.

"Oh, I . . ."

I should've told her how I felt. But after witnessing Tyler around Dani, I knew it didn't matter.

Instead I kept my mouth shut. I cheered her on as she got ready for her first date, even though I was convinced he would move on to someone else quickly, just like he did with me. And then there was a second date. And a third. A one-month anniversary. Two . . . I had a front-row seat to their love story unfolding.

And it hurt. It was silly for me to have feelings for somebody who wasn't interested in me, but it made it harder that Tyler wasn't this player. He was a dream boyfriend. The one who said the right things. Who would surprise Dani with flowers just because. Who came to all our show choir performances to cheer her on.

With every kind gesture to Dani, I found myself falling harder and harder for Tyler. It became too difficult to be around them.

I finally met the guy of my dreams, and he was in love with my best friend.

So I buried everything down. I switched my schedule so we no longer had classes and lunch together. I tried not to be near them. I stayed numb as Dani would talk about Tyler. I pulled away from my best friend.

If I could snap my fingers and not have feelings for Tyler, I would. I did my best to turn that love into hate. Tyler became my enemy. I treated him like the kryptonite he was for me. I would bail anytime he showed up. I would be miserable whenever he was around. Openly glaring or rolling my eyes when he made any effort with me, which he did, a lot.

When I heard that he was joining show choir for our trip because they needed another guy, I was sick to my stomach. For a second—a teeny-tiny second—I contemplated not going. But I wasn't going to let Tyler Chen stop me from going to *London*.

I had already given too much because of Tyler.

I was losing my best friend.

And perhaps even worse, the person I used to be.

"I'm sorry," I say to Tyler now, but so softly he doesn't hear me.

"I just don't understand," he continues. "You were so awesome to me when we first met and then it's like I—I don't know—you looked at me like I was some mass puppy murderer. It kills Dani that the two most important people in her life can't be in the same room together. That she's torn between us. I don't want to be part of making her unhappy, so I don't know what to do. Because sometimes I think the only way to fix this, to have her not feel trapped, is to let you win."

"Let me win?"

His eyes are wet. "For me to end things so you can have Dani all to yourself and I can just . . . disappear."

I open my mouth, but I don't know what to say. For months, all I wanted was for Tyler and Dani to break up. For me to have Dani back and for . . . what? It's not like I can lay claim to Tyler. Or that he would want anything to do with me.

Tyler was never mine to begin with.

Seeing how devastated he is now, him shaking—probably from the height in addition to his surrender—makes me realize how much he truly loves Dani. It was obvious before, but now, I understand the monster who has been ruining everything was *me*.

"Don't." I kneel down so we're eye to eye. "This has nothing to do with you. It's all me, and I'm sorry, Tyler, I'm so incredibly sorry." As I say those words, I feel a lightness in my shoulders I haven't felt in months. I'd been holding on to an unattainable idea for so long, it wasn't serving anybody—especially me.

Tyler looks genuinely shocked by my apology.

"I really made a mess out of things," I admit with a groan.

Tyler shakes his head. "I don't understand."

I sit down next to him. "So you probably aren't going to believe this, but I had a crush on you when we first met."

If I thought Tyler was in shock before, that was nothing compared to now. His mouth is practically on the floor.

"Yep, and well, honestly for a while. Like a while, while."

"You . . . what?"

"Yeah, but you went and fell in love with my best friend."

"Oh," Tyler replies, before his eyes get really wide. *"Oh."*

I should be embarrassed, but instead I start laughing. "I mean, honestly, I don't know what I was thinking. Like, you walk into class and I was all, '*Oh my God, fresh meat.*' But you were so sweet and I became smitten and you are a really great guy, Tyler. But now that I think about it, we would've made a horrible match. Like, you're such a geek about comics, and half the time when you're going on and on and on about whatever manga you're into or whatever, my eye-rolling is because nobody—even Dani—has any clue what you're talking about."

"Yeah, I can get carried away sometimes," Tyler replies softly.

I vigorously nod. "But Dani thinks it's cute you're in your own world. *Although*—" A memory flashes in my head. "You never take social cues. Do you remember that time we were at Tiffany's house and everybody—and I mean *everybody*—was talking about that insane pop quiz in chemistry? Poor Sydney was practically in tears over it ruining her perfect GPA and you just started talking about a YouTube video about some weird contraption that made toast."

"Oh yeah!" Tyler perks up. "A Rube Goldberg machine."

"Yeah, whatever that is." I drop my head. Why hadn't I thought about this before? Instead of focusing on Tyler not choosing me, I should've realized we were never meant to be.

"And let's talk about—"

Tyler throws his hands up. "Okay, I get it! Crush is over. That message is loud and clear."

We both look at each other for a beat before cracking up.

"I'm sorry! It's just . . ." I stop when I realize we're at the top of the Eye. London is spread out all around us. A whole city filled with so many possibilities and people, not to mention cute boys with British accents. "I guess this is my long-winded way to ask you to forgive me."

Tyler's face lights up. "Are you kidding me? All I've wanted is for things to be cool with us, even though it's clear you have some opinions on my questionable social skills."

"Sorry!"

He lets out a groan. "Do you realize what this means?"

"That I'm a jerk?" Because I have been, especially to Tyler. He'd done nothing wrong but be charming and wonderful. *How dare he!*

"No, that Dani was right about locking us in this pod together."

"Aw man, we're never going to hear the end of this." While I love Dani with my whole heart, she likes to rub it in when she's right.

"No kidding," Tyler agrees.

Tyler and I look at each other and both say, "*Let me hear you say it.*" Something Dani loooooves to do.

"Well in this case, I couldn't be happier she's right," Tyler admits. "And look, I know how much you love London, so you and Dani should get high tea when we're done."

"Thanks, but you two should go. I'm happy just walking

around, and . . ." I can't believe I'm about to tell Tyler something Dani doesn't know. "I sort of need to see what it's like to be on my own, because I might be going to uni here."

"What?" Tyler gasps. "Dani didn't tell me."

"Only my family knows," I admit. "I didn't want to tell anybody I applied abroad because I would've been embarrassed if I didn't get in."

"Where are you going? Oxford?" Tyler asks. "Ah, what's the other big one?"

"Cambridge. But it's neither of those. I've been accepted at University College London. I'm taking a tour tomorrow to see if I love it in person as much as I do online."

"Oh, wow. That's really amazing, congrats!" he says, and I can tell he's truly happy for me. "You should be really proud of yourself. You're living your dream."

"Thanks." I am pretty—as the Brits put it—*chuffed* that I made this fantasy about living in London a reality.

Now I guess I need to find my prince.

And since I'm no longer holding on to something—or someone—I may just finally find him.

Tyler's focus goes off to the distance. "Oh my God, how high up are we?" His eyes are filled with panic.

I walk over to the window that looks out to the Thames. It's a clear day and as I squint, I can barely make out Windsor Castle in the far distance. "This is so cool." But then I remember one of us is terrified of heights. "Are you okay?"

Tyler shakes his head. "Um, yeah . . . I kinda want to look out, but ah . . . I'm also utterly terrified."

I think about how I am with snakes. How I flinch if one appears on a screen while watching TV. But this is *London*. It's not going to bite.

"How about I tell you what I see and then you can decide if you want to take a look?"

Tyler timidly nods.

"Okay, well . . . it's London. Super helpful, huh? Um, right below us is Big Ben and Parliament, Westminster Abbey, but if you look out you can see the Pall Mall, which leads to Buckingham Palace, then Hyde Park, and then it's all these gorgeous buildings and parks as far as the eye can see. You can even see Wembley Stadium in the distance. It's pretty cool and that's just this one direction. But it's the places you'd be most familiar with. Do you want to take a peek?"

Tyler nods again, but makes no motion to stand up. I walk over and hold out my hand. "I've got you. Nothing bad is going to happen," I say as I give his hand a squeeze. "Huh."

I look down to see his hand in mine.

"What?"

"Oh, it's just"—I gesture down at our entwined hands—"zero sparks."

"Oh my God, I get it, Morgan. You're physically repulsed by me now."

"I mean, I *think* I can put up with being in your presence. As a friend. And hey, friend, what do you think?" I gesture my chin out the window.

Tyler takes a small step to the glass. "Oh my God!"

"Are you okay?"

"Yeah, this is really cool . . . and so scary."

"Well, here, let me distract you with my amazing wit."

"Do you think you can manage that without the expense of my fragile ego?"

I pretend to consider it for a second. "I reckon I can give it a go."

For our remaining time in the pod, I hold Tyler's hand and point out all my favorite parts of London. Sharing something special with someone who is special. As a friend. That's all I want. While I could keep chastising myself for pushing him away, I have to let go of the past and focus on the future.

And I have to admit, the future is looking pretty great.

As we get ready to exit I give Tyler a big hug. "Thanks for being a great boyfriend to Dani and forgiving me."

"Thank *you* for the compliment. Can I quote you on saying I'm a great boyfriend? Maybe get it on a T-shirt or a mug: 'World's Best Boyfriend.'"

"Whoa, I didn't say anything about *world's best*," I reply with an exaggerated eye-roll. "You're competent . . . for an American."

"I'll take it!"

As we step out on the platform, Dani is nervously chewing on her thumbnail. There's a flash of relief that we're both alive and didn't go all Hunger Games on each other.

"Are you guys okay?" Dani's eyes dart back and forth between Tyler and me.

"Oi!" Tyler calls out to her. "We're brilliant. The view was pretty grand, innit?"

"Oi!" I reply in a cockney accent. "You're a legend for conquering your fear, mate."

Okay, so I may have given Tyler a rundown on some British slang as well.

Dani looks suspiciously between us. "What's going on with you two?"

Tyler puts his arm around me and I give him a nod. "You were right!" we say in unison. "You were right, you were right!"

"Wait, what?" Dani's mouth is hung open. "So that . . . worked?"

I pat Tyler on the back. "I'm going to let you deal with her gloating while I find a cuppa and a scone. Cheerio!" I bow down to Tyler and he does the same, leaving him to explain everything that happened.

"Wait!" Dani calls after me. "Are you really okay about what I did? You don't hate me?"

"Of course I don't hate you."

Relief floods her face. "I'm so sorry, but I have to say, it makes me happy to see you guys getting along, unless it's an act."

I give her a hug. "No acting, one hundred percent real. Tyler can tell you all about it."

"Okay, but I want to hear your version over fish and chips tonight. Just the two of us."

"Sounds brilliant," I reply before turning to leave.

I've got a boy to see.

I walk toward Westminster Bridge to spend some more time blatantly admiring that hunk, Big Ben.

"Watch it!" a female voice yells out, and before I know it,

I'm on the ground. Pain radiating off my leg. I look up to see a biker speeding away. She gives a little wave as she passes by a No Cycling sign. "Sorry!"

Great. Maybe *this* is a sign that being on my own in London wouldn't live up to the fantasy I've had in my head.

"You all right?" A hand reaches down to help me up.

I nod, my ego more bruised than my body. I brush the dirt off my jeans, before taking his hand and being pulled up.

Then I look up to find the most adorable boy standing in front of me. He's tall with rust-colored curly hair that's sticking up in different directions. And . . .

No, *nope*. No way this is happening to me. I must've really hit my head when I fell because there is no way on earth this is real. That *he* is real.

Then I hear a loud ringing noise confirming I clearly got a concussion in my fall.

"Do you hear that?" I ask as I check my head for any bumps.

He looks around. "Are you talking about the chimes?"

"So that's not in my head?"

"No." The boy rubs his hand around his messy hair, making him even more adorable. "That's Big Ben over there."

Oh my God, Big Ben *is* chiming. My heart is fluttering in time to its rapid bongs as I take in this British boy standing in front of me wearing a *University College London* T-shirt.

"Are *you* real?" slips out of my mouth. Because what are the chances?

Please be real, please be real, I wish upon a chime.

His entire face lights up. "I *am* real. And I take it you're

American?" I notice his accent is slightly different from the ones I hear in London.

"Yeah. Are you from Liverpool?"

"Aye, you've got an ear for the Scouse accent." He gives me a wink and I think I'm going to melt into a puddle right here and now.

"I mean, the Beatles," I reply, as if that's some sort of answer.

"Legends they are." He smiles and I notice he has the most adorable dimples in his cheeks, ones that put Tyler's to shame.

Tyler who?

"Do you go to UCL?" I find myself holding my breath. How amazing would that be? To meet someone—and that being a really, *really* cute British boy—who might be going to same uni as me.

"Yeah, I'm a fresher."

Oh, sweet Prince George, when did I get so lucky?

"That's amazing! I might be going there!" I exclaim a little too loudly. Then again Americans do have a well-earned reputation for being loud.

"Maybe?" His mouth turns down.

"Yeah, I got in and I'm touring tomorrow, and probably will be going, I just . . . haven't confirmed. Yet."

"Well, that won't do," he replies with a shake of his head. "Fancy a cuppa, and I can tell you all of the reasons you should be going to uni here?"

Do I fancy a cuppa with a cute British boy? Who wants to convince me to go to the same school as him?

This is the stuff of rom-com legend.

"That would be grand," I reply as heat radiates from my

cheeks. We walk toward Westminster Bridge and the ringing of the chimes, falling in step next to each other. I can practically feel a buzz between us. "I'm Morgan, by the way."

"Ben," he replies.

It appears Disney was right: Sometimes dreams do come true.

LIBERTY
(The Makeover)

ANNA-MARIE McLEMORE

TICK TOCK

1. *Noun—stunting move in which a flyer changes legs, right liberty to left, like it's nothing, like the possibility of falling has never crossed her mind.*
2. *Noun—the act of switching in the air so fast that everyone watching wonders if they really saw you do it.*

If Wren Miller hadn't left so last minute, I probably wouldn't have made the squad this year. But when a space opened up on a club team, our school squad lost Wren, and a flyer. They needed me. I knew it, and they knew it.

And unlike the first time I showed up at tryouts, I knew what they were looking for.

Back then, I thought I was ready. I had hyperextended jumps

(thanks to genetics) and almost enough flexibility to pull a scorpion (thanks to a hell of a lot of work).

So I put on my cutest shorts, and a cropped shirt that didn't have any grass stains (yet). Then I queued up the latest from my favorite (and massively underappreciated) beauty expert's channel.

Camila Sanchez was my age, with brown skin like mine. She was vicious toward brands with ridiculous ranges of foundation (a dozen ivory and only a few past tan) or blush (variations on cotton-candy pink, none of which showed up on our cheeks). But to her viewers, she was as encouraging as a best friend.

"*You're looking to catch the light, not turn it into a glare,*" she said while talking us through highlighting.

"*Hermanas, I hate to break it to you, but you're probably underlining as badly as you've seen the gringas overlining,*" she said while explaining how to find your true lip shape.

"*You'll get it, it just takes practice,*" she said as she told us why contour probably belonged higher than we thought it did.

The morning of tryouts, I followed along as she did a subtle liquid eyeliner (no wing, just enough to bring out my eyes). A light dusting of bronzer. Two soft blooms of blush on my cheeks. Waterproof (sweatproof) mascara. Thin coat of lip stain, just enough to look like I'd been eating a raspberry lollipop. Tinted lip balm over that (no lip gloss during practice unless you wanted your hair and everyone else's to stick to your mouth).

I smoothed my hair-sprayed ponytail, blew a kiss at the mirror, and decided Camila Sanchez would have been proud.

But I didn't make it.

And I knew before they posted the list.

I knew before tryouts were even over.

And I knew why.

It had nothing to do with how well I could dance, or my shapes during stunts.

That was the day I stopped watching Camila Sanchez's channel.

That was the day I started becoming someone else, someone who went by Mena instead of Ximena, someone who looked, to the white girls deciding the roster, a little more like a cheerleader.

It took me a year, and a dozen different beauty channels. But by the time the next tryouts came around, I was ready, really this time. I pulled on shorts that flattened my ass as much as physics allowed, and a looser T-shirt that downplayed my shape. I dragged my hair through a flat iron until it stayed straight and shined back at me. I put on foundation and powder as light as I could get away with.

And this time, that was enough to get me on the squad.

Well, that, and my hyperextended jumps, and the fact that they really needed a flyer.

DEADMAN

1. *Noun—a planned fall out of a stunt.*
2. *Verb—falling out of a stunt and hoping to God the people who are supposed to catch you actually do.*

I gripped my hands around my shoes, trying to let the tension out of my hamstrings.

"Keep stretching, but listen up," Emmie said.

"Can you pull on me?" Leah whispered, offering me her hands. I helped her go deeper into her stretch. She was new on the squad too, and one of the best bases I'd ever seen. The girl didn't move.

"So, exciting newwws," Zoe said, stretching out the last word.

Our two co-captains sounded nothing alike. Emmie's voice was as chilled as the ice-blond of her hair. Zoe's had the sparkle and bounce that made me think she'd been born to cheer. But they were both loud enough to command our corner of the practice field.

"We have an incoming transfer student, a new addition to our cheer family," Zoe said.

"And she's pretty much been cheering since she could walk," Emmie said. "So I want you to listen to her like you'd listen to either of us."

Brooke and Jenna tried to look focused on their heel stretches, but exchanged worried glances. I didn't blame them. From what I'd heard, last year's cocaptains had been unprecedented levels of terrifying, instituting the infamous Bagel Ban (no refined carbs within their sight), and (unconfirmed rumor) turning rookies away from practice if their eyebrows weren't tweezed.

Darcy and Cassidy and a few of the older girls were practically sneering, especially the seniors Zoe and Emmie beat out for captain.

Zoe scanned all of us stretching on the grass. "Cammie, where are you?"

With a flip of a dark, curly ponytail, a girl I'd never seen in real life sat up from a straddle stretch. And just like that, I was as unsteady as if I'd slipped out of an arabesque.

In this girl, I saw everything I had tried to either hide or change over the past year. The same brown as my own skin. The lips lined true, instead of underlined with concealer. The hair gelled back but the ponytail itself wavy and curly instead of straightened. Winged eyeliner, worn to practice. An outfit so meticulously planned that the neon-pink trim of her sports bra matched her shoelaces.

Everything that had looked like trying too hard when I did it, looked flawless on her.

"Not Cammie," the girl said, in a voice I'd only ever heard through a computer speaker. "Camila."

KICK SINGLE TWIST

1. *Noun—a dismount from full height with a full revolution on the way down.*
2. *Verb—using the momentum of your kicking leg to turn your body.*
3. *Noun—a spin fast enough that you can't see if your bases have you until they've either caught you or let you fall.*

"Stunt groups!" Emmie yelled.

I drifted over to our group's spot, still dazed from seeing the star of my once-favorite beauty channel in real life.

"Now, Your Highnesses," Zoe said to Cassidy and Darcy, who begrudgingly got up from their low lunges and half-splits.

Ever since group assignments, Darcy and Cassidy hadn't made a secret out of the fact that they didn't love basing me. They resented throwing me instead of Kaitlyn, Emmie's tiny younger cousin who didn't have her scorpion yet but was light enough that they could have tossed her into the sun.

I bounced to keep my body warm, ready to clench every muscle. Right now, Zoe and Emmie were trying us out as point stunt group, front and center. Cassidy and Darcy knew each other well enough that they could move as one organism, syncing so precisely it was like they shared a pair of lungs. And Erin, our backspot, could throw me hard enough that Darcy and Cassidy barely took my weight on the way up to full height.

So it didn't really matter if they liked me. They didn't have to. All that mattered was staying in the air.

Erin counted us through prep. I focused on keeping my body tight, but I could still tell the others girls in my year were eyeing Camila, sizing her up, realizing she was gonna be their main competition for captain senior year.

Even as Darcy and Cassidy were getting me to prep height, I could see Camila watching every stunt group. She was practicing her tumbling, but surveying us between passes. She came out of a standing tuck, and in a split second her eyes were back on us. Layout, stepout, and then she was telling Bethanne to lock her elbows. Roundoff, back handspring, and she was checking out our group in a way that made the inside of me wobble, even if I wouldn't let the rest of me follow.

I kept my elbows straight, core engaged, not making my teammates take any more of my weight than I had to. I locked out my standing leg, flashes of Camila Sanchez still in my field of vision. She was throwing handsprings to back tuck in a fearless way that told me she'd be our center tumbler, the one who kicked off our best routines.

"Wrists," Erin called up at me.

I straightened them. I extended my arabesque through my pointed toes just in time to see Camila practicing another run.

She was still bouncing out of the tumbling pass when she fixed her eyes on our group. It was the look of a captain, the same watchfulness as Zoe and Emmie.

Flyers didn't usually turn out to be captains, at least not in the squads I knew. Maybe it was because flyers had to focus on the tightness in our cores, and just trust that the catch was gonna happen. We had to tune out everything else. We had to ignore what didn't matter in that moment. Our safety and the safety of our bases depended on that.

But captains couldn't tune anything out. They had to watch everything at once.

Which is probably why, even as I threw my leg to spin out and down, the fact that something was wrong registered on Camila's face.

I was off. I could feel it. The way I spun out was a little too fast. I could picture the physics of it, the same way I thought of my velocity going to zero as I reached maximum height during a throw. Only instead of the thrill of that moment, that stillness right before falling, this was an unmistakable sense of being off-kilter, some error in angular momentum.

Erin tried to save me. I felt her trying. But a backspot, even a good one like Erin, couldn't catch someone spinning as fast as I was if the bases didn't pull in. And Darcy and Cassidy were pulling apart.

Being a flyer meant training some of your survival instincts out of yourself. You didn't fight the hands throwing you in the air as hard as they could. You didn't bend your knees to lower your center of gravity and reduce the chance that you'd fall. When something went wrong, I'd learned to pull in my limbs so they didn't knock out a base's tooth or give another a black eye. Bases got concussions and broken ribs as often as flyers, and it was as much my job to look out for them as it was for them to look out for me. So my self-preservation instincts fizzled away, leaving behind the learned reflex to turn my body so my full weight wouldn't hit Erin in the head or chest. Especially since Darcy and Cassidy weren't helping.

There's a very specific kind of alone you feel when you sense your bases coming apart, stepping back from the act of catching you.

Liberty

1. Noun—a pose that can be done at almost any level a base can get you to.

2. Noun—a pose that's a hell of a lot harder than it looks. Especially with a base who's under the impression that it's a two-person stunt at full height.

I went down, hard enough that Erin could only break my fall a little. Most of my weight hit the ground at once.

Pain rippled through my body as Erin talked at me, asking if I was okay, asking me what year it was.

Then came Camila's voice. At first I thought she was telling me not to give up, that it takes a minute to get the hang of liquid eyeliner, that sometimes eye shadow fallout is the eye shadow's fault, not yours.

But she wasn't talking to me.

She was bitching out Darcy and Cassidy.

"You do not do that." From where I was lying on the grass, her voice carried over the whole field. "You do not let that happen. You do not let her hit the ground."

"It's not our fault," Cassidy said. "She's gained weight since tryouts."

Shame added heat to the ache in my body. My mother and I didn't own a scale. I went by how my clothes fit and how strong I felt. So I didn't have hard data to refute Cassidy.

I pictured a current sparking through my body. I imagined the pain turning into energy, the heat of that shame into a fire. With pain along my ribs and pressure in my sternum, I made myself get to my feet.

Zoe and Emmie ran over.

"You do that"—Camila was still yelling at Cassidy and Darcy—"she will never trust you, and neither will anyone else you ever fly, got it?"

"I can go again," I said. My voice was weak, but the fact that I was up and talking was enough to stop Camila.

"Are you sure?" Zoe asked.

I brushed the grass off my legs, and ignored the red patches where I'd hit the ground. "I'm ready." I nodded.

Erin moved to get into position, but Darcy and Cassidy stayed back.

"You heard her," Camila said.

"Who made you captain?" Cassidy asked.

"Cassidy." Emmie sighed.

"Does she even base?" Darcy asked.

Camila gave them a withering smile. Then her eyes landed on me.

She took a step close enough to me to ask, "You really ready?"

"Yeah," I said.

"You're sure you're good?"

"Yeah," I said, wary now.

"Then I'm taking you up." Camila's voice was low enough that I was the only one who could hear her even though the whole team was gathered around now, watching. "Liberty. Full height."

"Us and who else?" I asked. Was she gonna knock Darcy or Cassidy out? Was she really gonna try to sync with the other? Or was she backspotting?

"Nobody." The sun caught the subtle shimmer in Camila's eyeliner. "You and me."

My throat went tight.

A liberty at full height wasn't a one-on-one stunt, not unless you had guys on the team, and we didn't. Camila Sanchez was about to loft me in the air, and I was about to get dropped, again, this time by the star of my former favorite makeup channel.

I may not have owned a scale, but I knew I had enough muscle on me to be heavier than I looked. Cousins took one look at me and assumed they could throw me around like I was nothing. Then they tried to pick me up, and looked as shocked as if they'd realized I was made of steel. If I didn't fully engage, like I always did for bases to keep my weight off them, I wasn't easy to handle.

And I didn't know how I was gonna engage when my heart beat harder every time I heard this voice I'd heard so many times through headphones.

"I don't think you get how heavy I am," I said under my breath.

Camila gave me an open-mouthed smile, like I'd insulted her, amused her, and challenged her all at once. "I don't think you get how strong I am."

Maybe I was humiliatingly starstruck, or pissed off about the whole team seeing my fall, or still rattling around from the pain of landing. But when Camila Sanchez looked at me that way, my heart flinched, and I was ready to do what she said. Like I was back watching her channel and she was telling me how to fix my lip liner.

"Don't try this at home, kids," Camila said, and for a second I heard it, the beauty channel voice again. But now she was talking to the whole team. "Or mere mortals of any age."

Even as she squatted low and offered me her hands, I knew

this was a bad idea Camila Sanchez was talking me into, just like neon eye shadow was a bad idea Camila Sanchez had talked me into.

The difference was that no one saw the neon eye shadow except my mother. The whole team, which had now halted practice, would see this.

Camila counted it out. Her counting made my flyer instincts kick in, and I followed. I put one foot into her cupped hands. As I pushed off her shoulders, she used the momentum of straightening up from her squat to boost me up. I swiveled as she turned me in midair.

I braced to fall out of it. I braced to crash to Earth.

But she stopped me turning. She caught my other foot. She had me, one girl holding me that high, like I thought only guys could.

"Go," she said.

I engaged everything, then did my liberty, arms extended and straight, one leg bent up. As fast as I pulled that leg up, she had both her hands under my standing foot.

For the minute Camila held me up there, I was a goddess, the kind she'd made me feel like once before when I learned how to use gold highlighter or glitter on my lips.

I was a comet, streaking right through the sky. Everyone saw it. The gold of the sun was my highlighter, my glitter, my blush, the glow filling me.

Camila counted me down. I lowered my raised leg back into her hand. She lofted me up and then forward just enough to guide me down by my waist. The pain of falling was gone, and everywhere Camila had touched me was lit up.

Zoe stood back, arms crossed, her thinking smile on her face.

"Nice," she told us both, then nodded at me. "I want you with Camila tomorrow."

"What?" I asked.

"You two are partnering," Emmie said.

Had they managed to hold a captains' conference about this in the space of me being up there?

"For group, it's gonna be you two with Leah and Morgan," Zoe said.

Now I felt like I was dropping out of a stunt again, crashing back toward the ground.

"What?" I asked.

But Zoe and Emmie were already calling us toward jumps.

Just like that, I was off point stunt group.

Camila Sanchez had made me a goddess, and then gotten me downgraded, in the space of one practice.

SCORPION

1. Noun—a real bitch of a move that involves pulling your leg up behind you and your foot as high as you can.

I swore under my breath—or really, under my mom's current reality-TV selection—as I wrenched my leg up.

"Careful," my mother said from the kitchen.

But I was seething, enough to ignore the soreness as I stretched. *It's not our fault.*

She's gained weight.

From whatever heights came all cheer wisdom was the general consensus that your nature-given anatomy decided whether you were a base or a flyer. But that didn't mean there wasn't a hell of a lot of pressure to keep my weight down, which is why I never ate my favorite cherry coconut granola bars until I got home.

"En serio," my mother said, getting down four glasses. Two for water, two for ice and our Diet Cokes. "Don't break yourself."

I let my leg fall. "Do I look like I've gained weight?"

"What?" My mother almost dropped the ice tray.

I breathed hard, shaking out my muscles.

"Where's this coming from?" she asked.

"I don't know." I looked over my shoulder. "Maybe the fact that my ass just keeps expanding the more I work out? It's like the fat refuses to go anywhere." I look back at it. "The muscle just adds a layer."

"That's a superpower," my mother said, raising a glass of water like a toast. "Be proud of your ass."

I stretched out the muscles of my arms, pulling on one with the other.

Weight wasn't everything. I knew that. Taller girls had a harder time as a flyer no matter how thin they were. The limb length that made almost any clothes look good on them was also limb length they had to manage on the way down from a stunt. The same height I was always envious of made their center of gravity higher, which made it harder to get a stunt up to full, harder to get it stable, harder to keep it in the air.

But I still had to work my poses—my scorpion had to get cleaner, and then I had to get my needle, and my bow and arrow—to prove I belonged on this team. I had to prove it wasn't just anatomy that had gotten me here. Or the sudden absence of Wren Miller.

My mother opened the fridge. "You want grilled cheese?"

I finished my arm stretch. "You are the worst cheer mom in the world."

"Sorry." She put on a stern expression. "Do you want"—she thought for a few seconds—"celery and electrolyte water?"

I sighed. "Of course I want grilled cheese. My ass is gonna stay big. I might as well enjoy it."

My mother handed me a glass and immediately knocked hers against it. "That's the spirit."

CRADLE CATCH

*1. Noun—a planned way for your stunt group to
stop you from hitting the ground.
2. Noun—an unplanned way to stop you from
hitting the ground when something goes wrong.*

I wanted to hate Darcy and Cassidy, or Emmie and Zoe, or Camila, for me being off point stunt group. But I hadn't realized what it could feel like to fly without having to fight your teammates to stay up. Camila called Leah and Morgan through the stunts, and they stayed in rhythm. Their arms were straight, locked. They fixed their grips, their hands holding all of my shoes, not just the toes and heels. They synced up, throwing on time. And when our stunt wobbled, they didn't step out. They pulled together.

With that secure of a base under me, I could focus more on my shapes, on twisting, turning, on giving the kind of big smile the captains always wanted. I could tune into the space between control and letting everything go. I moved like I was flying, not falling, even though half of flying was falling like you meant it.

I spun out of my arabesque, kick double twist this time. I fell. They caught me, absorbing the impact of me in the same moment I engaged everything in my body.

"Good," Camila yelled.

One more bounce, and I jumped onto my feet.

Camila looked at Leah and Morgan. "Nice work. You're talking to each other."

When Camila smiled, the sun caught the glitter on her cheekbone. Glitter. She wore glitter to practice. Of course she did.

Emmie called us into pairs, and my heart sped up.

Whatever I felt around Camila, I could tune it out when we were in groups. It was some stupid kind-of-celebrity crush, as shallow as the gold coating on my earrings, and I knew it. But when it was just me and her, it flared through my chest.

"Chairs, everyone," Zoe announced.

Camila groaned.

I whipped my head around. "Something wrong?"

"Nothing personal," Camila said. "This one's just not my favorite."

Even though I held myself back from saying *Huh?* I'm sure

my face said it. Camila had gotten me up in a stunt where it was just her hands under my feet. Compared to that, a chair was nothing.

But then when Camila got me up, she couldn't keep me there. Her hand kept shifting, trying to grab my thigh instead of settling where it belonged, between my legs, the awkward but inevitable placement for a chair.

"You've got to stop moving your hand," I said.

"I'm trying," Camila said, sounding more hesitant than I'd ever heard her, on her channel or in real life.

She shifted again, trying to get a grip on my upper thigh.

I fell out of it, too fast and too hard for her to bring me forward.

By instinct, I folded my body, pulled my legs together, straightened my knees, tensed my core, formed my body into a wide V.

Camila caught me, one arm under my back, one under my thighs.

"Sorry," she said, breathing hard.

I couldn't tell if my body was slick with sweat and sunblock or if her hands were damp, but she dug her fingers into me to stop my slipping.

She held on to me, my pulse hard in my neck and my fingertips.

"You okay?" she asked.

"Yeah," I said, nodding to signal she could put me down.

Even when she did, I was still close enough to smell her body splash.

Catching my breath was the only thing that stopped me from

asking, *What was that?* Cheer involved getting used to having your teammates grab your ass and breasts. It happened if you were a flyer, and your bases were trying to save you. It happened if you were a base, and your flyer or your fellow bases were scrambling. Cheer meant getting used to either having your hand under a girl's concha (if you were a base) or having a girl's hand under yours (if you were a flyer).

For Camila, the hesitation made no sense. Losing her center of gravity on a chair after the kind of tumbling and basing she did was like perfecting a chocolate soufflé and then panicking when it's time to make Pop-Tarts.

"Problem, Sanchez?" Darcy asked on the way by.

"Isn't that your favorite?" Cassidy asked. "Putting your hand in a girl's crotch?"

The fluttering through my body fell away. Rage floated up in its place.

Camila's eyes wavered on me, nervous, just a second, and then flew over to Cassidy and Darcy.

"Tell you what," she told them. She grabbed her water bottle off the ground, taking a long drink before continuing. "You two learn to do a layout with a full twist, and then go fuck yourselves, and then maybe you can talk to me again."

I couldn't tell what offended them more, her flicking her ponytail as she passed them, or the way she casually, right before leaving the field, did the full twisting layout she knew neither of them could.

Pretty Girl

*1. Noun—a basket-toss pose that calls for a
big smile more than maybe any other move in
cheerleading.
2. Noun—a pose that makes you feel ridiculous but
looks good from a distance.
3. Noun—a pose that requires you to commit
completely.*

There was a reason I stopped watching Camila Sanchez's makeup tutorials. And it started with the first time I tried out for the high school squad.

I didn't realize until I walked onto that field that it didn't matter if I had the form, the strength, the flexibility, the bizarrely open hip turnout. It didn't even matter if I'd shown up with the perfect glowy no-makeup makeup.

The older girls weren't heavy with muscle like the best tumblers on my junior high team, their middles thick with the power and strength of their abs. The girls ruling this squad were willowy and small-waisted, even the bases. Most were blond and most who weren't had identical honey-gold highlights. The two girls of color I could place who were already on the team had perfectly straightened hair, straighter than I ever managed to get mine.

The girls of color who weren't on the team yet had the same kinds of ponytails I did, slicked back against our heads with hair spray or gel, the tails wavy or curly, a look that I'd always thought was cute but that I now realized did not fit on this team.

The other girls knew it too. They looked as uncomfortable as I did. We didn't have the skinny ponytails, either naturally straight or meticulously straightened. We were all wearing clean, wrinkle-free clothes that made us look painfully earnest alongside the older girls' pajama shorts and cut-up T-shirts.

Any makeup the older girls were wearing was a messy afterthought. A swipe of highlighter but no blush. Or the worn-off color of lip gloss applied hours ago. They didn't care. They didn't have to. The point was showing that they didn't have to.

I was the definition of trying too hard. And yet, in my makeup that brought out my Latina features in all the wrong ways, I also hadn't tried hard enough.

I should have underlined my lips.

I should have gone for a lighter shade of powder, exactly like Camila Sanchez told us not to do. *(That white girl helping you pick a foundation may mean well, but she's probably gonna steer you too pale. It's not her fault. It's the white beauty industrial complex.)*

I shouldn't have tried to be the shiniest, perkiest version of myself.

I should have tried to be paler, more casual and haphazard.

I should have tried to be just about anyone else.

That night, after practice, for the first time in a year, I went back to Camila Sanchez's channel. And in with her tutorials about contouring and eyebrow shaping were a couple of posts of her talking to the camera about thinking she might be queer. Then being pretty sure she might be queer. Then claiming the word *lesbian*, followed by a tutorial using the colors of the lesbian flag.

Everyone wanted to seem real online. But something about Camila was past real and into raw. When she cried, she didn't flap her hands at her face to stop her makeup from running. Her makeup bled. Her mascara ran. She was beautiful in a way that her makeup going ugly didn't lessen. When she did her lesbian flag tutorial, she had to stop and start over when she got teary and messed it up, and she joked about it. She laughed loud and without apology.

I hadn't claimed any particular label, at least no label more specific than thinking maybe I was queer. But her claiming her label, the nervous but unhesitating way she looked into the camera and said *"I'm a lesbian,"* that was more beautiful than the most flawless smoky eye.

"Ximena?" My mother squinted into my room, glowing from screen light. "You sleeping anytime soon?"

"Yeah," I said. "In a minute."

I watched them all. The tutorials where she turned her eyelids into pride flags. The video where she tried out a blush palette while talking about coming out to her mom. The post where she showed the look she wore to cheer at games at her old school, an update on her makeup routine that looked like she wasn't wearing makeup.

Whatever bubbly feeling came back, the one I used to have watching her videos, it now came with the shimmery feeling of her holding me, and a bitter sense of the distance between us.

Camila was everything I had to undo about myself so I could

be the kind of girl who belonged on the high school squad. The kind of girl who belonged at all.

But apparently, she belonged. With the muscles that made her an unshakable base, and the full-out eyeliner she wore even to practice, Camila belonged.

Apparently, it was just me who didn't.

I always thought the problem was that I was a brown girl with curves who liked makeup.

But the problem was that I was the wrong kind.

Camila was stunning and brazen, and she had the skill and strength to back it up.

I wasn't good for much of anything except getting thrown around.

NEEDLE

1. Noun—what you work your body toward after the scorpion.
2. Noun—the approximate width of the leeway you get as a girl of color.

I was still on the practice field as the sun was going down, trying to get my needle. But I was wobbling in it. If I'd been up in a stunt, I'd have already fallen.

"You still here?" Camila asked. She had her bag on her shoulder, like she'd just come back for something she'd forgotten.

I pretended I was too absorbed in straightening my leg behind me to answer.

"You don't have to work so hard, you know," Camila said.

That made me drop my leg. "Because you tumble like you do after *not* working hard?" I asked.

"I didn't mean cheer," she said. "You have to work hard in cheer. I meant"—she gestured at my face and body—"what you're doing. To look like them." She glanced over her shoulder like the team was still there.

I tried balancing my weight again to prep, and tried not to laugh.

On me, wearing lipstick when I was just gonna sweat during practice made me look like I was trying too hard. On Camila Sanchez, sweat added more glisten to her glitter.

On me, my high, hard cheekbones looked harsh, the very reason I softened the angles of my face with contour and highlight. On her, high cheekbones were fashion.

On me, my big ass made my cheer skirt ride up so much in the back that some of the white girls side-eyed me like I was committing an obscene act. I wanted to say, *I don't know what to tell you, these are the skirts, and this is my ass.*

But on Camila Sanchez, her ass was another perfect contour on her body, the natural continuation of the muscles in her thighs. The width of her hips and the exaggerated bow of each calf were the perfect balance of curvy and solid. She was a base no one could move.

I grabbed behind me for my shin.

"You're not breathing," Camila said.

I tried to breathe, but not show I was thinking about breathing.

I fell off balance again.

"Tell you what." Camila adjusted the strap of her bag. "You let me give you a makeover before the first game of the season, I'll help you get your needle."

My heart skipped like it was stumbling. Once, I would have thought I was the luckiest girl who ever picked up a blush brush.

But now Camila wasn't just a face and voice on a screen. She was a reminder that she and I were very different kinds of queer brown cheerleader.

If Darcy and Cassidy knew I liked girls, if I'd had a label I was ready to declare, they'd have made comments about how much I liked being in a chair lift too. If they knew the fizzy feeling I got whenever Camila's hands were on my waist, if they knew how the sweat on her skin looked, to me, like a million tiny crystals, they'd get in any hits they could when Zoe and Emmie were out of earshot.

Whatever they said to Camila, they'd do worse with me. I wasn't grounded and steady like she was. I'd gotten used to yielding, to getting thrown around. As a flyer, that was my job, to go where other people's hands sent me.

"I don't need help." I prepped again. "I almost have my needle anyway."

"And I'll help you get your bow and arrow," Camila said.

I stopped, and squinted to make her out against the orange light.

"Before first game," she said.

I thought of that girl on the screen who talked me through metallic eyeliner, who looked beautiful in mascara streaks as she said the word *lesbian* like it was the most powerful spell in the world.

I thought of her turning me into a comet, a firework, my heart bursting open in the air.

If I kept worrying about what the Darcys and Cassidys on the squad thought of me, I'd lose that spark, that light.

Whatever I'd kept of that spark gave me an idea.

"Only if you let me help you with something," I said.

"What?" Camila asked.

I gave her a look.

Her eyes widened. "No."

CHAIR

1. Noun—possibly the most dreaded lift for a cheerleader who likes other girls.

"I fucking hate this," Camila said.

"Why?" I asked.

"Because I'm a lesbian cheerleader, and because queerphobic people exist, and because that makes me a little hesitant to put a hand in a girl's crotch even when she gives enthusiastic consent," she said.

"Okay," I said, "this is beyond enthusiastic consent. I don't want you to drop me."

"I am a lesbian cheerleader," she said again, slowly, "putting my hand in a girl's crotch."

"And it's cheerleading," I said. "Backspots push on my ass constantly to get me into the air. I've gotten my boobs grabbed to stop me from hitting the gym floor, and I've said thank you."

"But do you get how I feel like the jokes are inevitable?" she asked.

"And when you're cocaptain, queerphobic jokes will get fifty push-ups."

"I'm not gonna be cocaptain," Camila said. "There are gonna be five of us going after it."

"Four," I said. "I don't want it. And you'll get it, trust me." I got closer to her. "Now quit stalling. If you haven't gotten my shorts deeper into my ass crack, you have failed."

"I know, I know." She sighed. "Let's get this over with." We bent down and then she shoved me up. I propped one knee, but she was still moving her hand.

"Okay, no," I said. "Actually under my crotch."

"Are you sure—"

"Crotch, Sanchez!" I yelled down at her.

Maybe it was that she'd never heard me yell. Maybe it was that the first thing she was ever hearing me yell was the word *crotch*. But she shifted the heel of her hand, and I stopped wobbling.

"See?" I asked, locking my arm pose. "Aren't I easier to keep in the air?"

She brought me down, hands on my waist. One misstep, and I fell back onto her.

She caught me, wrapping her arms around my rib cage.

"Sorry," I said. If it had happened during a routine, we could have recovered without anyone noticing.

But I didn't move.

And she didn't move me. She didn't let go. She didn't bounce me back up to standing straight, the buoyant rhythm we were always following, like our bodies were balloons.

I looked back at her. Her mascara-ed eyelashes brushed my cheek. The glitter on her temples refracted through the sweat along her hairline, turning to crushed diamonds.

Technically, she caught my lips. But I made it easy, my raspberry lip balm meeting her lip stain that tasted like birthday cake.

Her fingers grazing my cheek felt as soft as a highlighting brush. They followed the curves of my cheekbone and browbone as she kissed me, like she was reminding me of all the best parts of my face.

But in that moment, she wasn't the Camila who filmed my favorite makeup tutorials, and I wasn't the girl who followed along with an eye shadow brush.

I was a girl, kissing another girl.

In cheerleading, you learned to ignore a base's hand in your crotch. You learned to ignore the boob and ass-grabs that either help you fly or keep you from crashing. When Camila had me in the air, I barely felt the heel of her hand pressing into me. It was just part of the lift.

But now, leaning back against her, a heat stirred between my legs, like that spot was just now registering that she had touched me there.

For these few seconds, Camila wasn't the tumbler who intimidated us all, or the backspot whose counts I followed. And I wasn't just a flyer, my heart pulling in to make itself smaller the same way my body did.

I was Ximena, kissing Camila.

BOW AND ARROW

1. Noun—a position in which the curves and angles of your body become your fiercest weapon.

Camila Sanchez taught me to do everything right.
You have to get used to your center of gravity on every new move, or you're not gonna be able to keep it in the air.
Don't pop your hip.
Really, I mean it, breathe.
Grab the middle of your foot, not your toe.
Don't let your chest drop.
Camila Sanchez taught me to do everything wrong.
Again.

I stopped straightening my hair. I gelled it back but let the tail go like I used to. I went back to being Ximena instead of Mena. Camila ate bread, real bread, during long practices, and I wasn't all the way there yet, but I pulled out my granola bars in full view of the senior girls.

I stopped underlining my lips. I stopped trying to round out my cheekbones to hide the angles of my face (*Having angles means you're sharp*, Camila told me. *Never let them forget it*).

I stopped wearing elastic shorts under my practice shorts to change the shape of my ass (*Wear it with pride*, my mother said).

Once, I'd learned that flying was the art of locking every muscle in your body while making your face look relaxed, happy, energetic, excited. Now I was remembering how to do that again, how to show my face—my own face, not a version of it paled by the wrong foundation or rounded off by contouring—as I shaped my body into the curve of the scorpion. The line of the needle. The tense beauty of the bow and arrow I'd been working on for months.

As I worked into those poses, I got Camila used to the idea that the awkward grabbing of each other's bodies was part of this sport we loved. I got her used to it by showing her the distance between her hand in my crotch to lift me, and her hand up my skirt in my room, how touching me on the field and off were two separate languages.

I still hadn't worked up the nerve to tell her that I'd known her before she walked onto the field that day, that I was·one of those views on her channel.

I would. Eventually. Maybe. Once I could actually look at her without that shimmery feeling going through me.

But the night of the first game, when I looked in the mirror, I looked like me. Lipstick. My favorite eyeliner. Blush. Coats of mascara. Everything most of the other girls never did, but that made me feel as beautiful as the word *lesbian* sounded on Camila's tongue.

I got looks about that, about being exactly the kind of girl who didn't make the team freshman year.

But when I hit my jumps, I took my space on the ground.

When I got my scorpion and my needle, I took my space in the air.

When I showed off my bow and arrow, I proved I earned them, that I was both a girl who belonged on this earth, and a firework.

THE SURPRISE MATCH
(The Matchmaker)

SANDHYA MENON

I wonder if this is the first time someone has actually, full-on *danced* through the parking lot of Game and Fortune, the mega-arcade near our neighborhood. I have my hands thrown up in the air, my slightly sweaty face bathed in the gentle spring night breeze, my smile more brilliant than the orange streetlights that shine down on me and my best friend, Easton.

"Oh my god, Rosie." He rolls his eyes and shoves me lightly. "You *do* know that people can see you, right? With their eyes?"

I laugh, the sound boisterous in the night. A young boy walking with his dad turns to stare at me and I flash him a big smile. "You're just mad I beat you at *Tekken* again, my dude." I sling my arm around Easton's waist. I used to be able to sling it around his shoulders, but he's grown a lot since we were first friends. And I've . . . not grown a lot.

He mock-glares down at me, his blond hair hanging in his eyes. "Okay, but I beat you at DDR."

I splutter in outrage as we reach my car, a tiny white hand-me-down Camry. "You have to be joking, Easton Cooper." I unlock the doors and we both get in and turn to face each other. I search Easton's light brown eyes for a hint of teasing. "Right? You're joking. You're making fun of me."

"I don't know what you're talking about, Rosie Gupta." His tone is casual, light, but because we have four years of friendship under our belts, I know he's mocking me. Trying to get under my skin. And it's totally working. "I beat you by about ten thousand points."

I burst out laughing at the utter absurdity of the thought that *Easton* might beat *me* at any game.

"Okay, okay, maybe I didn't beat you." He pauses. "You know what's weird, though? I don't know your favorite DDR song." Frowning, he adds, "I think that's, like, the *only* thing I don't know about you."

I pause in my laughter, realizing he's right. I know Easton's favorite songs to listen to, no matter his mood (happy, sad, or existential crisis), his favorite movies, his favorite anime, his favorite pair of underwear (that's a long story we don't have time for right now). But I don't know his favorite *Dance Dance Revolution* song to play to. "I don't know yours, either. How is that possible?"

"I know, right?" He shakes his head. "Our friendship is clearly not as deep as we'd thought it was."

"Clearly." I roll my eyes. "Hey. Wanna say our favorites on the count of three?"

He smiles, his teeth bright white in the dim light. "Sure. One . . ."

"Two . . ."

"Three."

We take a breath and then both say, "'Paranoia KCET.'"

This time, we both laugh. Easton holds out his fist to bump and I do. "Well," he says, "I guess we can continue being friends."

I snort. "I guess so. Can't get rid of me that easily." I start up the car, we buckle in, and I begin to drive back home.

"Thanks for treating me to Game and Fortune," he says, when we've been driving and vibing to some BTS for a bit. "Maybe next time we can go to karaoke at that place by the mall."

I hit him in the chest with the back of my hand. "Never say that word to me."

"'Mall'?"

I narrow my eyes in his direction before turning back to the road. "'Karaoke.'"

Easton laughs. "I don't understand why you hate it so much! You're not even *that* bad a singer."

"Wow, thanks," I say wryly. "That's such a ringing endorsement of my talents. I'm not sure *why* it doesn't ignite me to get up in a room full of judgmental people and belt out a tune."

He grins. "I'll never stop trying to make you a karaoke nut. You know that."

Easton *loves* karaoke. It helps that he sounds like Nick Jonas, though. "Yeah, I know."

"I think you could do a rousing rendition of 'Can't Take My Eyes Off You.'"

"'Can't Take My Eyes Off You'? *That's* what you think my karaoke song should be? What am I, eighty?"

Easton scoffs. "Stop trying to act like you haven't watched

Ten Things I Hate About You thirty-eight times. And I happen to know that the part when Heath Ledger sings that song to Julia Stiles makes you cry every single time."

I punch him on the arm. "You're not supposed to talk about that! Ever!"

When he's stopped laughing, Easton squeezes my arm. "But seriously, thanks for paying my way. You know you didn't have to."

"Don't thank *me* for that." I glance at him. "Thank my customers."

"How much are you making now, BTW?"

"Three hundred dollars this week. I think Shore Creek High might be the most matchmade school on the entire planet."

He chuckles and shakes his head. "I can't believe you just wrote a program that would find people's best romantic matches using info trawled from their social media profiles. Like, how do you even come up with an idea like that? And then how do you execute it?"

I wave a hand in the air, secretly pleased at his compliments, as I come to a stop at a red light. "Ah, I saw an opportunity for money to be made. That's all."

"Just don't forget me when your billion-dollar company goes public." Easton studies me for a moment. "So . . . have you run the program on yourself to find *your* best match?"

"Pah! As if. I already know I'm a walking romantic disaster. I don't need my own code to tell me that."

"Right . . ." He continues to study me.

"What?" I squint at him. "What's that look about? Spit it out, Cooper."

The light turns green and I begin to drive again.

"I was wondering if you'd run it on me."

My eyebrows shoot up off my face. "Wait, what? On *you*? I thought this was going to be the year you went girlfriend-less."

Easton picks at an invisible thread on his jeans. "Yeah . . . I'm thinking that might not be a great idea." He cuts his eyes at me, and there's a long pause, like he's weighing something in his mind. Then he sighs. "Asking girls out is terrifying."

I drum my fingers on the steering wheel. "So . . . is there anyone in particular you're hoping to match with?"

He begins to answer before I'm even done asking the question. "Ro . . . Ronan Chang." Easton clears his throat. "Yeah, Ronan." He sits staring resolutely ahead.

There's a strong prickle of some feeling I can't identify in my chest. I push it away quickly. It's annoyance, I decide. "Ronan Chang? I've never even heard you say two words about her."

Easton shrugs. "Come on, Rosie. You know I've been in a slump since Marie and I broke up two years ago. I was wrong about being girlfriend-less." He cuts his eyes at me again and swallows audibly. Is he *nervous*? Of what—that I'll say no to this? He should know better. I've never been able to say no to Easton.

I sigh as I turn onto the street that will take us both home. "Fine."

Easton reaches over and hugs me around the shoulders, which prompts a lot of indignant squawking from me (even though he smells really good, of the mint gum he's always chewing and something soft and yet sturdy, like a well-worn leather jacket). "Thanks, peanut. Love ya."

He has me wrapped around his little finger and I'm not even mad about it. Le sigh.

The next morning, Saturday, I sit on my bed in my fleece pj's and comfy socks and fire up the program on my laptop. I haven't decided what to call it yet, but I know the perfect name will come to me in time. While it loads, I pick up the steaming mug of coffee on my nightstand and take a sip, checking out my reflection in the mirror opposite my bed.

I usually have a Lilly Singh x Lady Gaga vibe going on—you know, combat boots, a collection of colorful wigs, neon blazers worn over crop tops and miniskirts. But here's a secret only my parents and Easton know: When it comes to pj's, I like supergirly, almost-bordering-on-childish stuff. Case in point: I'm currently wearing a fleece nightdress (shut up) with a Hello Kitty on the front, and HK's holding a mug of hot cocoa with *heart-shaped marshmallows* in it. If anyone at school (except Easton, naturally) saw me in this, I would *die*.

The program pings, ready for me to upload someone's social media profiles so it can go trawling. I copy and paste links to Easton's Instagram, TikTok, Snapchat, Tumblr, and Twitter accounts. Because Easton's straight, I tell the program to only match him with girls. I have 98 percent of the school already uploaded in here, including Ronan Chang, so I'm confident it'll find someone to match him to. And then I sit back and sip my coffee.

It only takes a few minutes for the program to analyze his

profile and then match it. When the "Result found" bell dings, I set my coffee aside and check the screen.

EASTON COOPER has been matched to . . .
ROSIE GUPTA

I stare at the screen, a hollow laugh bursting out of me as my brain finally registers what I'm seeing.

What? What?!

I read the results over and over again, shaking my head. Then I tell the clearly broken program to run itself again.

I uploaded my own profile in the early stages of development, when I wanted to test the program and find bugs. I also uploaded my parents' profiles. But all three of those were just for R&D purposes. It isn't supposed to *actually* match us to anyone.

Least of all me to Easton.

The results bell chimes again.

EASTON COOPER has been matched to . . .
ROSIE GUPTA

What . . . the . . . actual . . . fuck.

"This makes no sense," I mutter to myself, tapping away at the keys, checking the code, rechecking the results. Everything looks right; the program did what it's supposed to do, what it always does.

In a separate window, it tells me the reasons it's matched me to Easton and vice versa.

1. On February 22, 2018, Rosie and Easton both posted the same quote from the book *Six of Crows* that they were buddy reading. ("I will have you without armor . . . or I will not have you at all.")

2. In summer 2018, Easton and Rosie both made a Spotify playlist, with sixteen out of twenty-five song matches.

3. In winter 2019, Easton and Rosie both expressed dismay at the commercialization of Christmas while allowing that they secretly loved the way the country transformed into a "glowing Christmas tree" (quote from Rosie Gupta's Twitter).

And on and on and on the reasons went, from small to large, from political to whimsical and every place in between.

I stare at the screen. Easton and me? Me and *Easton*? I mean, I knew we were compatible. It's why we're best friends. But a *romantic* match?

My cell phone beeps.

Easton: Hey, Rosie. How's it going. Ah . . . nice weather we're having, huh?

I narrow my eyes at my phone. It pings again.

Easton: So, just wondering totally casually . . . did you run it yet?

And there it is. Oh my god. My palms instantly turn sweaty and I wipe them on my soft nightdress and try not to panic.

Rosie: Um, yeah! Trying to!

Easton: Okay, cool! Do you want to meet up in an hour at the park and talk about it? Maybe shoot some hoops?

I can practically see him bouncing from foot to foot as he waits for my response. Because he wants to know if his love match is Ronan Chang.

Rosie: Yes to the talk, no to the hoops

Easton: You got it, maestro!

Rosie: Your nicknames for me have got to stop.

Easton: But they won't tho

Easton: It's only one (1) of the many things you love about me

I smile weakly and send him a thumbs-up emoji that I'm sure he'll interpret as sarcasm when really it's just me being tongue-tied for the first time in my life.

Holy shit. What am I going to tell him?

An hour passes by wayyyy too fast and before I know it, I'm at Holt Park waiting in the sunshine by the lake. I try to watch a peaceful family of ducks paddling around in the late spring sunshine, but I keep thinking of their little orange feet churning away underneath the water, just like how my brain is churning away underneath the surface of my skull.

What? I never said I was a poet.

I even wore my power outfit for a confidence boost: pale pink wig, black leather moto jacket over a lime-green crop top and paper bag–waisted shorts, paired with my favorite Doc Martens. Nothing is helping. My palms are dripping sweat. Uggghhh.

"It's Ridiculously Ravishing Rosie!"

I swivel to see Easton jogging up to me, dressed in a blue T-shirt and black shorts, his blond hair catching the sunlight like gold thread. He bends to give me a quick hug and then bounces from foot to foot. See? Told ya.

"So? Who'd I match to?" His Adam's apple bobs as he swallows.

I nibble on my lip for a second. "Um, let's walk." We begin down the trail that leads in a big loop around the lake, passing families and couples and older people, all of whom smile at us. "So . . . the program is still running. I'm sure it'll have a name for me soon." I hold up my phone. "It'll send it to me via email. But before all that, let me ask you: What happens if the result isn't what you're expecting?"

Easton frowns. "What do you mean?"

"Just . . . you know. What if it matches you with someone you haven't ever thought about in *that* way?"

A blue jay flies overhead, chittering at us, drunk on sunshine. We both ignore it.

"I don't know." Easton's eyes bore into mine. "Why are you asking me this?"

I glance up at him, his broad shoulders, his easy smile. I know it like my own; somewhere along the way, I've memorized it. And if I told him the truth . . . what would happen to our friendship? Would he ever be able to be this easy, this comfortable with me again? "Just answer the question."

He shrugs and rubs the back of his neck. "I don't know, Rosie. It's hard to say. I guess it depends on who it is."

Meaning: Yes, it might ruin our friendship. If he doesn't even know how he might react, I'm not going to chance it. No way. Turning to face forward, I say, "Right." A second later, I make a show of checking my phone screen. "Oh, and here's that email. Looks like you did match with Ronan after all." I smile up at him.

There's a long pause, and I can't quite read his expression.

"Really? I matched to Ronan? The exact person I named last night in the car?" He sounds hella suspicious, his light eyes narrowed. "Let me see."

I slip my phone hurriedly into my back pocket. "Don't you trust me?" I laugh as if it's all a joke to me, even though it feels like I have a thorny burr stuck inside my rib cage. How annoying. What do I care if Easton wants to match to Ronan? Have at it, I say. "Anyway, so that's the all-clear you wanted. You can tell her the program thinks you should be together and I'll back you up."

There's a long pause, and Easton keeps studying my profile while I do my best to ignore him. Then he clears his throat.

"Okay, then . . . great. Thanks. I'll Venmo you the money." He seems unsure or unhappy or something, which makes no sense. This is what he wanted . . . isn't it? Of course it is. He was the one who brought up wanting to be matched to Ronan.

But he keeps glancing at me, as if he wants to ask something and doesn't know how. Maybe I'm the one bringing his mood down, I realize, with the way I'm acting.

I force a smile and squeeze his elbow. "Hey, I'm really happy for you. This is great. Now you can take Ronan to the prom next weekend. I don't think she has a date; I heard she was going to go with a group of friends."

"The prom, right." Easton gives me a half-hearted smile.

Probably nerves, now that he actually has to make his move. "I didn't even think about that." He pauses and then turns to me. "So you really want me to ask Ronan? To the prom?"

"Of course I do. Why wouldn't I?" Still smiling in a slightly frozen way, I turn away from my best friend and change the subject. "So, do you want to go get some gelato? I saw they have a new flavor: black char and rose."

He's almost mumbling to himself when he replies, "Hell yes. I need some sugar."

I stop by my friend Charlotte's house after gelato with Easton. She answers the door in her sweatpants, a video game controller in her hand, her lanky brown hair in a messy braid that hangs over one bony shoulder. "Hey!" Charlotte steps aside so I can walk in.

We're at each other's houses often enough that her brothers don't even look up from their game when I walk in. The living room smells like Cheetos and Coke, and her parents, as usual, are off working at their family-owned hobby and crafts store. Charlotte and her brothers probably have shifts there later on.

I sit on the couch next to her youngest brother and watch the game for a moment. They're playing *Children of Morta*, one of my favorites.

"Want me to get you a controller?" Charlotte asks.

"Nah. I'm good."

She watches me for another minute and then kicks my boot with her shoe. "Okay. What's up?"

I look up at her. "What?"

"You just *slumped* in here and I've never heard you refuse a round of COM. So what's going on with you?"

I frown at her. "Nothing's going on with me. I have no idea what you're talking about." I sigh and lean my head back, staring up at the ceiling. My phone beeps and I scrabble for it, wondering if Easton's having second thoughts about the program or Ronan or prom. But it's just Duolingo, threatening me with bodily harm because I haven't practiced my Spanish in four days.

I sigh again and continue my study of Charlotte's ceiling. "Do you think there's someone for everyone?"

"What?"

"It's what we're told from when we're little, right? I mean, take my own matchmaking program, for instance. It's predicated on the theory that there's one perfect match for everyone, right? But what if that's not true? What if I'm—I mean, some of us are—meant to be alone forever?"

Charlotte doesn't answer my questions. Instead, she continues watching me in silence for another minute. "You know, if I didn't know better, I'd think you were acting lovesick."

I sit up so quickly my teeth clack together. "What?" I bray laughter. "Lovesick? How do you even know what that looks like?" Charlotte, like me, is vitamin L deficient. (Vitamin L, obviously, is the love vitamin.)

She points a thumb over at her sixteen-year-old brother Leo. "This guy acted exactly like you're acting when Jenny Bowles dumped his ass. The sighing, the staring off into space, the stumping from one place to another, the utter lack of interest in video games, the existential-type questions about love. It's identical."

"It's true," Leo says without looking over from his game. "I was a total bummer for, like, three weeks."

I stare at him. And then I stare at Charlotte. And then I stare at my reflection in the mirror next to the TV. The wan face, the dark circles under my eyes, the downturned mouth.

Oh my *god*.

They're totally right, I realize in a whoosh.

I'm lovesick. I'm sickeningly jealous. Of Ronan Chang.

I clap a hand over my mouth and look at Charlotte. "Holy shit."

She grins and nods knowingly. "Mm-hmm. Thought so. So. Who's the guy?"

Two days later, Charlotte and I have dissected and redissected and overdissected every single feeling I have for Easton, our friendship, and the situation. And no matter how we come at it, I can only arrive at one logical conclusion: There is no way in hell I'm going to disrupt our friendship by telling Easton how I feel. I do *not* want to be the one to reduce what we've built over the last four years into a smoking pile of ash and rubble. No way. Nuh-uh.

Charlotte, of course, thinks I'm a total idiot. She says I should shoot my shot, tell Easton how I feel before he takes Ronan to the prom, before the train leaves the station.

But that's what I've been trying to tell her. There *is* no station. We're friends. We'll always be friends. Because Easton can't see me as anything else. He's into Ronan; he told me so himself—and if he felt even an inkling of what I feel, wouldn't he be, I don't know, *not* into Ronan?

In these intervening two days, Easton and I haven't really talked much, either at school or on text. If I'm being honest, I've kept my distance a little bit while I come to terms with the total bizarreness of my feelings. And I guess he's kept his distance because he's got a new girl now.

Not that I was ever his girl, of course.

I sigh and continue my aimless scrolling of Instagram. I'm sitting on a bench near the pier in the bright sunshine, waiting for Easton to show up, dressed in my usual uniform of a short skirt, Doc Martens, and a neon-colored top (fuchsia this time).

He and I meet up several times a week just to walk around or take pictures of ducks to post to Instagram or whatever. And this is one of those days. I considered canceling, but figured it'd raise too many questions. If I have to swallow my feelings until they assimilate into my digestive system and stop making me sick, that's what I'm going to do.

I look up and catch Easton's eye as he walks toward me in loose jeans and a *Dragon Ball Z* T-shirt. My heart instantly melts into a puddle of goo. A boyfriend I could watch anime with? A boyfriend I could play arcade games with? A boyfriend who already knows every single irritating and/or weird thing about me and still sticks around? How perfect would that be?

Easton waves. "Yo."

I force the questions away from my mind. *Stop it*. He's not my boyfriend. He's never going to be my boyfriend. I stand and slip my phone in my pocket. "Yo yourself."

Easton wraps me in a hug like he always does, except this

time, I make the mistake of inhaling deeply, my nose pressed against his chest. He smells like spring—sunshine and a light dusting of flowers. *Mmmm.*

He laughs. "Rosie, I think you're sucking my T-shirt up into your nostrils."

I pull back, my cheeks flaming to the temperature of a preheated oven ready to roast potatoes. "Uh, sorry. Just . . . have a stuffy nose or something. Allergies. Pollen." I sniff a few times for good measure.

Easton frowns at me in concern as we begin walking down the length of the pier, our shoes clacking on the wooden slats. "Really? Do you want to do this or do you need to go home?"

I look up at him, squinting in the sunshine. The warm air wafts around us, smelling of water and salt. "Go home? For what?"

"Do you need to rest or take allergy meds or anything?"

I laugh, softening at his troubled expression. "I'm totally fine, I promise."

Easton relaxes beside me, both of us enjoying the sunshine and the looming end of the school year. There's promise in the air.

For a moment, I'm completely unburdened, truly happy. School's almost done! Summer's almost here! But in the next second, I remember my current predicament again. The boy I like—my best friend—likes someone else.

"So." I keep my voice casual as we stop to watch the water a few feet away from some dude who's fishing off the pier. "Did you ask Ronan to prom yet?"

The breeze blows Easton's blond hair into his eyes and he

tosses his head in that familiar, heart-tugging way I've seen so many times. "Not yet, no." His voice is subdued, an under-current of . . . something in it.

I glance up at him in interest. "Why not? I thought it'd be a done deal by now." It was part of the reason I was avoiding him; I didn't want to hear it, not when I'm still licking my own wounds. Maybe that makes me a shitty friend, I don't know.

He chews on his bottom lip, brown eyes looking across the water at nothing in particular. Then, half turning to me, he says, "Do you think Ronan and I are a good match?"

Oh. I know what's happening. He has cold feet. He's nervous because Ronan's cool and beautiful and has summer homes in Hong Kong and Belize and is *still* one of the nicest people at school.

I tuck my hair behind my ear and say what it genuinely, legiti-mately pains me to say. Because Easton deserves happiness more than anyone else I know. "Dude, yeah. You should just ask her. She's totally into nerdy jocks like you. Remember when she went out with Graham in eighth grade?"

His gaze lingers on me for a long moment and then he nods. "Yeah. Cool. Okay." There's something he's not saying. His tone is damp; he looks like a daffodil caught in a spring shower.

Curious, I attempt to wait him out, but he continues to stare at the sparkling water. Then he points to something in the dis-tance. "Look. A dolphin."

I follow his pointing finger and there is, indeed, a lone dol-phin cresting the waves, its pointy gray nose reaching up toward the cloudless sky. "Cool."

"They say dolphins are a sign of hope."

I paste on the shiniest smile I can. "Awesome. Maybe it means good things for you and Ronan."

Easton doesn't respond.

Prom night arrives just a couple days later, balmy and full of the scent of freesia and hormones, but I can't bring myself to scoff at it or proclaim loudly how glad I am to be in sweats lounging on Charlotte's bed. That was the original plan, but now all I can think of is what Ronan Chang might be wearing and how sexy and elegant she probably looks and how Easton's going to hold her close all night and kiss her and . . .

"Ugh." I cover my face with my hands, my popcorn untouched in a bowl on my lap.

Charlotte looks over at me from her side of the bed, her mouth full of popcorn. She's been watching *How I Met Your Mother* like we'd planned to. Pausing the TV, she sighs. "You're torturing yourself, aren't you?"

"Little bit," I say, my voice muffled behind my hands. "I know he's going to look so *good*, Char. There's no way he and Ronan aren't going to become a thing after tonight. He texted me pictures of his tux and asked my opinion on the shoes he should wear and everything. He didn't say anything about Ronan specifically, but I heard he promposed at the away game on Friday and it was totally romantic and Ronan accepted on the spot." I let my hands fall and look at Charlotte.

"How do you know that?" Charlotte frowns. "I didn't hear that."

"I just kept an ear out in the halls. Everything Ronan does gets broadcast. You know that."

"It could just be a stupid rumor."

"It's not." I can feel it in my marrow.

Sighing, Charlotte falls back against her headboard. "I'm sorry, dude."

"Me too." I have never felt more like a loser in my entire life.

What's our friendship even going to look like now? I thought telling him we matched would be catastrophic to our friendship, but I don't think I thought this through all that well. Will Easton want to bring Ronan everywhere we go now? Or maybe he won't even want to hang out anymore. Which, you know, I get. But it still hurts like hell.

"You look like your appendix just burst or something."

"Yeah, it kinda feels like that."

Setting her popcorn bowl aside, Charlotte suddenly stands and stares at me. There's a bit of popcorn in her hair, but I don't say anything because she looks super intense at the moment. "You need to go."

"What?" It's like she embedded an ax in my skull. I don't know how much more pain I can take. "Am I really that much of a bummer?"

She waves an impatient hand. "No! I mean you need to go to prom. Come on, I'll drive you."

I sit up. "What? Why? I don't need to torture myself by watching Easton and Ronan all night. I hate to tell you this, but you're kinda violating the best friend code right now by even suggesting it."

Charlotte leans forward, her palms on the bed. "Oh, for—You

need to tell Easton how you feel, Rosie. Tonight. ASAP. Before it gets too serious with Ronan and you regret it for the rest of your life. Come on, let's go."

She heads to her closet and pulls on a pair of sneakers.

"Seriously?" My palms are instantly covered in sweat. "I—I can't do that!"

"Oh yes, you can," Charlotte says. "And you are. You can't just sit around waiting to be invited to your own life. You've gotta make stuff happen."

I knew I shouldn't have gotten her that Amy Poehler memoir for her birthday.

I hop off the bed and begin to pace the tiny room in little panicked circles. "But what if he says no? What if he's aghast?"

Done with her shoes, Charlotte comes over and takes me by the shoulders. Looking me straight in the eye, she says, "Then you'll know. And you won't need to keep torturing yourself wondering what if. If he says he doesn't feel the same way, you can move on. But you can't let your feelings just putrefy inside you, Rosie. It'll kill you."

I take a deep breath, my hands trembling. I press them into my thighs. "Are you right? Yeah, I think you are. Okay. You're right. Okay."

And we bound down the stairs and out to Charlotte's Jeep, my heart fluttering so fast I'm practically flying.

I am SO scared. More scared than I've ever been in my entire life. Even more scared than that time I fell in the lake at Holt

Park and this giant duck began to peck at the knot headband on my head. The duck was a freak of nature; so monstrous it blocked out the sun. I thought I was terrified then. Ha.

The prom is at the Wentworth, a really fancy five-star hotel with gold ceilings and marble floors so shiny they look like glass. I would usually never set foot in all this glamarama voluntarily, but Charlotte's right. I need to come clean to Easton so I can lay the soul of this feeling down to rest and move on.

I walk up to the table where people are being checked in, although there are just one or two stragglers now that prom has started in earnest. I can hear the music thumping behind the heavy double doors a few feet away.

There's a sophomore who looks vaguely familiar at the check-in table, dressed in a bow tie and a sweatervest. He's kind of adorable, and gives me a smile that slowly fades as he takes in my sweatpants, graying sneakers, and messy bun. "Um . . . can I help you?"

"I don't have a ticket. But I really need to get in there." I point to the double doors, behind which the stragglers have now disappeared. "I'm not planning on staying or anything. There's just something I have to do. Please."

"What do you need to do?" He eyes my pockets suspiciously, as if I may have a wayward carton of eggs in there, or maybe some TP.

I take a deep breath. "It's about a boy. And . . . my . . . um. Well, my feelings." Gross. I've never said "my feelings" to anyone before. "I have to do this now or I'll probably regret it for the rest of my life. You're the only one standing between me and cold, sad, lifelong regret." I stare at him meaningfully. "Do you want me to curse your memory thirty years from now?"

"N-no?" The poor kid looks like he's wishing he'd stayed in and played chess against himself instead of volunteering for check-in duty.

"Exactly." I give him a brilliant smile. "I knew you were cool. Thanks, dude." And then, my smile fading, I stride past him and push open the wooden doors.

It's dark inside the hall, with just a few neon strobe lights illuminating the dance floor. I look around as I make my way farther in. A couple of people turn and look me up and down, but for the most part, I'm going unnoticed. The adult chaperones are at the far end of the big space, so I'm safe for now.

I dodge around a group of seniors who are wayyyy too animated to be sober, my eyes roving the crowd, looking for Ronan's long, shiny black hair or Easton's tall form. But there are too many people here, and I'm too short. I'm never going to find them like this.

What if they left? What if they've gone off somewhere more . . . private?

The thoughts fly into my head unbidden and now I can't unthink them. Oh god. What if it's already too late? Should I just text Charlotte to come pick me up now?

No, come on. Don't be so weak, Rosie. Give this your best shot.

I came this far. I might as well do it right.

Before I can think too much about it, I rush toward the stage at the front of the room, where the DJ is playing his music and where, later, they'll announce the prom royalty. I climb the steps to the side and stand on my tiptoes on the stage.

"Hey!" the DJ calls over his music. He isn't using a mic, so only I hear him. "What are you doing?"

"This'll just be a minute." From this vantage, I can see the entire room pretty clearly.

At first it really does seem like Easton and Ronan have left. My heart starts to sink . . . and then I see her. Ronan Chang. She's breathtaking in a formfitting ice-blue dress with a lace back. And she's standing with Graham, her old boyfriend, her arm around his waist.

Wait, what?

Frowning, I continue to scan the room.

"Listen, miss, you need to get off the stage." The DJ sounds really annoyed now.

"Yeah, in just a minute. I promise." I flash him a quick smile that doesn't seem to assuage him at all because it's probably not nearly as charming as I'm imagining in my head.

Where the hell is Easton? People are beginning to notice me on the stage, and a few are pointing and smiling unsurely, as if this is some kind of skit I'm putting on for their entertainment. I don't have much time before one of the chaperones sees me and ushers (read: kicks) me out of here.

And then I finally see Easton. He's dressed in the tux I helped him pick, surrounded by other guys in suits. Those are his friends from the basketball team, I realize. Did he . . . He came to prom with his buddies? But they're all heading for the door. In fact, Easton's hand is already on the door handle. There's no way I can jump off the stage and race across the enormous hall in time to catch him. By the time I get outside, he's probably going to be gone.

For just a second, my heart sinks. I don't know what's going on here—why Ronan's got her arm around Graham or why Easton's leaving without her—but I do see my only chance to tell Easton how I feel slipping away from me. I know me; if this doesn't happen now, in an indisputable, can't-take-it-back way, I'm not going to do it. I'm going to wimp out.

And that's why I run across the stage and grab the mic, turning it on before I have a chance to think about what I'm doing.

"Can you pause the music?" I ask the DJ, my voice echoing into the room.

Everyone goes quiet and still. Easton's group stops at the door and Easton turns around slowly, as if he can't quite believe that he's hearing my voice from the loudspeakers. He meets my eye and my heart jumps like a wild animal in my chest. I can't read his expression; I have no idea what he's thinking. Well, it's too late to stop now.

My eyes dart to the adults in the room; the chaperones look a little dazed, and I wonder if they've imbibed a bit tonight as well. The DJ looks unsure, but after a moment, he nods and cuts the music like I've asked.

I turn to look at Easton again. "You tell me all the time that I'm the smartest girl in the world."

Oh, shit. Everyone's listening. A few people even have their cell phones out and are recording me. But I want to do this. I *need* to do this.

My throat clicks audibly when I swallow. "But I'm the stupidest. I'm an idiot because I didn't see what was right in front of me all these years. Easton Cooper, I've fallen in love with you. This entire time I thought it was just friendship, and it is— it definitely is—but at some point friendship began to blur into like and like into love and now I'm all turned upside down and inside out.

"I don't know if I'm ruining everything by telling you how I feel. God, I hope not. But I guess it doesn't matter because I know if I held this in another day—another minute, even—I would probably die." I pause. A few people are snickering. But Easton's staring at me without blinking, without moving, and still without the tiniest flicker of expression on his handsome face. "Shit, that sounds dramatic AF. But okay. That's what I wanted to say and I've said it." The chaperones are beginning to make their way toward me, as if the cursing broke their paralysis. "Now there's only one thing left to do."

I clear my throat. And then I begin to sing.

> "You're just too good to be true
> Can't take my eyes off of you
> You'd be like heaven to touch
> I wanna hold you so much
> At long last, love has arrived—"

"Off the stage!" one of the chaperones, a middle-aged lady who's probably someone's mom, shouts. She's running at me now, surprisingly quick in her heels. "Right now!"

Fuck, fuck, fuck. I don't have time for the whole song, so I launch into the chorus. Easton's mouth is twitching.

"I love you, baby, and if it's quite all right, I need you baby—"

But now the chaperone has leaped onto the stage and she bum-rushes me. I hand over the mic without complaint. Then I take a bow as the entire hall bursts into applause, and hop off the stage, my heart pounding a thousand miles a minute.

"You need to leave," the male chaperone, who has just reached the stage and is huffing and puffing with the effort of speed-walking, says. "I'm guessing you don't have a ticket."

"Nope. And don't blame the kid at the desk. I kind of forced my way in here."

The chaperone glowers at me. "You need to leave," he says again.

"Hear you loud and clear." I walk to the double doors. Easton's group isn't by them anymore, and I try to spot him, but now that I'm off the stage, he's swallowed by the crowd and it's impossible.

I walk out into the night and wrap my arms around myself as I stand alone in my sweats on the sidewalk of this glittery, gilded hotel. "Well," I say to no one in particular. "That happened."

Fuck. That *happened*. And Easton . . . he had absolutely no expression the entire time. I screw my eyes shut, telling myself that I will *not* cry until I get home. This might be the saddest, most pathetic thing I've ever done. And people have *video evidence*. Oh god. How am I going to go back to school on Monday?

I reach into my pocket to pull out my phone and text Charlotte to come get me ASAP, when I hear the sound of footsteps. And then a voice as familiar as the inside of my own eyelids.

"Rosie."

My mouth is suddenly completely dry. I turn slowly, the cool night air enveloping me like a silky shawl. Easton is coming down the stairs of the hotel, looking like he belongs in a movie. One hand is in his pants pocket, the other in a fist by his side. His eyes are serious, probing, as he strides toward me.

"H-hey." My own voice is high and thin, on the knife-edge of hysteria.

He comes to stand in front of me, closer and closer, no more than a foot away. We are breathing the same air. "I can't believe you did that."

Welcome to the club, I want to say, but instead I say this: "You didn't bring Ronan. To the prom."

He blinks. "No."

"Why not?"

"She wasn't right for me."

"But I heard you did a promposal at an away game that she accepted on the spot."

Easton shakes his head once, impatient. "That was Graham."

Graham. Ronan had said yes to *Graham*. Charlotte was right; it was all just a rumor that Easton had been the one to prompose.

There's a long pause as I process what he's told me. We don't look away; we're barely breathing. We're staring at each other so hard and so intensely I'm afraid we'll light each other on fire. "Who did the program really match me with, Rosie?" Easton asks this last question in a voice so low, it shimmies slowly up my spine and whispers into my ear.

I have goosebumps when I answer, my voice dry and husky. "Me. It matched you with me."

He smiles. Actually smiles. "I knew it," he says, more like he's talking to himself than me.

I stare at him. "You knew it? But you told me to run the program because you wanted to match to Ronan. I thought you were going to ask her to prom."

He shakes his head. "I asked you to run the program because I was hoping it'd match me to you. And then maybe you'd start to see me as more than just your friend. The Ronan thing . . . I was about to slip up and say *your* name, and the only other 'Ro' name I could think of was hers." He laughs softly. "Don't you see, Rosie? I was never going to ask her. I was never into her. I'm into you."

I have no words. They've all evaporated out of my mouth.

Easton continues, "But why didn't you tell me the program had matched me to you?"

I step closer. "Because I was scared. I was stupid and scared. I didn't want to lose you."

He steps closer, too. His hands are on my face, smoothing a strand of hair away from my cheek. "You could never lose me."

"Never?" My face is tipped up to his, a flower seeking sunlight.

"Never, never."

And then he kisses me.

It's like the launching of a thousand fireworks, like a million string lights coming on in my brain. It's like the first morning there ever was, or a sunset you can taste. I wrap my arms around his waist and press myself into him, closer, feeling his warmth, the hard length of his torso. His hands slip from my face to my shoulders and then my waist and he cinches me in, as if he can't get close enough, either.

We kiss until my mouth is raw, until my cheeks sting from the rub of his stubble. And then I pull away and grin up at him.

"That smile," he says softly, rubbing a thumb across my lower lip. "It always gets me."

"I love you, Easton."

He gazes into my eyes. "I love you, too, Rosie. By the way, killer rendition of 'Can't Take My Eyes Off You.' I knew it was your song."

I snort. "And the best part is, I have a name for my match-making program now. I'm calling it VALLI after Frankie Valli, who first sang that song. It stands for Very Accurate Love Link Interface."

We laugh together for a minute and then Easton gets serious again. "I have a very important question to ask you, Rosie Gupta."

My heart thumps. "Yes?"

"Will you go play *Tekken Seven* with me at Game and Fortune?"

"Easton Cooper, I would be honored."

Matching grins on our shining faces, we walk hand in hand down the street, the moon shining down on us like a lucky penny.

ABOUT THE AUTHORS

ELISE BRYANT is the author of *Happily Ever Afters*. For many years, she had the joy of working as a special education teacher in South Los Angeles. Elise now lives with her husband and two daughters in Long Beach, where she spends her days reading, writing, and eating dessert. elisebryant.com.

ELIZABETH EULBERG is the international bestselling author of more than a dozen novels for young readers, including *The Lonely Hearts Club*, *Better Off Friends*, and her latest, *The Best Worst Summer*. Her acclaimed middle-grade detective series, The Great Shelby Holmes, has been on dozens of state reading lists across the country, including the prestigious Texas Bluebonnet list. Elizabeth currently lives in London, where she gets constant inspiration walking around (and eating scones) and is looking forward to her own meet-cute with a British bloke.

LEAH JOHNSON is an editor, educator, and author of books for young adults. Her bestselling debut YA novel, *You Should See*

Me in a Crown, was a Stonewall Honor Book, the inaugural Reese's Book Club YA pick, and named a best book of the year by *Cosmopolitan*, *Kirkus*, *Marie Claire*, *Publishers Weekly*, and New York Public Library among others. Her sophomore novel, *Rise to the Sun*, is now available from Scholastic.

ANNA-MARIE MCLEMORE (they/them) grew up hearing la llorona in the Santa Ana winds, and now writes books as queer, Latine, and nonbinary as they are. They are the author of *The Weight of Feathers*, a Morris Debut Award finalist; Stonewall Honor Book *When the Moon Was Ours*, which was longlisted for the National Book Award in Young People's Literature; *Wild Beauty*, a Kirkus, School Library Journal, and Booklist Best Book of 2017; *Blanca & Roja*, one of Time Magazine's 100 Best Fantasy Books of All Time; *Dark and Deepest Red*, a Winter 2020 Indie Next List title; *The Mirror Season*, a Junior Library Guild Selection; and the forthcoming *Lakelore* and *Self-Made Boys: A Great Gatsby Remix*. annamariemclemore.com.

SANDHYA MENON is the *New York Times*–bestselling author of *When Dimple Met Rishi*, *Of Curses and Kisses*, and many other novels that also feature lots of kissing, girl power, and swoony boys. Her books have been showcased in several cool places, including the *Today* show, *Teen Vogue*, NPR, BuzzFeed, and *Seventeen*. A full-time dog servant and part-time writer, she makes her home in the foggy mountains of Colorado. sandhyamenon.com.

MARISSA MEYER is the #1 *New York Times*–bestselling author of The Lunar Chronicles series, the *New York Times*–bestselling

Renegades trilogy, as well as the graphic novel *Wires and Nerve: Vols. 1 and 2*, and *The Lunar Chronicles Coloring Book*. Her first standalone novel, *Heartless*, was also a #1 *New York Times* bestseller; her most recent standalone novel is the bestselling rom-com *Instant Karma*. She lives in Tacoma, Washington, with her husband and their two daughters. marissameyer.com.

JULIE MURPHY lives in North Texas with her husband who loves her, her dog who adores her, and her cats who tolerate her. After several wonderful years in the library world, Julie now writes full-time. When she's not writing or reliving her reference-desk glory days, she can be found watching made-for-TV movies, hunting for the perfect slice of cheese pizza, and planning her next great travel adventure. She is also the #1 *New York Times*–bestselling author of the novels *Dumplin'* (now a film on Netflix), *Puddin'*, *Ramona Blue*, *Side Effects May Vary*, *Faith Taking Flight*, *Dear Sweet Pea*, and *If the Shoe Fits*.

CALEB ROEHRIG is a writer and television producer originally from Ann Arbor, Michigan. Having also lived in Chicago, Los Angeles, and Helsinki, Finland, he has a chronic case of wanderlust, and has visited over thirty countries. A former actor, Roehrig has experience on both sides of the camera, with a résumé that includes appearances on film and TV—as well as seven years in the stranger-than-fiction salt mines of reality television. His young adult novels include *Last Seen Leaving*, *White Rabbit*, *Death Prefers Blondes* (a Popsugar Best Novel of 2019), and *The Fell of Dark* (a 2021 American Library Association Rainbow Book List Selection).

Cartoonist **SARAH WINIFRED SEARLE** originally hails from spooky New England but currently lives in sunny Perth, Australia. Her graphic novels include *Sincerely, Harriet*, a quiet middle-grade tale (Graphic Universe, May 2019), and a fictionalized YA memoir from First Second coming in 2022. Find her around the web: @swinsea/swinsea.com.

ABIGAIL HING WEN is the *New York Times*–bestselling author of *Loveboat, Taipei*, a romantic comedy following the journey of Ever Wong in her summer in Taipei, and continuing in the companion novel, *Loveboat Reunion*. *Loveboat, Taipei* and *Loveboat Reunion* have been optioned for film by ACE Entertainment. Abigail holds a BA from Harvard, a JD from Columbia Law School, and an MFA from the Vermont School of Fine Arts. When she's not writing stories or listening to her favorite scores, she is busy working in artificial intelligence in Silicon Valley, where she lives with her husband and two sons. @abigailhingwen/abigail hingwen.com.

Thank you for reading this Feiwel & Friends book. The friends who made *Serendipity* possible are:

Jean Feiwel, Publisher

Liz Szabla, Associate Publisher

Rich Deas, Senior Creative Director

Holly West, Senior Editor

Anna Roberto, Senior Editor

Kat Brzozowski, Senior Editor

Dawn Ryan, Executive Managing Editor

Kim Waymer, Senior Production Manager

Emily Settle, Associate Editor

Erin Siu, Associate Editor

Foyinsi Adegbonmire, Associate Editor

Rachel Diebel, Assistant Editor

Michelle Gengaro, Designer

Helen Seachrist, Senior Production Editor

Follow us on Facebook or visit us online at fiercereads.com.
Our books are friends for life.